TRUE LOVE

#9

BRENDA JACKSON

TRUE LOVE

ARABESQUE®

TRUE LOVE

An Arabesque novel published by Kimani Press/March 2009

First published by BET Books, LLC in 2000.

ISBN-13: 978-0-373-83127-2
ISBN-10: 0-373-83127-7

www.kimanipress.com

Printed in U.S.A.

Acknowledgments

To the love of my life, Gerald Jackson, Sr.

To my family and friends.
Thanks for being so supportive.

To the Prominent Women of Color Book Club.
You are a special group of ladies.

To Brenda Simmons. Once again, your helpful feedback on the finished product kept me on track.

To Keshia Chenault. This one is for you.

In memory of my good friend and classmate
Elliott Russell Gamble, better known to all as Shine.
You are gone but not forgotten.
The William M. Raines Class of 1971 misses
you deeply.

To my Heavenly Father. I'm everything
I am because you love me.

THE MADARIS FAMILY AND FRIENDS SERIES

Dear Readers,

I love writing family sagas, and I am so happy that Kimani Press is reissuing my very first family series, the Madaris family. It's been twelve years and fifty books since I first introduced the Madaris family. During that time this special family, along with their friends, have won their way into readers' hearts. I am ecstatic to be able to share these award-winning stories with everyone all over again—especially with those who have never met the Madaris clan—up close and personal—in this special-edition collectors' series.

I never dreamed when I penned my first novel, *Tonight and Forever,* and introduced the Madaris family, that I was taking readers on a journey where heartfelt romance, sizzling passion and true love awaited them at every turn. I had no idea that the Madaris family and their friends would become characters that readers would come to know and care so much about. I invite you to relax, unwind and see what all the hoopla is about. Let Justin, Dex, Clayton, Uncle Jake and their many friends transport you with love stories that are so passionate and sizzling they will take your breath away. There is nothing better than falling in love with one of these Madaris men and their circle of friends and family.

For a complete list of all the books in this series, as well as the dates they will be available in a bookstore near you, please visit my Web site at www.brendajackson.net.

If you would like to receive my monthly newsletter, please visit and sign up at www.brendajackson.net/page/newsletter.htm.

I also invite you to drop me an e-mail at WriterBJackson@aol.com. I love hearing from my readers.

All the best,

Brenda Jackson

THE MADARIS FAMILY

Milton Madaris, Sr. and Felicia Laverne Lee Madaris

Milton Jr. (Dora)
- Milton III (Fran)
  - Blade and Slade (Skye)⑭, Quantum, Jantzen

Lee (Pearl)
- Lee Jr. (Alfie)
  - Lee, Kane, Jarod

Nolan (Bessie)
- Nolan Jr. (Marie)
  - Nolan, Corbin, Adam, Victoria, Lindsay

Lucas (Carrie)
- Lucas Jr. (Sarah)
  - Lucas, Reese, Emerson, Chance

Robert (Diana)
- Felicia (Trask)⑦

Jonathan (Marilyn)
- Justin (Lorren)①, Dex (Caitlin)②, Clayton (Syneda)④, Tracie (Daniel), Kattie (Raymond), Christy (Alex)⑬

Jake (Diamond)⑧

KEY:
( ) — denotes a spouse
◯ and number —denotes title of book for that couple's story

① Tonight and Forever
② Whispered Promises
③ Cupid's Bow
④ Eternally Yours
⑤ One Special Moment
⑥ Fire and Desire
⑦ Truly Everlasting
⑧ Secret Love
⑨ True Love
⑩ Surrender
⑪ The Best Man
⑫ The Midnight Hour
⑬ Unfinished Business
⑭ Slow Burn

THE MADARIS FRIENDS

Maurice and Stella Grant
|
Trevor (Corinthians)⑥,
Regina (Mitch)⑪

Angelique Hamilton Chenault
|
Sterling Hamilton (Colby)⑤,
Nicholas Chenault (Shayla)⑨

Kyle Garwood (Kimara)③

Ashton Sinclair
(Netherland)⑩

Drake Warren
(Tori)⑫

Trent Jordache
(Brenna)⑨

Nedwyn Lansing
(Diana)⑭

KEY:
( ) — denotes a spouse
◯ and number —denotes title of book for that couple's story

① Tonight and Forever
② Whispered Promises
③ Cupid's Bow
④ Eternally Yours
⑤ One Special Moment
⑥ Fire and Desire
⑦ Truly Everlasting
⑧ Secret Love
⑨ True Love
⑩ Surrender
⑪ The Best Man
⑫ The Midnight Hour
⑬ Unfinished Business
⑭ Slow Burn

Most important of all, continue to show deep love for each other, for love overlooks a multitude of faults.

—*I Peter* 4:8

Chapter 1

The distinctive scent of a man's aftershave alerted Shayla Kirkland that she was no longer alone in the interviewing room. She had glanced up, thinking the fragrance was smooth, hypnotic, and sexy…very much like the tall, remarkably good-looking man who had walked in.

"Ms. Kirkland?"

"Yes," she'd responded, rising to her feet and parting her lips in a wry smile. She had known Nicholas Chenault was extremely handsome. Her extensive research of Chenault Electronics had prepared her for that fact. But the photographs she'd seen of him had evidently been of poor quality, because they'd failed to capture the vibrant coloring of his light brown skin and the brilliant gold of his eyes. He had taken her hand in a businesslike handshake. She'd let out her breath slowly, realizing that she'd been holding it since he had entered the room.

"I'm Nicholas Chenault. I appreciate your interest in my company. Please take a seat and we'll begin the interview."

Shayla sat down again, forcing herself to remember that this would not be an ordinary interview. She was here with a purpose. She was here with a plan. But first she had to get her foot in the door.

Now, Ms. Kirkland," Nicholas Chenault said in a deep husky voice as he sat behind the desk, "what exactly do you know about Chenault Electronics?"

If only you knew, she thought. Lifting her eyes to meet his directly, she wished she hadn't. His eyes were brilliantly gold, and they were brilliantly intelligent, sharp, and assessing. She wondered how good he was at reading people. For a brief moment an uneasy feeling swept through her. Knowing this was not the time to rethink her decision about what she was doing, she straightened in the chair and met his gaze. He had asked a common interview question, and thanks to her in-depth research she had an answer, one that was appropriate. She would tell him some of what she knew about his company, but not everything.

She would not tell him about her plans to destroy it.

"I can give you a historical summation dating back to the day Chenault Electronics was first formed by your father, Alan Chenault, thirty-five years ago, and how he transformed it from a corner store operation into a relatively neat and tidy electronic company. Unfortunately, he lacked vision, which is evident in his failure to tap into numerous domestic and international markets." She paused, giving him her best businesslike, professional look. Although she had just openly criticized what had been his father's narrow strategy for running the business, it had been the absolute truth. "However, I believe what I know about your present-day operation is what I'd like to address."

At his nod, she continued. "Under your leadership, Mr.

Chenault, this company has emerged as a powerful force within the global economy. Your expansion into the overseas market is phenomenal, as well as timely. Sales for this year are expected to exceed thirty million. You've even gone one step further. You've capitalized on the failures of your competitors—who can't see the advantages of putting out new products and diverse technology—especially in the development of total wireless communications and advanced electronics that will ultimately replace the need for electrical outlets throughout the world."

When she stopped talking, a slow smile touched Nicholas Chenault's lips. "Please go on," he said, not hiding the fact that he was clearly impressed with her accurate summation of his company.

"Chenault Electronics was the first to deploy a wireless telephone network in Benin, Africa. This helped to provide the first telephone service in the area, providing a long overdue means of communication to hundreds of remote customers."

Feeling confident that she had the interview under control, Shayla relaxed. She was more determined that ever to convince the man sitting across from her that she was everything his company was looking for.

Nicholas Chenault was impressed with Shayla Kirkland's wealth of knowledge about his company. To say that she had done her homework and was fully prepared would be an understatement. So far they had been in the interview for over an hour, and each question had been answered in a way that definitely displayed her knowledge and her intelligence. She was now expounding on her educational background.

It was a good thing he'd already done a number of interviews that week, so that it required little thought—his mind was focused on the woman.

He glanced down at the notes he had jotted down on the evaluation form. The first category listed on the form was appearance. He'd written *neat, dresses with good taste, professionally.* He glanced back up to look at her and decided not to add that the fit of her navy blue, tailored, business suit was chic, precise, and enticing. Then there was her hair—short, black, and cut in a trendy style that didn't take away from her professional image. Her almond-colored skin had a light touch of makeup. The berry tone of her lips highlighted the glow of her cheeks and the sultry, dark, brandywine coloring of her eyes. Nicholas inhaled deeply, forcing his mind to concentrate only on those of Shayla Kirkland's assets that were important in terms of employment.

"Ms. Kirkland, why did you move back to Chicago?" he asked, trying not to notice her crossing her long gorgeous legs. Nicholas had to tighten his grip on the pen he held in his hand to keep his imagination from taking over.

"My mother passed two weeks ago, unexpectedly. Now that I'm here, I feel this is where I belong, and have decided to stay."

The deep sadness in her voice gripped Nicholas. "My condolences for your loss."

"Thank you."

Nicholas decided to move on to the next interview question. "Tell me about some of your other achievements, and how they can benefit us here."

When she began speaking, he couldn't help but zero in on her poise. She was definitely at ease, composed, and had a self-confident manner. She wasn't hesitant in providing eye contact. The dark coloring of her eyes was compelling and magnetic, and he found his gaze pulled back to them time and time again. He couldn't help wondering what color her eyes were when they glowed with passion and inner fire. How would they look when they became heated with pleasure?

"Ms. Kirkland, what do you see in this position of manager of international affairs that you did not have in your last position?" he asked in an effort to keep his mind on track.

As she began answering, he glanced down at the evaluation form. The next category on the list was personality. As he sat there watching her and listening to her, there was no doubt in his mind that she would be a perfect fit for his company. If first impressions were to be believed, she was friendly, but not overly so. That was good, because she was a single woman of twenty-six—a very attractive one at that—and he had a number of single men working for him. The last thing Chenault Electronics needed to deal with was a sexual harassment lawsuit.

After asking her a few more questions, for which she provided concise and informative answers, he leaned back in his chair and said, "That ends your interview, Ms. Kirkland. Is there anything you'd like to ask me about the position?"

"No, Mr. Chenault. You've told me everything I needed to know. However, I'd just like to add that I believe I can be an asset to your company."

Nicholas nodded, thinking that she could be an asset in a number of ways. He stood. "This was a very pleasant interview, Ms. Kirkland. I hope to make a decision within a week."

Shayla stood and offered him her hand. "Thank you for giving me the opportunity to interview with your company. Good day, Mr. Chenault."

Nicholas walked her to the door, then stood and watched as she walked away. He let out a deep breath, thinking that everything about Shayla Kirkland was real class, even her walk. The graceful sway of her hips was enough to bring a comatose man back into the world.

Walking back to the desk, Nicholas sat down and looked

over the evaluation form. Her communication skills were superb. She had expressed herself eloquently. Her answers had been clear, fluid, and organized, and her information had been accurate and informed. Her educational background was outstanding—an MBA from Harvard—and her fluency in four languages—Chinese, Spanish, French, and Swahili—was more than impressive. Her letter of recommendation from Howard University spoke volumes, and nearly glowed on the page.

He sighed, knowing he didn't have to cover the other categories of the interview evaluation form to know that Shayla Kirkland was the ideal person for the new Chicago office. She would definitely bring a lot of experience and diversity to the table. He would be a total fool not to hire her.

Yet he was contemplating that very thing.

Nicholas stood and walked over to the window. Since buying this building six months ago, he had decided he liked the location because it provided a stunning view of downtown Chicago. The metropolis was totally different from downtown Jacksonville, Florida, where his home office was located. Here in Chicago, the buildings surrounding his were tall and impressive, but the areas surrounding those structures were crowded and congested. One of the things he appreciated most about the location of his office building in Jacksonville was the beautiful view of the St. Johns River and the land space that came with it. Jacksonville had more land space than any other city in Florida. And with the revitalization plans the city had underway, it wouldn't be long before downtown Jacksonville boasted structures that were just as tall and impressive, a scenic river view that would continue to be breathtaking, and surrounding buildings that would still provide space.

Space was something he appreciated more than anything, especially personal space, which was why he was thinking seriously about not hiring Shayla Kirkland.

For the first time since taking over Chenault Electronics after his father's death three years ago, he had been totally captivated by a woman. He had definitely not expected the rush of pleasure that hit him square in the solar plexus when he'd taken her hand in his to shake it. He had been overcome with a weird feeling, and—although he had been able to downplay it and get through the interview session with Shayla Kirkland without any hint of the turmoil he'd been in—it had been there, just the same. He had noted everything about her, things he had needed to notice and things he had not—like the perfect coloring of her pantyhose against the flesh of her smooth legs, and the fullness of her lips, and how those lips seemed to have been begging for a kiss even while she was in her most professional mode. For the first time in his life he had felt cramped and closed in.

Threatened about his space.

All the time she had been talking to him, telling him about her extensive travels abroad before she'd finally taken a job as manager of the Business Department at Howard University, he had been thinking that any man would have designs on her. She was definitely a woman who deserved a man's complete attention. And if that thought hadn't been bad enough, at another time during the interview, when a small wisp of hair had fallen out of place and brushed her forehead, he had been tempted to reach over and tuck the strand back in place. There was no way he could work as closely with her as he would need to for the next six to eight months without feeling devoid of space…and of sane thoughts and body control. Shayla Kirkland might be well-qualified for the position she had applied for—to his way of thinking maybe even a tad overqualified—but she would also be a threat he didn't want to deal with. And with the security surrounding his company's development of the mangolid chip, better known as the MC Project, he didn't need anything or anyone around him that could challenge his focus. The last thing he needed was to be in the constant company of a woman he consistently thought of taking to bed.

Nicholas sighed before walking back over to the desk and sitting down. He leaned back in his chair, trying to remember the last time he had been intimate with a woman, and coming up with the conclusion that it had been too long. Because of his vigorous work schedule he'd been too busy to carve out time for a personal life, and he'd never gone for the idea of having sex just for the sake of doing so. At the age of thirty-two he had an intense sexual drive, like most men his age. However, he knew how to control it. Marriage and children were the last things on his mind. Although he much preferred a long-term relationship to a short-term one, he also preferred a relationship in which the two individuals knew up front what to expect and what not to expect. The one thing any woman he became involved with could not expect was an invitation to become a "live-in"—he allowed no one to invade his space—or share it, for that matter.

His last long-term affair had been with Olivia. They had lasted nearly a year before she began dropping hints that it was time for their relationship to move to another level. Since the level they'd been operating on had suited him just fine and he'd seen no reason to change it, she had decided to move on. That had been more than a year ago, and he hadn't been intimate with a woman since. Of course, since the press conference ten months ago—when it had been announced to the world that he was the half brother of superstar movie actor Sterling Hamilton—women from everywhere had been coming on to him in droves, but he'd been too busy to appreciate his newfound popularity. Not that he would have, anyway, since that wasn't his style. His mind had been filled with thoughts of mangolid chips and micron-controllers, not silken sheets, naked bodies, and hot sex.

Until today.

For the first time in over a year he had obsessive thoughts of sleeping with a woman—Shayla Kirkland. No, he quickly corrected, he had more than just thoughts of sleeping with her. During the interview, he'd had visions of her in his arms, the scent of her entrenched in his skin, the taste of her on his tongue, and the feel of him hard and solid as a rock inside of her. Lucky for him he'd been sitting behind a desk.

He was smart enough to know that Shayla Kirkland was a disaster just waiting to happen. She would tempt him to break his own personal rule of not dating any of his employees. Making a quick decision, he checked the block on the interview evaluation form for *Do not hire.* He would release her file to his secretary, so she could send out the customary *Sorry, but you did not get the job* letter.

He had to do whatever was needed to protect his space and his peace of mind.

Emotions too numerous to name swept through Shayla as she entered her home. Her world was tilting, and she was experiencing the movement right along with it. Leaning against the closed door to get her balance, she breathed in deeply to take a mind-clearing breath.

The interview had tense moments for her. Although Nicholas Chenault had been the epitome of a professional throughout the process, she had felt a tingling in the pit of her stomach every time she had looked into the depths of his golden eyes. Eyes that color were a rarity among African-Americans unless they wore color contacts. It was obvious his eye color was natural. It was perfectly in sync with his skin tone.

A glimmer of warmth flooded through her as she remembered sitting across from him during the interview. In the beginning it had seemed as if she had no defense against her attraction to him. His startling good looks had nearly taken the wind out of her sails, leaving her body feeling as if it were being heated.

Shayla pushed away from the door, walked across the room, and dropped onto the sofa. Although she had gotten off to a shaky start, she believed she would get the job. Then she would make Chenault Electronics pay for what they had done to her mother nearly twenty-seven years ago. First, she would deal with Chenault. Then she would find a way to take care of Thomas Jordache, the man who owned TJ Electronics. She would have taken care of him first if he had not been out of the country on business. According to his office, he would not be returning for another three weeks or so. That would give her time to put together a plan to deal with him, since he had been the initiator of her mother's woes back then.

Sitting up straight in her seat, Shayla reached over to pick up a book from the coffee table in front of her. It was her mother's diary. She had found it last week when she'd been in the attic going through her mother's things. The information she had uncovered after reading the diary had tilted her world, had literally rocked it. According to what her mother had written, Glenn Kirkland, the man Shayla had grown up believing was her father until his death two years ago, had not been. Glenn had married her mother when she was ten weeks pregnant with another man's child, willingly giving the unborn child his name, his love, and his protection. It had all come about because of a web of deceit and lies.

Shayla closed the diary and placed it back on the table. Twenty-seven years ago her mother suffered an enormous amount of humiliation for nothing. She had been stripped of her dignity and her pride, as well as her job, because of Chenault Electronics and Thomas Jordache.

Shayla stood and walked over to the window and gazed out. "Both of them will pay for causing you undeserved pain, Mama. I'll see to it."

Chapter 2

Nicholas was roused by a knock on his office door. He looked up as Paul Dunlap opened the door and stuck his head in. "Can I talk to you for a second, Nick?"

Nicholas pushed the papers he was working on aside. "Sure."

Paul had been head of security at Chenault Electronics for nearly thirty years. Now, at fifty-two, Paul claimed he would hold the position for just one year before retiring. Nicholas didn't know what he would do when that day came. Paul was much more than just head of security at Chenault. He had been Nicholas's father's good friend and trusted confidant. And now Paul was those same things to Nicholas. Paul was also a father figure, and as much a part of Chenault Electronics as Nicholas was. Paul was a highly intelligent man who took his job seriously. He always had. And now, with the high security measures surrounding the MC Project, Nicholas depended on Paul's skill and expertise even more. The world of technology was a very competitive one, and the ability to emerge as a leader within the industry could mean the difference between success and failure. Some people, those without scruples, would stop at nothing to get that success.

Nicholas watched as Paul walked in carrying an envelope in his hand. He placed the envelope before him on his desk. "Would you like to explain this, Nick?"

Nicholas glanced down at the envelope, which was addressed to Shayla Kirkland. He shrugged. "What's there to explain, Paul? She didn't get the job." Nicholas raised an eyebrow. "Is she someone you know?"

Paul shook his head. "No, but she's someone I wouldn't want to take a job with one of your competitors, especially TJ Electronics. They would just love to get their hands on a person of her caliber."

Nicholas leaned back in his chair and looked up at Paul curiously. "And just what do you know about her caliber? You weren't in on the interview."

Paul sighed. "I didn't have to be. I saw a copy of her résumé for security clearance. After reading it, I figured you'd grab her up. I was totally surprised when I saw Leanne typing up this letter."

Nicholas nodded. Leanne was his secretary. "What if I told you she wasn't a good fit?"

Paul sat down on the edge of Nicholas's desk and gazed at him pointedly. "After reading her résumé, I'd ask you this question—she wasn't a good fit for what, this company, or your bed?" A smile touched the older man's lips when he saw the deep coloring flush Nicholas's features. "In fact, I'd bet she was a very good fit for both this company and your bed, and that's what has you worried."

"I'm not worried about anything," Nicholas grumbled, pushing the envelope aside.

"Then maybe you're just a tad bit horny, son."

Nicholas couldn't keep from grinning. For as long as he had known Paul, and that had been forever, the man had been blunt, and straight to the point. It had been Paul who had taken on the chore of explaining the birds and the bees to the fourteen-year-old Nicholas when Alan Chenault had become flustered with embarrassment while attempting to do so.

"I'm glad you're finding humor in all this," Paul said, frowning. "The statement was not meant to be funny. It was said in all seriousness. I'd hate to think we're losing a prime candidate for employment because you don't think you'll be able to keep your pants zipped whenever you're around her."

Nicholas stopped grinning and sat up straight. "That's not it."

"Then what is it, exactly? Shayla Kirkland is looking for a job. Her credentials are excellent. Just imagine how her expertise could be used here. If we won't give her an opportunity to come work for us, who's to say that JT Electronics won't be her next stop? I told you I thought we'd be making a mistake by opening another company in the same city where Thomas Jordache is also doing business. We can barely tolerate the likes of him in Jacksonville."

As Nicholas studied Paul he heard the venom in his tone. It was there every time he mentioned Thomas Jordache's name. Although Jordache was their major competitor and had proved to be a pain in the butt more than a few times, Nicholas knew why there was more to Paul's immense dislike of him. It had a lot to do with Paul's sister, who had been married to Jordache for a short while. Paul had been against the marriage. But that wasn't the only reason. Over the years Nicholas had heard other rumors about why Paul disliked Jordache. He'd heard that over twenty-seven years ago Jordache, in an attempt to obtain classified information from Chenault Electronics, was said to have bought off one of Chenault's female employees, who'd been willing to give him what he wanted. It was a case of underhanded industry theft, or at least that's what they'd thought initially. It had been Paul, as head of security, who had uncovered the plot. Months later, after the woman had been fired, Paul had also discovered that the woman had been falsely accused. She had been an innocent pawn in one of Jordache's ruthless games.

Nicholas sighed, knowing Paul was right regarding Shayla Kirkland. He had been thinking with the lower part of his body rather than with his brain. Somehow and someway he would have to maintain an iron-fisted amount of sexual control around her even if it killed him…and it just might. There was only so much a man could take, especially a man who hadn't slept with a woman in over a year. He picked up the envelope and ripped it in two, knowing Paul was watching him with keen interest.

"Is she that much of a temptation, Nick?" Paul asked, cocking a curious eyebrow at him.

Shayla Kirkland's beautiful face and shapely body flashed through Nicholas's mind. "Yes, but I'll deal with it for the sake of the company. My relationship with Ms. Kirkland will be strictly professional, and nothing more."

Shayla watched her aunt take a sip of coffee, then put her cup back down on the table. As usual, she thought Callie Foster, her mother's younger sister by four years, was a beautiful woman who wore her age of forty-seven well. She could pass easily for a woman in her thirties. Shayla knew her aunt credited her good eating habits and her policy of staying in shape as the reasons for her young appearance.

"So, sweetheart," her aunt said cheerfully, interrupting Shayla' s thoughts. "What did you do today?"

Shayla sighed inwardly. Now was as good a time as any

to tell her aunt about the phone call she had received an hour ago. "I had an interview earlier today, and got a call before you arrived making me a job offer."

Shayla saw the happiness that lit up her aunt's entire face. She knew Aunt Callie had been hoping that she would move back to Chicago permanently. Callie reached across the table and captured Shayla's hand in hers. "Oh, honey, that's wonderful. Now that your mother is gone, you're all the family I have." Her aunt's smile widened as she released her hand. "Did you take that job as manager of the business department at the hospital?"

Shayla sighed and deliberately watched her aunt's reaction when she answered. "No. I've taken a job as manager of international affairs with Chenault Electronics."

Callie Foster nearly choked on the piece of pie she'd just put in her mouth.

"Aunt Callie, are you all right?" Shayla asked, genuinely concerned. Her aunt' s reaction was a dead giveaway that she knew something.

"Yes, I'm fine," Callie said, trying to regain her composure. "Wh-what made you want to go to work for Chenault?"

Shayla put her coffee cup down as she decided just what she would tell her aunt. There had always been complete honesty between them in the past, and Shayla knew she would tell her the truth—all of it. "I came across Mom's diary, Aunt Callie, while packing up her things. It was in the attic." Determined to bring everything out in the open, she added, "And I know."

Shayla could tell from the way her aunt was nibbling on her lower lip that what she had read in that diary was something she was never, ever supposed to have known.

Aunt Callie cleared her throat "You know *what,* Shayla?"

"I know that Glenn Kirkland was not my biological father."

Her aunt said nothing for the longest time. When she did

speak her voice was soft, almost weak. "You weren't supposed to find that out."

"Evidently."

Shayla watched as light tears formed in her aunt's eyes. Pushing her chair back, she stood quickly and walked over to the woman she loved so much. Reaching out, she took her aunt's hand in hers. "Come on, Aunt Callie, let's go into the living room. It's time for us to have a girls' chat, don't you think?"

Callie nodded and stood. The two of them left the kitchen and walked into the living room and sat down on the sofa.

"First of all," Shayla started off, "I want you to know that as far as I'm concerned Glenn Kirkland is, and forever will be, my dad. He was a wonderful person, and a fantastic father. I loved him so very much. If anything, finding out the truth makes me love him that much more, for giving me his love unconditionally."

Shayla felt a lump form in her throat and paused to steady her voice before continuing. "He was always there for me. He was the perfect dad, and I know he was a wonderful husband to Mom. Both Mom and I were devastated when we lost him two years ago."

Shayla took a deep cleansing breath as she remembered that time. She knew that during their entire marriage her mother and father had a close relationship. Evangeline Foster Kirkland, known to her family and friends as Eva, had taken her husband's death of lung cancer extremely hard. Shayla knew in her heart that no matter what had happened twenty-seven years ago between her mother and the man who was her biological father, in the end Eva had found true happiness with Glenn Kirkland. "Dad made Mom very happy," she said achingly, and she knew without a doubt that was true.

"Yes," Callie agreed softly as she reached over and

captured Shayla's hand. "And she made him very happy, too." She understood Shayla's need to know everything, but she couldn't help but remember all the promises she, Glenn, and Eva had made to conceal the truth.

She looked into Shayla's eyes, wondering just how much of the truth she could handle. After a few emotional moments, Callie tightened her hold on Shayla's hand. "When we were kids in South Carolina, Glenn and his parents lived across the street from us. I think he'd been in love with your mom forever, and I know that she'd always loved him, too. Age was always a major factor, since he was five years older than Eva. Glenn said he was just biding his time and waiting for her to grow up. Everyone knew how he felt about her, and figured he would pop the question when Eva finished high school. That would have been around the time Glenn was to come home on leave from the military."

Callie shook her head, remembering that time, before she continued. "But he never got leave. The army shipped him off to Vietnam immediately after basic training. In the meantime, Eva graduated from high school and left to attend college in Florida."

"Why didn't they get together when he finally came back from the war, or when she had finished college?" Shayla asked quietly.

Callie stared off in the distance as if trying to regroup her thoughts. "Things weren't the same for Glenn after the war. During his stint in Vietnam he had gotten an injury that robbed him of the ability to father children. He thought it wouldn't be fair to ask Eva to marry him, so he did what he thought was the honorable thing and broke things off between them. Eva was devastated by that."

"Did Mom know the reason he broke things off?"

"No, but I did, and he made me promise not to tell her. Eva believed he no longer loved her. A part of me will always regret keeping that promise. Things might have turned out differently if I hadn't. Anyway, Eva remained in Florida after finishing college, and went to work at Chenault Electronics. Glenn was discharged from the army and decided to go to medical school in Washington, D.C."

Aunt Callie released Shayla's hand and leaned back on the sofa. "While working at Chenault, your mother met Thomas Jordache. She was trying to get over Glenn. I don't know the specifics of their short affair. All I know is that she believed he was someone she could care about, and move on with her life with. Then one day she showed up unexpectedly at my apartment in Atlanta with her suitcases, saying she had been fired from her job. Glenn was in town attending a medical convention at Emory University, and was at my place when she arrived. Hurt and torn, Eva told us everything that had happened. She also told us that she'd found out a couple days earlier that she was pregnant. Glenn told her the truth about why he had broken things off between them, and convinced her to marry him. He promised to love Eva's child as his own. And as far as anyone knows, you're a child Glenn and Eva made together. The only ones who knew the truth were me, your mother, and Glenn."

Shayla nodded, knowing it would have been easy for everyone to assume that, since Glenn had married Eva during the very early stages of her pregnancy. "What happened after that? The last entry in Mama's diary was made the day she married my father."

There was a brief pause as Callie tried to gather her thoughts and her emotions. Everything she was telling Shayla had happened long ago, yet recalling those times made it seem just like yesterday. She looked up into Shayla's eyes and smiled. "What happened after that is that you were born, a beautiful little girl. Your arrival in the world made Glenn and Eva very happy."

Shayla nodded. Her parents had taken enough baby pictures of her to prove that. "Do you know if Thomas Jordache ever tried contacting Mom?"

Callie's eyes were somber when she said, "No, but he knew about her pregnancy. Eva said when she told him about it, he told her to get an abortion. As far as he knows, she did."

Shayla shuddered at the thought of all her mother had gone through.

"Knowing all of this, Shayla—especially how Chenault treated Eva when they thought she was passing classified information to Jordache, which she wasn't—how can you even think about going to work for them?"

"I'm doing it for revenge."

Aunt Callie looked at her for a moment, obviously trying to make sense of Shayla's statement. "What do you mean, revenge? That incident happened nearly twenty-seven years ago. Anyone who was working there at the time has retired by now. From what I understand, Alan Chenault, who was president at the time, is dead."

Shayla nodded. "Yes, he died three years ago. His son is running the company now."

"And you plan to make his son pay for something he probably knows nothing about, Shayla? Think about what you're doing."

"He still represents Chenault Electronics, and they humiliated Mama. She didn't deserve that. She'd been a loyal and dedicated employee, and in the end they chose to believe the worst about her. They didn't even listen to what she had to say in her own defense."

Callie Foster shook her head. "And I guess you plan to make Thomas Jordache pay, too?"

"Yes, that's part of my plan."

Callie took a deep breath, knowing Shayla wasn't thinking

straight. No doubt she was still in shock as a result of her mother's unexpected death two weeks ago in a car accident. She also knew that when Shayla made up her mind about something there was no changing it. Unfortunately, she had inherited a stubborn streak that could be a force to reckon with at times.

"Shayla, promise me you'll think about this, and not do anything foolish or vindictive that could get you into serious trouble. Please let what happened in the past stay in the past. Let it go, sweetheart."

"I can't do that. All the while I was reading Mom's diary I could feel her pain, her humiliation, and her frustration. I could feel her loss of pride and dignity at the hands of Chenault Electronics and Thomas Jordache. She didn't deserve what they did to her."

Callie captured her niece's hand in hers. "Be careful, Shayla. Sometimes revenge can be like a double-edged sword. You can taste a little of it yourself while you're trying to dish it out to someone else. I don't want you to be the one who gets hurt in the end."

Shayla met her aunt's worried stare. "I won't, Aunt Callie. I know what I'm doing."

Callie heard Shayla's words, but she was fearful that she really didn't.

"After reading Mom's diary I think she let Chenault Electronics off too easy."

Callie raised a brow. "What do you mean?"

Shayla released a long sigh. "I kept rereading the entry she made on the day she got fired. If I knew I was innocent of something I was accused of, I would stand my ground. There's no way I would have let them get rid of me without a fight on their hands."

Callie couldn't keep from smiling. Knowing Shayla and her stubbornness, she could see that happening. "Eva did speak up for herself, although I doubt she took it to the extremes that you would. She was a soft-spoken, easygoing person, Shayla. You know that. She never liked conflict of any kind. She was just that way. She was a peacemaker, and everyone loved her."

Shayla's smile was thoughtful, reflective, and filled with loving memories. "Yes, everyone did love her, didn't they?"

Callie shared Shayla's smile. "Yes, they did."

Chapter 3

Shayla sat cross-legged on her living room floor, mapping out in her daily planner all the things she needed to accomplish in the coming week. She was compulsive when it came to organization, and preferred doing things systematically by following a well-thought-out schedule. Although she could be flexible—if she had to be—she much preferred order to disorder, preparation to no preparation, and planning to last-minute decisions.

Those were the main reasons why at three o'clock Sunday afternoon, anticipating her first day on the job at Chenault Electronics on Monday, she was diligently planning the week ahead. No doubt her first week at work would be spent going through some sort of new employee orientation and a fast-paced management training program. However, the hours she spent away from work were her main concern at the moment. She needed to plan her meals for the week, get her clothes together, make a trip to the grocery store, squeeze in an appointment at the dentist, and arrange time for a repairman to come in and check out her washing machine. The spin cycle didn't seem to be working properly. Last, but definitely not least, she wanted to include spending time with Aunt Callie. They had decided to get together and enjoy dinner at some nice restaurant at least once a week.

Satisfied that she had covered all her bases for the week in an organized fashion, Shayla closed her planner. At that exact moment her phone rang. She reached over and grabbed it. "Hello."

"Ms. Kirkland?"

"Yes."

"This is Leanne Johnson, Mr. Chenault's secretary. I'm sorry to bother you at home, but Mr. Chenault asked me to call you to discuss your reporting to work tomorrow."

Shayla frowned. "Yes?"

"He apologizes for this last-minute change, but he's been called out of town on a very important business trip, and would like you to join him as soon as you can. He feels you can most definitely be useful to him right now."

Shayla's frown deepened. "I don't understand. Useful in what way? And where exactly am I supposed to join him?"

"China."

"China!" She thought she had misunderstood the woman.

Leanne Johnson's response assured her she hadn't. "Yes, China. There seems to be a glitch in some business negotiations, and he needs your help. Your résumé indicates you speak fluent Chinese."

"Yes. But what about my first day on the job tomorrow, here in Chicago?" *Whatever happened to new employees' orientation or management training!* She wanted to scream.

"Well, now it seems that your first day on the job will

be in Hong Kong. Mr. Chenault has been placed in a bind, and really needs your help with some very important negotiations." As if that explanation were enough, Leanne Johnson added, "I just got off the phone with the airlines. Your tickets are ready. I hope your passport's in order."

"Yes, it is, but this is totally unexpected," Shayla implored.

"I know, and Mr. Chenault apologizes for any inconvenience, but he hopes you'll come through and meet him there. A courier will deliver a package containing information about the Ling Deal to you before seven this evening. He wants you to study it and become familiar with it. May I relay a message back to Mr. Chenault that you'll be joining him?"

No, no, no! Shayla wanted to scream. What gave Nicholas Chenault the right to mess with her well-ordered life? Taking a deep breath, she forced herself to remember why she had sought employment with Chenault Electronics in the first place—revenge. A major part of dishing out that revenge was getting to know as much about the company as possible, and what better way than to have firsthand knowledge of Chenault's business dealings? She released a deep sigh. She wasn't crazy about the idea of going anywhere, especially out of the country, on such short notice. At the university where she had worked for the past two years, business trips were planned far in advance, especially those that took her out of the country. Evidently in the private sector things were different. They were fast-paced, competitive, and last-minute.

"Yes, tell Mr. Chenault I will be joining him there."

"Thank you, Ms. Kirkland, and I hope you have a nice week."

After hanging up the phone Shayla looked down at the planner in her lap. All her well-thought-out plans for the week had just been cancelled—big-time.

* * *

Shayla had not given much thought to the mistake she might be making by going to Hong Kong until she began packing later that night.

After her conversation with Ms. Johnson, she had immediately called her aunt. Callie owned one of the most exclusive clothing stores in Chicago, and she was a lifesaver, helping Shayla get ready for her trip, opening the store that evening just for her. Shayla had met her aunt at Callie's Fashions and shopped to her heart's content.

Now they were in her bedroom, while Shayla packed.

"Are you sure you're doing the right thing, Shayla?" Her aunt's question interrupted Shayla's thought. She decided not to tell her that she was beginning to have second thoughts. Instead she said, "Yes. I have to do this, Aunt Callie. I know you don't understand, and I respect that, but there's no way I can let Chenault Electronics or TJ Electronics get away with what they did to Mama."

"Things worked out fine in the end for Eva. If you ask me, they did her a favor. If things hadn't turned out the way they did, she would never have married Glenn. Have you thought of that?"

Shayla nodded. Yes, she had. But still, their treatment of her mother was inexcusable, unforgivable.

"Tell me about Nicholas Chenault," Callie said quietly.

Shayla continued packing, hoping her aunt would not notice the tint that colored her face. For some reason just the thought of Nicholas Chenault did that to her, and that wasn't good. "What do you want to know?"

"Well, is he good-looking?"

Shayla turned to her aunt. The eyes that met hers were filled with curiosity, knowledge, and understanding—a woman's understanding.

"Yes, he's good-looking."

There was a moment of silence before her aunt spoke

again. Her voice was thick with caution. "Shayla, don't go," she pleaded in a soft voice. "I don't think you understand what you might be getting yourself into. A week in Hong Kong alone with Nicholas Chenault may not be such a good idea."

Shayla turned back around and pretended to be totally absorbed in her packing. "It's just a business trip, Aunt Callie, nothing more."

"Yes, sweetheart, but even things of the most innocent nature usually start off that way."

Shayla chuckled to shake off her feelings of uncertainty. "I know all about the birds and the bees."

Callie caught Shayla's wrist before she could place another piece of clothing in her luggage. "I'm not talking about the birds and the bees, Shayla. I'm talking about your heart."

"My heart?" Shayla asked, frowning.

"Yes, I'm talking about your heart, and the risk of losing it. Don't you see?"

Shayla really didn't see at all. She couldn't help wondering what her heart had to do with anything. Over the years she'd had her share of dates, but none had ever come close to having any effect on her heart. She'd decided long ago to hold out for that special kind of love her parents had shared, and would not settle for anything less. She'd always known her parents had a close relationship. Now, after reading her mother's diary and having her long talk with her aunt, she understood why. In everything they'd done, love had governed their actions. Despite all their trials and tribulations, things had worked out for them in the end. It had been meant for them to be together. Even when Glenn had been robbed of the ability to father a child, a twist of fate had given him her. He had loved her and accepted her as if she'd come from his own seed. Not once had he held her mother's brief affair with Thomas Jordache against her. Love that pure and that true was hard to find with a man.

Shayla glanced down at the hand that was holding her wrist gently. They were the hands that had often braided her hair when she was a little girl. They were hands that had wiped away tears from her eyes when she'd discovered that a boy she had a teenage crush on was more interested in her best girlfriend than in her. They were the hands that had comforted her when she'd lost her father, and most recently they were hands that had held hers throughout her mother's funeral services. They were loving hands, caring hands.

Shayla didn't want her aunt to worry about her. She reached out and hugged her. She had always been there for her, and always would be. "Trust me, Aunt Callie, my heart wili have nothing to do with it. Although Nicholas Chenault's not directly to blame, it was his father's decision to fire Mama without taking into consideration that she might have been innocent. I won't be able to overlook that."

"But still, sweetheart, you may not know all the facts. Eva's involvement with Thomas Jordache may have been guilt enough in Chenault Electronics' eyes. He was their biggest competitor back then. Besides, you don't know how thick Thomas Jordache's web of deceit and lies was."

"Pretty thick, if you ask me," Shayla said with all the venom in her voice that she actually felt for the man who had fathered her. His day was coming, as well. His downfall would be even greater than Chenault's.

"Shayla, since you're intent on going, promise me you'll be careful."

Shayla nodded. "I promise."

The long flight from Chicago to Hong Kong was a rather relaxing one, Shayla thought. She had used that time to read the report she had received about the Ling Deal, taking naps in between. Although Nicholas Chenault was her enemy, she had to hand it to him for his expertise in negotiating a deal. From the one hundred plus pages she had read, what he was offering the Chinese government was a win-win situation. It would be a tremendous win for the people of China, as well as a financial win for Chenault. She wondered what had been the last-minute glitch.

She rested her head against her seat. Nicholas had some financial heavy hitters backing him on the deal. She had recognized some of the names immediately. There was Kyle Garwood of Garwood Industries, Jake Madaris, a wealthy rancher from Texas who had recently announced his marriage to movie star Diamond Swain, and Nicholas's half brother Sterling Hamilton, the superstar movie actor.

Shayla closed her eyes and hoped and prayed that she could handle being around Nicholas Chenault for a week. Whenever she felt herself weakening, she would remember what her mother had gone through. Doing that would guarantee she would be able to keep him at a distance.

A very safe distance.

Nicholas had been waiting for his gut to settle down ever since his secretary had called to confirm that Shayla Kirkland would be joining him in Hong Kong. He didn't understand why his stomach was tied in knots—she was just a woman.

Yeah, right. But when was the last time he had actually let a woman invade his dreams? In his dreams he had kissed her, tasted her lips and other areas of her body, as well. The perfume she had worn the day of the interview had been seductive, overpowering, captivating. He wondered if she would be wearing that particular fragrance again. If she did, he didn't know how he would handle it.

Pull yourself together, Chenault, he thought. *Your thoughts are bound to get you in trouble. Trouble you don't need.* Still, he couldn't help remembering everything about Shayla Kirkland, and it had been almost two weeks since he had seen her.

He nervously glanced down at his watch. Her flight from the States should be arriving at the Hong Kong International Airport about now. He had sent a limo to pick her up and deliver her to the Conrad International Hotel, where he had reserved an entire executive floor. He needed space for his fax machine and computer set-up, and two private meeting rooms where he would hold his business meetings. There would be three suites on the floor—one for him, one for Shayla, and one for Paul when he arrived at the end of the week. As with any big business deal, security measures had to be taken, and that required Paul's expertise.

Nicholas walked over to the minibar in his room and poured a cup of percolated coffee. He wanted something stronger, but always made it a rule never to drink before noon. A few minutes later, after determining he still had too much nervous energy and the coffee was only adding to it, he decided to go to the health club and endure an extensive workout. A good hour of physical exertion should eradicate Shayla Kirkland from his mind for a while. At least, he hoped that it would.

Chapter 4

The Conrad International Hotel was known to be one of the most luxurious in China, and Shayla could see why. It was evident that it was designed for both the business and leisure traveler. All the hotel's guest rooms had sweeping views of the Hong Kong harbor, Victoria Peak, and the city's skyline.

The panoramic view outside her window was nothing short of majestic. Shayla had been surprised to discover she was housed on the executive floor and that her suite was across the hall from Nicholas's. In fact, the only three suites on the floor shared a huge lobby that also served as a sitting area. She fell in love with an oversize bathroom tub that just seemed to be calling her name.

She decided to take a long leisurely bath and relax. She doubted Mr. Chenault would need her services today. Surely he would have pity on her and give her this day to rest and recover from jet lag. *Maybe not,* she thought when the phone rang.

Walking across the room, she picked it up. "Yes?"

"How was your flight, Ms. Kirkland?"

Shayla's heart thudded in her chest. Nicholas's voice was deep and husky. Against her will she remembered his features, seeing them clearly in her mind, especially his gold eyes. She tightened her hold on the phone, knowing she had to get a grip. "My flight, Mr. Chenault, was nice, although it was rather long. Luckily I had some interesting reading material to pass the time."

"The report on the Ling Deal?"

"Yes."

She heard his soft chuckle. "Not what you'd preferred to read, I'd imagine."

Shayla couldn't keep from smiling. "No. Not even close."

"I see. But you did complete it?"

"Yes."

"Good. We have a meeting with the Hong Kong people first thing in the morning. The meeting room is on this floor."

Shayla nodded. "Is there anything else I need to know?"

"Yes, and I'd like to go over those things with you. How about if we get together for a business dinner tonight?"

Shayla was quick to pick up on the fact that he'd made it clear that it would be nothing more than a business dinner. "All right. There are a few things I need clarification on."

"Will seven o'clock be a good time for you?"

"That's fine. Should I meet you downstairs?"

"No, I'm right across the hall. I'll walk over and escort you down."

"All right."

"I'll see you then, Ms. Kirkland."

Shayla wanted to check her appearance one more time before Nicholas Chenault arrived. The dress she had chosen to wear had been deemed a "must buy" by her aunt. Even with the generous discount she had received, it had cost plenty. But then, she thought as she looked in the mirror and saw how the soft material fit her body, it had been well worth every cent she had paid for it. In fact, Aunt Callie had made sure everything she had brought along with her was first class.

Because her aunt had always owned a clothing store, Shayla had been blessed to grow up having nice clothes. She had been the envy of most of the girls in high school and college with her stylish, chic, and sometimes expensive wardrobe.

She glanced back at her reflection in the full-length mirror, hoping the dress was not too sophisticated for a business dinner. Deciding that it wasn't, she turned away from the mirror. At the same time, there was a knock on her door. She smiled. Nicholas Chenault evidently believed in being on time. Good planning.

Seeing no reason to invite him into her hotel room, Shayla grabbed her purse and the envelope containing the Ling report from the table and walked over to the door. She took a deep breath before she opened it.

The deep breath got caught in her throat. Nicholas Chenault stood before her, displaying everything that was male. He was dressed in a gray suit, every part of him sensuous and sexy. His eyes appeared to be a liquid gold, and held hers within their depths. Then his gaze began moving over her slowly, beginning at the crown of her head and ending at the tips of her shoes. His eyes captured hers again, trapping her gaze. The huge lobby outside her door seemed to shrink before her eyes as the image of him became larger, almost bigger than life. She tried suppressing the hot sensations that shot through her body, frazzling her nerves and playing havoc with her mind.

She forced herself to breathe, then breathe again, when

she realized that the attraction was mutual. The look he was giving her said as much. The sensuous vibes flowing between them were thick as deep fog.

Although she wasn't overjoyed about the sexual tension radiating between them, she wasn't put off by it, either. After all, business or no business, he was man and she was woman…and certain things were just unavoidable. Physical attraction between the opposite sexes was one of them. However, it could be controlled, which was what she intended to do.

She watched as Nicholas Chenault's mouth tightened. Evidently he wasn't overjoyed with the prospect of being attracted to her any more than she was about being attracted to him. Then she noticed a sudden softening of his mouth, and decided he'd reached the same conclusion that she had. This attraction between them could be, and would be, controlled. They were professionals. This was a professional evening, and they would handle it as such. She had a very strong idea that he had no more intention of getting caught up in a personal involvement with her than she with him. He was her boss and she was his employee, and while they worked together they would handle themselves accordingly.

They both relaxed somewhat. Without saying a word they'd somehow reached an understanding.

She decided to be the one to break the tense silence. "Mr. Chenault, I'm ready."

He straightened and stepped back when she walked out of her room and closed the door behind her. "You look nice, Ms. Kirkland."

"Thank you." She couldn't help but note how close he was as they walked together to the elevator. The heat between them still simmered. When they entered the empty compartment and the doors shut behind them with finality, every muscle in her body was on edge. So much for thinking she'd be able to relax around him now that an understanding had been reached.

"Did you take a nap?"

Shayla blinked a couple of times before Nicholas's question registered in her hazed mind. "Yes."

"Good. It helps with jet lag."

It was on the tip of her tongue to tell him that jet lag was the least of her problems. They continued their ride down to the eighth floor, where the restaurant was located. When the elevator stopped and the doors opened, they stepped out quickly, needing to be out in the open and around others; needing to breathe again and get their minds back on track.

"This way," Nicholas whispered close to her ear as he captured her elbow in his hand. His touch sent sparks flying all the way from Shayla's head to her toes. She wondered if he had felt them. Taking a quick glance up at his face, she saw his mouth had tightened. It was a dead giveaway that he had.

They kept walking, ignoring passersby's whispered comments that the two of them made such a striking couple. Some of the comments were spoken in Chinese, and Shayla hoped Nicholas had not understood them.

They finally reached the entrance to the elegant restaurant. As they stood together and waited for the host to seat them, Nicholas leaned over and whispered, "I hope you like Chinese food." A smile tilted his lips.

Shayla couldn't help returning his smile—it seemed to be contagious. "There's a Chinese proverb, Mr. Chenault, that says, 'Food is heaven—especially when it's Chinese,'" she whispered back to him.

His smile widened. And so did hers.

Nicholas knew he was in trouble as they followed the host to their table. Shayla was wearing "that" perfume again, and the scent of it was driving him insane. It was the same scent she'd worn the day of the interview—sultry, seductive. It was meant to captivate, dazzle, bewitch. It was working on him full force.

He took a deep breath when he pulled the chair out for her, inhaling deeply and forcing his mind and his body to get a grip. He could hardly think standing this close to her. He quickly stepped back and took his own seat.

"So, you like Chinese food?" he asked for lack of anything else to say.

"Yes." Then, leaning over the table toward him so as not to offend their host, who was busy opening their menus, she whispered in a serious tone, "But I like Japanese food just as much."

Nicholas could not stop the deep chuckle that escaped his lips. He'd been right. Shayla Kirkland had an amazing personality. He waited until the host had left after pouring their wine before saying, "I must personally apologize for whisking you away from Chicago on such short notice. I do appreciate your coming. Your help with the negotiations will definitely be needed."

Shayla raised a curious brow. "Why is that? I thought this was basically a done deal, with only a few loose ends to tie up. The report I read on the plane alluded to that."

Nicholas smiled. "We're hoping that's true. But as a businessman I've learned to always look for surprises in the last stages of negotiations. One of the men who'll be at tomorrow's meeting has never attended any of the others. It's my understanding he's a smooth Chinese businessman, and someone I need to watch out for. I also understand he doesn't care much for doing business with Americans."

Nicholas sat back in his chair. "That's enough discussion of business for now. We'll resume that after we've ordered dinner. Can you suggest something for me to try?"

During dinner the conversation between Shayla and

Nicholas centered more on the professional than the personal, and the mood was comfortable.

"I hope this last-minute trip to China didn't upset your significant other," Nicholas said smoothly, taking a sip of wine. He was abruptly shifting the subject matter, and they both knew it.

Shayla lowered her lashes, attempting to hide her surprise. Up until that moment, he hadn't inquired about anything having to do with her personal life. She lifted her gaze to meet his. "I don't have a significant other, unless you want to count my Aunt Callie, who's my mom's younger sister. She's all the family I have, and the only person who's important to me."

Talking about family reminded Shayla of the reason she was involved with Chenault Electronics in the first place. Deciding to shift the topic of conversation back to business, she said, "So, what do you think our chances are of the Ling Deal being closed tomorrow?"

Shayla stepped into the huge bathtub, submerging herself in the hot bubbly water. The heat felt nice, and the bubbles smelled good. She leaned against the back of the tub and closed her eyes, remembering how well the night had gone. Except for the time Mr. Chenault had asked her about a significant other, the conversation had remained strictly business.

But still, that hadn't stopped her from appreciating his good looks. It had been hard sitting across from him feigning absolute nonchalance when she'd been attuned to every aspect of him. Everything about him had been sensuous: the way he drank his wine, the way he ate his food, even the way he held his eating utensils. But nothing was more sensuous than the way he lifted his eyebrow when he didn't quite understand something. His lifting that brow did things to her insides. It had been so hard for her to keep a firm grasp on her impulses.

She had to hand it to both of them. They had handled things extremely well when they read a fortune cookie message that said, *"Your destinies will be entwined from this moment on."* They'd shrugged it off without making any comment about it. Later when he had escorted her back to her room, he had remained professional and businesslike. He had turned and quickly walked across the huge lobby to his suite.

But now, back in the privacy of her own suite, in the intimacy of her bathroom, Shayla wanted to indulge a little in fantasy, knowing nothing would ever come of it. That would make it easier to get down to business tomorrow. She needed to get thoughts of him out of her system. The information he had divulged at dinner about the Ling Deal indicated that he had put a lot of his company's funds into it, not to mention those of his financial backers. His hopes were high about this deal going through. Setting the Ling Deal into motion had connections to another project he had in the works, a project he'd avoided discussing with her. She couldn't help but wonder what it was. But still, without knowing it, Nicholas Chenault had placed in her hands a way to destroy him financially. And she could do so as soon as tomorrow. She could effortlessly ruin things for him at that business meeting in the morning.

But she didn't want to think about that. She wanted to fantasize. For just a few exhilarating moments, she wanted to pretend he was not her enemy, that he was her lover—a lover like no other, which wouldn't be hard to imagine since she'd never had a lover. For just a few moments, she wanted to wonder how things could be with him.

Closing her eyes, she could imagine his long experienced fingers caressing their way from the peaks of her breasts to the heels of her feet, making her whimper—a little like she was doing now, just thinking about it. She could imagine the feel of his kiss, hot and moist as it captured her mouth with frantic hunger—a hunger that she reciprocated.

Shayla opened her eyes. Fantasizing about the enemy was a lot less harmful than sleeping with the enemy, which was something she would never do. She was on a mission, and because of it Nicholas Chenault would suffer.

When she got out of the tub and began toweling dry her body, she did not feel good about that thought.

Nicholas couldn't get Shayla out of his mind. *Unbelievable,* he thought.

He had spent practically the entire evening with her discussing the Ling Deal, yet he'd hungered for her as he sat across from her, soaking in her beauty, inhaling her scent. He wasn't sure how he had managed to last through their meal. Never in his thirty-two years had he wanted a woman so much.

The last thing he needed was a distraction from the business at hand. At tomorrow's meeting he had to stay focused. There was more than just his money at stake. Three men he admired and respected were counting on him. They had combined their monies with his because they had faith that he could make it work. They believed in the mangolid chip that his company had developed as much as he did. Closing the Ling Deal was just one part—a very major part—of the big picture.

As Nicholas prepared for his shower, he knew he had to do whatever it would take to put Shayla Kirkland out of his mind.

Chapter 5

The following morning Nicholas discovered that putting Shayla out of his mind wouldn't be easy. The woman had too much of a sensuous draw about her. He wasn't the only one to pick up on it. When she walked into the meeting room, looking completely businesslike and professional, every man took notice. Her presence demanded their attention.

Paul had arrived very late the night before. Standing beside Nicholas, he whispered, "I can see why temptation was nipping fast and furious at your heels. She's a good-looking woman."

Nicholas frowned. For some reason he did not like nor appreciate the male attention being lavished on Shayla. "Let's get this meeting underway," he grumbled, ignoring Paul's soft chuckle.

"Feeling the sharp bite of primitive male possessiveness, Nick?"

The look Nicholas shot at Paul spoke volumes. He then

shifted his attention from the older man back to Shayla. As efficient as she was beautiful, she had not waited for him to make introductions. A born diplomat, she was making her way around the room, speaking in fluent Chinese and conducting herself with culturally acceptable decorum. It was easy to see that the businessmen were just eating it up.

"Didn't I tell you she'd be an asset to us?" Paul asked, smiling. "Look how easily she's working that group."

Nicholas nodded. They both knew that it was expected for Westerners doing business in China to have a mastery of the given language. Although Nicholas's knowledge of the language was limited to a few words, Shayla, who was representing his company, was laying it on very smoothly with her vast knowledge of it.

He also observed her exchanging business cards with each man present. He knew from past experience that in China the exchanging of business cards was like shaking hands. It was part of the business etiquette. He had forgotten that major detail, and wondered where Shayla had gotten the cards. His company had not yet printed any for her.

By the time Shayla had made it over to where he and Paul stood, Nicholas was completely overwhelmed with her, as the others were. "Ms. Kirkland, I'd like you to meet Paul Dunlap, head of security at Chenault."

Shayla's gaze quickly left Nicholas and looked into the eyes of the tall handsome man standing beside him. She remembered the name from her mother's diary. He had been the security person to uncover Thomas Jordache's plot, and had brought it to the attention of Alan Chenault, resulting in her mother's firing. Knowing what she knew about the man, Shayla forced herself to offer her hand to him and pasted a smile on her lips. "Mr. Dunlap."

Paul took the hand in his. "Ms. Kirkland, welcome to Chenault Electronics." With his observant gaze, he studied her. "You look somewhat familiar. Have we met before?" he asked, releasing her hand.

Shayla quenched the panic that rose inside her. She hoped there was nothing about her that reminded him of her mother. Surely he couldn't remember that far back. "No, Mr. Dunlap, I don't think we have," she heard herself saying. "Unless we saw each other when I came in for my interview. Perhaps it was then."

Paul nodded as he continued to study her. "Perhaps."

Not wanting to give the man time to dwell on it, she said to Nicholas, "Everyone is ready to begin. How do you want the seating arranged?"

"Whichever way is comfortable for them."

Shayla nodded, agreeing with Nicholas's decision. Often, Chinese people saw Westerners' quick decisions as signs of suspicious behavior. It was imperative to be patient in any business negotiations with them. "I think that all of us sitting around the table will work out fine. Paul needs to sit on your left side, and I'll sit on your right."

Nicholas nodded, deciding not to ask why she'd suggested such an arrangement. He did want to ask her one thing before they began. "The business cards. Where did you get them?"

"After I went to bed I thought about the importance of having them. I got back up and used the computer in the office next to my suite to make them. I hope you don't mind."

"No, I'm very glad you thought of it. We don't need to get things off on the wrong foot." He glanced across the room at a Chinese gentleman standing alone near the window. "I take it you've met Mr. Ho Chin."

Shayla nodded. "Yes."

"We need to be cautious around him. He's the one I was talking about last night. The one who could sway the negotiations another way."

Shayla nodded again. She almost wanted to tell Nicholas

that Mr. Ho Chin was not the only one who could sway the negotiations. She had the ammunition to destroy him herself, and that was her intent.

"If you're ready, Mr. Chenault, we can get things started."

"I'm ready."

Shayla walked off to deliver that statement to each man in the room.

"There's something about her that's familiar," Paul said to Nicholas as they moved forward to sit around the table.

Nicholas raised a brow. "Perhaps you saw her photo in her personnel file. I'm sure one was there when your department did their background check."

Paul nodded, his gaze still on Shayla. "Perhaps."

When the golden opportunity presented itself for Shayla to ruin Chenault Electronics, she discovered she couldn't do it.

Negotiations were tense, and had been all morning. They were going into their fifth hour, and what had seemed like a done deal earlier was anything but that now. All because of Mr. Ho Chin. There was something about him that Shayla didn't like, and she found herself wanting the deal to go through just so Nicholas could best the man. His arguments were nothing more than stalling tactics, and everyone in the room knew it. Up until this hour, the other Chinese businessmen in the room were still leaning toward closing the deal, but now things didn't look quite that way. Mr. Ho Chin was trying to discredit Nicholas in the only way he knew, and that was to question his sincerity in doing business with their country.

Shayla shook her head. None of this made any sense. True, the Ling Deal would be good for Nicholas's company, but it would also be good for the Chinese people. Ever since the sovereignty of Hong Kong had reverted back to

China, the people of the Republic were trying to catch up in ways of advanced technology, and were doing an astounding job of it. What Nicholas was proposing in his plan was to put them on top, escalating them to a higher playing field than even Japan.

"May I try something, Mr. Chenault?" Shayla whispered, when it appeared the talks were momentarily at a stalemate.

"Anything is better than nothing," Nicholas grumbled softly for her and Paul's ears only.

Nodding, Shayla began speaking fluent Chinese, addressing her words to the men sitting across from them. They fully understood what she was saying, if their expressions were any indication. Nicholas frowned, wondering what she was saying to them. Whatever it was had their rapt attention. And whatever it was made Mr. Ho Chin not a happy camper. He suddenly spoke up in a loud voice, and Nicholas could tell he was angry about whatever Shayla was saying.

Keeping her voice soft and even, Shayla acknowledged Mr. Ho Chin's comments before turning to address the entire group again. After a few minutes, one of the other Chinese gentlemen began speaking. Shayla nodded, smiling. She glanced over at Nicholas and smiled again. Then she gave a reply to the man.

"What in the world's going on?" Paul had leaned over and whispered the question to Nicholas. "What's she saying to them?"

Nicholas shrugged. "I have no idea. She could be giving away the company, for all I know."

"Aren't you going to stop her?"

"No, I'm going to follow my gut instincts and trust her."

Paul lifted a brow. That might be Nick's inclination, but it sure wasn't his. Although he had pushed for her hiring, she had not worked for the company long enough to develop any sense of loyalty. This was just her second day on the job.

A part of Nicholas, the one ruled strictly by business sense, knew he should try to figure out, as best he could, just what Shayla was saying. But he was too caught up in listening to the sound of her voice as she spoke to the men. He doubted she realized it but her voice sounded soft, husky, and sexy. She might not be aware of it, but every man in the room was.

When the Chinese gentlemen at the table all nodded their heads except for Ho Chin, Nicholas knew he *had* to know what was going on. Before he could ask, Shayla turned to him. "All right, it's over."

Nicholas frowned, clearly not understanding. "What's over?"

Knowing that a few of the men in the room, Mr. Ho Chin especially, could understand the English language, Shayla chose her words carefully. "The negotiations. Everyone is ready to sign."

Nicholas felt his head spinning. "To close the deal?" he asked, incredulous.

"Yes."

He shook his head, clearly dazed. "But how? Why? What did you say to get them to change their minds?"

Shayla reached across the table and captured Nicholas's hand in hers. To everyone observing, it was definitely not a businesslike gesture. Nicholas lifted his eyebrows, wondering what she was doing. Instead of pulling his hand back, as he had an inclination to do, he decided to let it stay put. According to her earlier announcement, the deal was about to be closed. Somehow she had placed the ball back in their court, so he was willing to let her continue to play it as she saw fit.

"I explained things to them, Nicholas," she said softly, meeting his eyes.

"What things?" Nicholas asked, still not comprehending.

The look in her eyes pleaded with him to pretend that he did, and he hadn't missed her calling him by his first name.

"I explained why you had turned down Mr. Ming's invitation to the dinner party Friday night."

Nicholas lifted another brow. He knew why he had turned down the man's invitation to dinner—he intended to be on a plane headed back to the States on Friday. "Really? And just what did you explain to them?"

"I explained that you and I had made personal plans, and that you thought you would be disappointing me if you were to break them. However, in light of everything, I assured Mr. Ming that we would be honored to change our plans and attend the dinner party at his home."

She smiled tentatively at him, staring into his eyes. "Trust me on this one, sweetheart."

Nicholas blinked at her term of endearment. He then met her stare head-on. "I am, *darling*."

As if grateful for that, Shayla released his hand and turned her attention back to the gentlemen and gave them a smile that made all of them blush, except Mr. Ho Chin. She then placed the documents to be signed in front of them. Each of them signed, even Mr. Ho Chin, although he did it grudgingly. Nicholas was more than anxious to put his own signature on the paper.

With the business concluded, the men stood and walked out, leaving only Shayla, Nicholas, and Paul in the room. When Nicholas was sure the gentlemen were inside the closed elevator and couldn't possibly hear a thing, he turned to Shayla. "What the hell was that about?"

Shayla let out a deep sigh as she began gathering up the papers from the table. "That, Mr. Chenault, was about saving face. When Mr. Ming invited you to a dinner party at his home Friday night, you turned him down, not realizing the repercussions."

Nicholas frowned. Before he could ask the question, Paul did. "What's wrong with not going to the man's house for dinner?"

Shayla met Paul's inquisitive gaze. "Everything. In China, an individual's reputation and social standing are based on the complex concept of saving face. By turning down a dinner invitation to a Chinese associate's home, you can cause that individual to lose face simply because you're not available, or evidently think he's not important enough for you to make yourself available. To save face for him, as well as for yourself, if you can't accept the invitation you must apologize for not being able to do so, then propose an alternative plan that is palatable to the person who extended the invitation. Although you apologized for not being able to attend the function, you did not offer an alternative solution."

Nicholas shrugged. "I didn't know."

"Evidently you didn't, and your lack of knowledge was what Mr. Ho Chin was using to get the others to back out of the deal. He was trying to make it seem that you had intentionally delivered Mr. Ming an insult. He was carrying it a little bit further, too, by claiming you had no knowledge of their culture, and it would not be wise to do business with your company."

"So what did you tell them?" Nicholas asked quietly, trying to absorb it all.

"When I saw what Mr. Ho Chin was trying to do, I simply explained to the other men that you and I had recently gotten engaged, and that you wanted to get back to the States to look for a ring. That way I made them think that love had caused your thoughtlessness, not intentional rudeness."

Nicholas looked at her for the longest time, not saying anything. Paul, he noticed, had covered his mouth to smother his laughter. "Let me get this straight. You told them you and I are engaged? To be married?"

Shayla shifted uncomfortably from one foot to the other under Nicholas's intense stare. "Yes. I had no choice. I could have told them you were in a hurry to get to some other woman back in the States, but that would not have soothed them. They had met me and were impressed with my command of their language and customs and culture. They figured that as your future wife, I would make up for what you lack. And when I told them we would change our plans and attend the dinner party, that clinched things and took the wind out of Mr. Ho Chin's sails. Without any other argument, he had to go along with everyone and sign the papers."

"You seem to have understood the situation well," Paul said, clearly impressed.

"I did. Believe it or not, most Asians credit blacks with understanding their culture better than whites, especially in the field of literature. They feel we're quicker to understand and appreciate the value of their writing, and take it more seriously. Howard University has a history of publishing books by Asian-American authors."

Both Nicholas and Paul nodded at what Shayla had told them. After taking it all in, Nicholas couldn't keep from beaming. He was more than happy that the Ling Deal was closed, and was extremely happy that Shayla's ingenious thinking had pushed things through.

"I'm curious as to what they'll think when the two of you don't get married," Paul said, still clearly amused.

Shayla met Paul's grin. "They'll think nothing of it. They're aware that Americans break engagements all the time."

She then turned her attention back to Nicholas. "I hope your remaining in this country for another day won't pose a problem for you, Mr. Chenault—or for your significant other back in the States."

Nicholas raised an eyebrow as he looked at Shayla, remembering he'd posed the same question to her last night at dinner. He drew in a shuddering breath when her questioning eyes met his. His lips tilted into a smile, and she felt the intensity of his gaze. “I don’t have a significant other back in the States, Shayla. But it seems I do have a fiancée while I’m here in China, doesn’t it?”

Chapter 6

Nicholas declared that Chenault Electronics had cause to celebrate, and invited Shayla and Paul to dine with him.

Shayla made an excuse as to why she couldn't go. The last thing she wanted was to be in Paul Dunlap's company for any long period of time. The man was too observant for her peace of mind. Besides, she needed to think things through, to understand why she had intentionally blown her golden opportunity to ruin Chenault Electronics.

"You have to come, Ms. Kirkland. What if I run into any of those gentlemen again? What will I tell them if they inquire about my *fiancée?*" Nicholas asked, a teasing grin touching his lips.

"Tell them I had a headache and decided to go to bed early."

Nicholas's smile immediately vanished. "Are you not feeling well?"

Shayla shook her head. "I'm just extremely tired. It's been a long and tense day. If the two of you don't mind, I prefer to go back to my room and order room service."

Nicholas nodded, concerned. "Is there anything I can get for you before Paul and I go out?"

"No, I'll be fine. I hope you enjoy your evening." With that said, she gathered her purse and walked out of the meeting room.

After taking a nap Shayla felt somewhat better, but the feeling that she had let her mother down by not keeping her promise weighed heavily on her. Feeling the need to talk to someone, she placed a long-distance call to her aunt.

"Aunt Callie, I failed. I had the chance to do it, and didn't."

"Oh, sweetheart, I'm glad you didn't."

"But I still want to. I owe it to Mama. I feel I let her down by not taking the opportunity I had."

"Now you listen to me, Shayla Glenn Kirkland. Don't you dare try convincing yourself that Eva would want you to embark on this madness. Your mother was a loving and forgiving woman. I refuse to believe that sometime in her life she didn't forgive everyone involved with what happened to her back then. She and Glenn loved you very much, and no matter what, they'll always be proud of you. They wouldn't want you involved with what you're intent on doing to Chenault and TJ Electronics. Take my advice and catch the next plane back to the States."

Shayla wiped the tears from her eyes. "I can't. I have to stay here for the party on Friday. They think Nicholas and I are engaged."

"What are you talking about, Shayla? Who thinks that?"

Shayla took a long shaky breath. "It's a long story, and I can't explain it right now, but we'll talk when I get back."

"And when will that be?"

"Nicholas and I'll be flying out late Saturday or early Sunday."

"Shayla, sweetheart, get out of this mess while you can, before you get hurt."

Shayla glanced up at her reflection in the mirror above the desk where she sat. Her hair looked a mess, and her eyes were slightly swollen from crying. "I'm fine, really I am. I just needed to talk. But, Aunt Callie, nothing's changed. There'll be another opportunity."

"Shayla, listen to—"

"Goodbye, Aunt Callie. I love you." Shayla hung up. She knew her aunt didn't understand, but then, she had not been the one to read her mother's diary. She had not been the one to feel her pain.

Shayla stood and was about to run the water for her bath when there was a knock on the door. She walked over and looked through the peephole. It was Nicholas, and he was dressed to go out for the evening. She was not ready to see him right then, and decided not to answer the door. If she didn't answer, he would assume she was asleep. She backed away from the door when he knocked again. After a few moments, the knocking stopped, and she knew he had gone away.

Going into the bathroom she began running water for her bath. After adding a generous amount of bubble bath, she began removing her clothes. Knowing there wouldn't be any fantasies of Nicholas awaiting her in the tub, as there had been last night, she stepped into the hot bubbly water and sat down. Leaning against the back of the tub, she closed her eyes. As she'd told her aunt, she would have another opportunity to ruin Chenault. The next time, she would not be such a weakling.

When Nicholas returned from dinner with Paul, he looked across the lobby at Shayla's door, wondering if she was feeling better. Knowing it was too late to check on her, he entered his own room. Although he hated admitting it, he had missed her at dinner. Last night he had greatly enjoyed her company. She had looked so beautiful sitting across from him at the dinner table. And then today, when she had walked into the meeting room, all gazes had turned her way. He had been just as spellbound as the other men in the room. With her striking beauty, he was beginning to accept she had that effect on most men. And he had to grudgingly admit that she was the first woman who'd had that sort of effect on him. It seemed Shayla Kirkland was a first for him in a lot of ways. Paul had been right. He had felt a moment of primitive male possessiveness, and had not liked the idea of other men finding her as desirable as he did.

He began preparing for his bath, adjusting the water temperature. He removed his clothes while the tub began filling nicely with warm water. He felt good about what had transpired today. Finalizing that deal would keep Chenault Electronics on top, and would assure that the dynamics were in place when he revolutionized the mangolid chip.

Stepping into the tub, he lowered his body into the water and leaned back against it. Because of his height, he was grateful that the huge tub provided more leg room than most. He closed his eyes, and an image of Shayla immediately formed in his mind. He saw her as he wanted to see her—in his bed, without any clothes, in his arms, with the hardness of him inside of her, while she shuddered with the force of her climax, triggering his own.

Nicholas knew it was too dangerous to have such thoughts of a woman he barely knew. He tried switching his thoughts elsewhere, deciding that as soon as his bath was over he would place a call to Sterling, Jake, and Kyle. As his financial backers, the three men would want to have their own celebration, and no doubt they would do so with the women in their lives.

Nicholas wondered how his niece was doing. She was only a little over a month old, but she ruled the Hamilton household. Sterling and his wife, Colby, were overjoyed with their daughter. A part of him envied their happiness. Just being around them made him want to believe in the power of true love. He hoped to find a woman who would be his soul mate, who would give him children to continue the Chenault dynasty, but he was in no hurry for that to happen. He could very well sit tight and not become a family man for another five to six years, maybe more. When he was ready to become a father, he hoped that he and his wife would have at least two. He had been Alan and Angeline Chenault's only child, and he'd missed not having a sibling while growing up. He had not found out about Sterling until he was thirty. Since then he and his brother had made up for lost time, and were forging a very special and solid relationship. Sterling, Colby, and his niece, Chandler, were a few of the people whom he allowed to invade his space.

Nicholas tried clearing his mind of thought. He just wanted to relax in the tub with his eyes closed and think about nothing or no one in particular.

After a few minutes he gave up trying.

It seemed there was one person whom he could not stop thinking about no matter how much he tried.

Shayla.

Paul Dunlap tried to keep his concentration on the television screen, and it wasn't working. For some reason, he could not get Shayla Kirkland out of his mind. There was something disturbing about her, and it had started the moment she had been introduced to him.

Although she had taken his hand in a firm handshake, she had paused for a quick second. The hesitation had been so fleeting he doubted Nicholas had noticed it, but he sure had, and it had thrown him. Why would someone who was meeting him for the first time feel…what? Intimidation? Wariness? Anger? Immediate dislike? Then there had been her smile. He had picked up on the effort she had put behind it, and the sudden stiffness of her posture and the cutting edge of her gaze when Nicholas had said his name.

Why?

He shook his head. Although there was something about her that looked familiar, he was certain they had never met before. And that was really confusing him.

Paul couldn't help the rueful smile that suddenly touched his lips. One thing was for certain—she was doing a lot more than just confusing Nick. The woman tied him in knots. He was smitten with her big-time, and didn't even know it. Nick had been working extremely hard since Alan's death, and it was time he got interested in something other than microchips. He needed a life outside Chenault Electronics. It was interesting to watch him lose his grip on being in absolute control, and it was long overdue.

It seemed that Shayla Kirkland was going to be good for Nick. She was going to be good for the company, too. She had single-handedly convinced those Chinese gentlemen to honor the terms of the Ling Deal. The woman was almost too good to be true.

And, Paul thought, that was what had him worried. In his line of business he had discovered that anything that seemed too good to be true usually wasn't.

He shook his head. Maybe at his advancing age his overly cautious mind was working overtime. Yeah, that had to be it. Other than her initial reaction to him, there was nothing noteworthy about Shayla Kirkland…other than her astounding beauty. He would let Nick concentrate on that aspect of her. He seemed determined to do that, anyway.

Paul couldn't help grinning. It would be entertaining to watch Nick behave like a smitten nitwit for the first time in his life.

Shayla heard Nicholas call her name just seconds before she was about to enter the elevator. She had hoped she would not see him at all today. That had been the main reason she had risen early, ordered room service for breakfast, and gotten dressed. She was determined to spend a day at the upscale shopping mall that was just an elevator ride away from the hotel.

She forced herself to turn toward the sound of his voice, then wished she hadn't. She swallowed against a suddenly dry throat when her gaze settled on him. He was dressed for a workout in the health club in a pair of running shorts and tank top. His solidly built body and masculine presence were more overpowering than anything she'd ever been up against. To say the man had a nice body would be an understatement. Just looking at him made her feel trembly, hot, and bothered.

"Are you feeling better today, Ms. Kirkland?" Nicholas asked, easing into the confined compartment with her and then watching the door close on them. He punched the button for the floor where the health club was located after she had made her selection.

"Yes, thanks for asking." Although the elevator was roomy enough for both of them, she was very conscious of Nicholas's closeness. He was standing so near to her that when she looked up she thought she could see her reflection in the shining gold of his eyes.

"So, what do you plan to do today?" he asked. His voice, she thought, sounded too sexy for early in the morning.

"Shopping. I plan to do a lot of shopping today. Unless, of course, you need me for something."

"No, no. You deserve the day off. I'm taking it off, too."

Forcing herself to breathe evenly, she replied, "All right." Although she was looking straight ahead, she felt Nicholas's gaze move slowly over her hair, her face, and her mouth. Heat swept through her when she realized his gaze had stopped at her mouth and settled there. That wouldn't have been so bad if he hadn't been standing so close. The musky manly scent of him was engulfing her and making every part of her body acutely aware of his presence.

"Will you have dinner with me this evening?" he asked in a husky whisper.

Shayla drew in a deep breath. She didn't dare look at him. She couldn't. But then, she couldn't turn down his invitation. She convinced herself that going out to dinner with him was all part of her plan. "Yes, I will."

She all but gulped in a huge surge of air when the elevator suddenly came to a stop. It was her floor, and she couldn't get off fast enough.

"I hope you enjoy your day of shopping," Nicholas said when she stepped out. "I'll come to your room to get you around seven."

Without looking back she tossed the words, "Thanks. I'll be ready," over her shoulder and kept walking.

He couldn't believe he had asked her to dinner.

When the elevator closed, Nicholas shook his head in disbelief. Just that morning he had made up his mind that until he and Shayla had to put in an appearance together at Mr. Ming's dinner party tomorrow night, he would avoid her like the plague.

He sighed in exasperation. So much for having made up his mind about anything. It seemed that when it came to Shayla Kirkland he had little, if any, resolve. And that wasn't good. Over the years he had made it a point not to get romantically involved with any of his employees, but since meeting her that was all he'd thought of doing. He thought of her all the time, and he hadn't known he could be so imaginative.

When the elevator came to a stop, Nicholas stepped out. The health club was really a high-tech gym that combined the convenience and state-of-the-art fitness equipment with traditional Asian hospitality.

He glanced around the facility and saw Paul. The older man was hard at work on the treadmill, running in place at top speed. Nicholas couldn't help but admire Paul's devotion to staying in shape. He thought he looked good for his age, and wondered why he'd never married, though he did date occasionally.

Nicholas had been in the club for almost an hour before Paul had the chance to take time from his vigorous exercise routine and come over to join him in the sauna.

"So what are your plans today?" Paul asked him as he leaned against the wall. The expression on his face indicated he thought the steam felt good after his strenuous exertions.

"I'm planning to take it easy. What about you?"

"The same. I checked in with Jacksonville and Chicago this morning. Things are okay, so I guess Stockard hasn't driven anyone crazy yet."

Nicholas nodded. Carl Stockard, one of the security men, wanted to be Paul's replacement when he retired. To Paul's way of thinking, the young man of twenty-seven was too eager to do a good job and impress Nicholas. If left up to Stockard, everyone on Nicholas's payroll would be under suspicion of wrongdoing. "He does take his job seriously, doesn't he?"

"Too blasted serious, if you ask me." Paul snorted. "I just wish he'd slow down and think things through before he acts."

Nicholas shook his head. He knew Paul would find fault with any man who was eager to replace him. Paul was used to doing things a certain way—not always by the book. Often he went by his gut feelings. Carl Stockard operated altogether differently, often before fully thinking things through. "If you feel he's not up to snuff, why don't you consider putting off leaving next year? Give yourself another couple of years to groom him."

Paul returned Nicholas's grin. He knew his game. "As much as I'm going to miss Chenault, this time next year I'm out of here. I plan to spend the rest of my days taking it easy on the water."

Paul spent a lot of his free time boating. Besides his spacious house in Jacksonville, he was also the owner of a nice yacht, which he occasionally used when the huge house got too lonely for him.

"Do you plan to check out the sights while you're here?" Paul asked as he shifted positions.

"Why, you?"

Paul nodded. "I thought I'd do it today. Maybe you ought to consider taking Ms. Kirkland with you."

Paul's words claimed Nicholas's attention. "Take her where?"

"Sightseeing."

Nicholas raised a brow. "Why would I want to do that?"

Paul shrugged at Nicholas's question. "For lack of anything better to do. That way you can spend time with her under pretense."

"Pretense of what?"

"Of not really wanting to spend time with her."

Nicholas frowned. "What's that supposed to mean?"

Paul shrugged his massive shoulders again. "It means just

what I said, Nick. I have eyes, and I see things. Especially your interest. You're single, she's single. Why not go for it?"

"Because she's an employee, Paul, and you know I don't date my employees."

"Then fire her. If you fired her you wouldn't have to be concerned about her being your employee."

Nicholas turned a scolding glance in the older man's direction. "Your logic astounds me sometimes. I think Stockard isn't the only one in my security department that I need to worry about."

Getting up, Nicholas left the sauna, ignoring Paul's laughter behind him.

Chapter 7

She needed to formulate a plan.

Shayla knew that it was imperative that she stick to that plan and allow nothing to sidetrack her from it. Especially something like the huge larger-than-life arrangement of cut flowers she had received from Nicholas just minutes after returning from shopping.

A sigh broke from her lips as she looked at the exquisite floral arrangement. It was so large that it had taken two hotel clerks to deliver it to her room. The card that accompanied it was impersonal, and simply read, I appreciate your hard work, loyalty, and dedication. It was signed with his initials.

Shayla opened her daily planner to the current date. She tapped her pen against her chin in thought. The first thing she needed to do was to find out everything she could about this new project Chenault was working on. The Ling Deal was just a small part of a bigger picture, and she was determined to find out just what that bigger picture was. To accomplish that, she would have to gain Nicholas Chenault's trust. She would start there. She jotted down in her planner the words, *I'll do whatever I have to to get Nicholas to lower his guard and trust me. Tonight at dinner I'll put my plan into action, and begin working toward that goal.*

Then, after finding out whatever was being kept a secret at Chenault Electronics, she would use that to her advantage. When she was in the position that she wanted to be in, she would go about her original plans to destroy the company.

Shayla was pleased that she had some definable goals established. She would be operating under the principle of the three *D'*s: *deceive, discover, destroy.* She was already working under an air of pretense, and would use that deception to discover what she needed to know. Finally, she would use what she discovered to destroy the company.

She closed her planner, feeling a whole lot better than she had yesterday. For just a little while she had let Nicholas Chenault get next to her. His masculine charisma had momentarily captivated her, and had made her lose sight of her purpose, her goal, and her plan. She would not let it happen again. As she had told her aunt, she was on a mission, and she was determined to see it through to the end.

Nicholas closed the hotel room door behind him and paused before walking across the lobby to get Shayla for dinner. She was a woman through and through, and he always found his control wavering around her. There was no way he should be taking her out to dinner tonight. They had no reason to come in contact with each other until the Mings' dinner party. She was free to do her thing until then, and he was free to do his. But a part of him was determined that they do their things together. To put it more bluntly, he had an overpowering desire to be in Shayla Kirkland's company whenever possible.

And that wasn't good.

Glancing down at his watch, he began walking across the lobby to her room. A knot was pulled tight in his stomach. Shayla Kirkland held a certain appeal he could not resist. Oh, there was that strong sexual appeal he came up against each time he saw her. But then she possessed another sort of appeal on a totally different level. She had an intellectual appeal that was playing havoc with his mind. The woman was as smart and intelligent as she was beautiful and seductive. It seemed that everything about Shayla Kirkland had the ability to turn him on. Did she have any clue as to the effect that she had on him whenever they were together?

He had precious little time to ponder that question as he stood before her door. He knocked once, and then the door opened. Soft light from inside her suite illuminated the section of the lobby in front of her room. Another knot pulled in his stomach when his eyes feasted on her. She was dressed in a chic mint-green pantsuit, and as usual she looked great. A mixture of desire and longing tried overpowering his senses, but he refused to let it.

"You look very nice tonight, Ms. Kirkland."

"Thank you."

"Ready?"

"Yes."

He took a step back when she moved out into the lobby, closing the room door behind her. "I hope you're hungry," he said, leading her toward the elevators.

"I am. I worked up quite an appetite while shopping."

When Nicholas reached up to push the elevator button, Shayla couldn't help but stare at his large hands. They appeared to be strong. His fingers were long, and the dark hair that dusted the back of his hands appeared in sharp contrast to the dark brown hair on his head. She realized that was because of the dim lighting in the elevator. His coloring, which she would have described as light almond, somehow added an air of supreme sensuality to him.

When the elevator opened, Shayla quickly withdrew her attention from his hands. "Will Paul be joining us?" she asked. A part of her hoped that he wouldn't.

"No. He grabbed something to eat earlier."

Shayla nodded. Good. It would only be the two of them. She was determined to put her plan into action tonight. "Thanks for the flowers. They're beautiful."

"I'm glad you like them. You're most deserving." He reached out and wrapped his fingers around her arms to assist her in taking a step back when the elevator stopped and others entered. The heat from his hands, those hands she'd just been so attentive to, made her tremble deep inside. She glanced up at him, searching for some sign that he had felt her reaction to his touch, then relaxed when she didn't notice any. They continued the elevator ride in silence.

Nicholas cursed silently. He had felt her tremble from his touch. He couldn't keep from imagining how she would react if he caressed her bare skin. For a moment, he wished he had the chance to find out. He inhaled deeply as he tried willing those disquieting thoughts away, then discovered he couldn't—especially when he was totally consumed by her scent.

Shayla's perfume, he thought, was downright alluring, sensual, and provocative. He leaned over, stopping a mere few inches away from her neck. At that close range he was getting the full potent effect of it. "What's it called?"

Shayla looked up at him, suddenly caught off guard by his closeness and the sharp coloring of his gold eyes. "What?"

"The perfume you're wearing. What's it called?"

She held his gaze. "Seduction."

She watched as the color of his eyes deepened. "I can understand why."

Shayla was spared having to respond when the elevator door opened.

When they stepped into the lobby, Nicholas couldn't resist placing his hand in the center of her back as he led her down the stairs and through swinging glass doors to a waiting limo.

Shayla turned to him, surprised. "We're leaving the hotel?"

"Yes, do you mind?" he asked when he noticed she had slowed her steps.

Yes, she minded. Since the day she had arrived, the hotel had served as her safety net. Instead of telling him her true feelings about the matter, she shook her head and said, "No."

Nicholas smiled. "Good. I thought it would be nice to get away from the hotel for a few hours. Besides, you and I need to get our stories straight."

Shayla waited until she was seated comfortably in the backseat of the limo with Nicholas before asking, "What stories?"

"The ones about our engagement. I understand Ming is not hosting some short-order dinner party. A number of Chinese dignitaries and quite a few important American businessmen will be attending. News of my engagement may surprise some, and I want to at least know something about my fiancée, in case I'm asked."

Shayla blinked at him. She hadn't thought her little white lie would cause this much trouble, and said as much.

"As you told Paul yesterday, you had to do what you had to do. I don't have a problem with the story you came up with. Engagements can easily be broken. And I'm not concerned about my business associates from the States. I can deal with them later. I just don't want Ming and the others to think they were deliberately deceived in any way. I have a feeling Ho Chin will be there, and I'm not sure he fully bought the story of our engagement. He may try his hand at digging holes in it."

Shayla nodded, and the limo made its way through the streets of Hong Kong to the restaurant.

Shayla's hand tightened around her wineglass as she answered another round of Nicholas's questions. The evening was not going as she had planned. She was supposed to be asking the questions. However, he was determined to find out everything he could about her for the dinner party.

"So let me see what information I have so far," he was saying. "Pink is your favorite color. You like jazz music. You have a weakness for chocolate. You prefer seafood to steak. Your most favorite place is the Islands, and doing volunteer work with charities is important to you."

Shayla nodded. "Now I think I deserve answers from you to those questions, as well."

Nicholas took a sip of his wine. "Believe it or not, you and I enjoy a lot of the same things, although pink is not my favorite color. Green is," he said, smiling. "Like you, I prefer jazz music. I enjoy chocolate, although I wouldn't go so far as to call it a weakness. I prefer a plate of plump fried shrimp to a T-bone steak any day, and I've enjoyed my visits to the Islands, too. My favorite place is St. Thomas."

He took another sip of his wine. "And I also firmly believe that a person should help those less fortunate. I've always devoted my time and money to a number of worthwhile charities. My favorite is Dream Maker—a group of other businessmen and I work closely with a foundation that helps fulfill the dreams of terminally ill children. I'm chairman of the board of that particular one."

Shayla didn't like this, finding out about the personal side of him. She preferred sticking to the business side. She didn't want to think of him as a separate individual, one with a life that wasn't connected to Chenault Electronics. She decided to move the conversation to one that was more to her advantage.

"Now that you have the Ling Deal, what's next?"

Nicholas smiled. He was still pleased with the way things had turned out. "Chenault is involved in a number of projects, some more important than others. Once you get back and get settled, I'll go over all the ones you'll be working on."

"Anything major?"

Fortunately for Shayla, Nicholas did not pick up on the eagerness to know in her voice. "All my projects are major. The most important ones are being worked on at the Jacksonville, Florida, office. However, there are a number that will be handled out of both Jacksonville and Chicago."

Two hours later Shayla and Nicholas had returned to the hotel. Although Shayla didn't feel the evening had been a complete waste, she did wish she could have obtained more information about Chenault's major projects.

When Nicholas walked her back to her suite, she turned to him after retrieving her key from her purse. "Thanks for dinner, Mr. Chenault."

Nicholas's gaze swept her face. "Considering the fact that we're supposed to be engaged, don't you think we should get into the habit of calling each other by our first names for tomorrow night's affair?"

A frown drew Shayla's eyebrows together. She didn't like the idea. Calling him "Mr. Chenault" had kept things on a business level. But still, she had to agree with his suggestion. "Yes, I suppose that makes sense, Mr. Chen—I mean Nicholas."

"We don't want to take any chances, do we?"

Shayla nervously gnawed on her bottom lip. She immediately stopped when she noticed Nicholas's gaze fasten on her mouth. "I guess not." She then held her hand out to him. "Thanks again for a nice evening."

Nicholas looked down at the hand she was offering him. A part of him knew he should take it and remove himself from her company immediately. Another part, though, wanted to do something he'd been dying to do since first meeting her. He glanced up from her hand to her face. "I don't think it's proper for an engaged couple to shake hands, Shayla. What happens if we're placed in a position where we'll have to kiss?"

A knot formed in Shayla's throat and heat settled in the pit of her stomach at the very thought of that possibility. The lump in her throat tightened, and the heat in her stomach grew more intense when she saw Nicholas's gaze had again fastened on her mouth. "I doubt that'll be necessary. The Chinese aren't big on public displays of affection."

"That may be the case, but Americans are, and a number of them will be there. I think we should get in a couple of practice sessions," he said, leaning toward her.

When Shayla realized his intent, she went still. How on earth would she be able to survive his kiss? Before her mind could provide an answer and before she could catch her next breath, Nicholas's lips captured hers. He tasted of the wine they'd had at dinner and the heat of desire. The mixture was intoxicating. On a sigh, her mouth opened under his, inviting the invasion of his tongue.

His kiss was possessive and urgent as it began mating rhythmically with hers. Automatically, instinctively, her tongue began moving with his as her emotions whirled and skidded out of control. Something in the back of her mind told her that she desperately needed this—the deep urgent mating of his tongue with hers, the release of the emotional turmoil within her, and the fierce heat that was totally consuming her.

From somewhere else, the voice of reason flashed through her delirious mind and tried convincing her that she did not need this. But when Nicholas's kiss deepened, becoming even more demanding, and his arms tightened around her, bringing her even closer to the muscled breadth of his chest, she thought that even if she didn't need this, she wanted it, anyway. She eradicated all thought from her mind, languidly content to be in his arms, savoring the heady taste of him.

The sound of a door opening and closing startled Shayla from the sensuous insanity possessing her. Since they were on a private floor with only three suites, the person who opened the door had to have been Paul. No doubt he had been a witness to their torrid kiss. Although her body was still somewhat out of whack, she forced her mind back on track, broke from Nicholas's kiss, and took a step back.

"Nicholas," she said breathlessly, "that was enough practice. I think we'll get it right if the time comes."

As Shayla's gaze settled on Nicholas's features, she saw that his lips were moist and glistening. His eyes had a glazed look that made the pupils appear a fiery gold. She also noted that they were both breathing hard.

"Yeah, I think you're right," he responded softly in a deep husky whisper. His gaze glued to her lips, he was ready to practice some more if she let him.

"Good night, Nicholas." Shayla opened her door and hurried inside, quickly closing it behind her.

Chapter 8

Later that night Nicholas discovered that no amount of physical exertion could remove the fierce desire be felt for Shayla. After she'd entered her room, he had gone to his own, changed into a jogging outfit, and left for the health club. Luckily for him, the facility stayed open all night.

After an hour of nonstop running around the inside jogging track, he returned to his room, took a shower, then crawled into bed completely exhausted, only to remain awake with his mind filled with thoughts of Shayla and the kiss they had shared. He had regretted kissing her the moment he had done so, but the softness of her lips and the sweetness of her taste had made him keep right on kissing her. She had felt so good, so right, so perfect in his arms. And now that he had savored her taste he wanted more.

She had returned his kiss with equal abandonment. Her tongue had mated furiously and urgently with his, withholding nothing. Shayla Kirkland was a passionate and sensuous woman. Even when she had abruptly brought the kiss to an end, a look of total surprise and wonder had flushed her features. Neither of them could deny the heat that had surged between them.

Seeing that he could not sleep, he got up and tried watching television. When he couldn't find anything that held his interest on the English channel, he tried one of the international stations. It only took a few minutes to discover that solution wouldn't work, either.

Nicholas turned off the television set. Since it was apparent that going to sleep was impossible for him, he decided he might as well get some work done. Earlier that day his marketing department had faxed him a report that needed his attention.

Less than thirty minutes later, when he'd failed to concentrate on what he was reading, he pushed the papers aside. No woman had ever gotten to him to the point that he could not focus on work. For the three years following his father's death, Chenault Electronics had been the main interest in his life.

He snorted, gave a choked laugh, and leaned back in his chair. Amazing. He had been involved with Olivia for over a year, and thoughts of her had never intruded on his work time. His yearnings had never been this strong and fierce. Ever since he had returned from dinner he had been filled with thoughts of Shayla.

Common sense was warning him to back off and to erase her from his mind, but that was easier said than done. He felt bewitched, even besotted. He tapped his fingers against the desk, feeling irritated and frustrated. He rolled his shoulders in an effort to ease the tension lodged there.

Nicholas stood, groaning as he rose and stretched his body. He might have overdone things at the health club. Having decided that soaking in a warm tub wasn't a bad idea, he'd begun walking toward the bathroom when the phone rang. He picked it up immediately.

"Yes?"

"Nick, this is Paul. I figured you wouldn't be getting much sleep tonight."

"How'd you figure that?"

"After seeing you and Ms. Kirkland wrapped up pretty tight in each other's arms earlier, I figured sleep would be the last thing on your mind."

Nicholas was determined to remain cool and unruffled by Paul's comment. "You surprise me, Paul. I never thought I'd see the day you'd resort to being a Peeping Tom."

The older man's chuckle made Nicholas scowl. "And I never thought I'd see the day that you'd make a public spectacle of yourself."

Nicholas rubbed the top of his head in annoyance. He did not need Paul reminding him of his unorthodox behavior around Shayla that night. "Was there a reason for this call, Paul?"

"Yes, I thought you'd want to know what I discovered today while I was out and about."

Nicholas frowned. "What?"

"Thomas Jordache is in Hong Kong."

Nicholas's frown deepened. "What's he doing here?"

"Your guess is as good as mine. We'll just have to wait and see what sort of game he's playing this time."

Shayla rubbed sleep from her eyes and blinked against the bright sunlight flowing into the window. She switched positions in bed, letting her eyes adjust to daylight before looking over at the clock on the nightstand. It was eight o'clock Hong Kong time. Her body was still trying to operate on Chicago time.

She closed her eyes when she remembered the kiss she

and Nicholas had shared. There was tightness in her stomach and an ache in her breasts just thinking about it. It had been a long time since she'd been kissed, and never like *that.* Sheesh, the man was an excellent kisser. He had made her head spin, and her body tremble. He had tortured her mouth with his tongue, and she had responded by pressing her body closer to him, coming alive and uncontrolled in his arms. The sensuous emotions that had surged through her had robbed her of any conscious thought. She had acted wantonly, behaved recklessly. How on earth would she face him today? Their kiss had been a mistake. Pretended engagement or not, she would not let it happen again. How had she allowed it to happen in the first place? While kissing him she had lost all sense of time and purpose. And to make matters worse, she had totally forgotten about her plan.

Tossing the covers back, she pulled herself out of bed and went into the bathroom. After taking a shower, brushing her teeth, applying light makeup, and combing her hair, she began getting dressed to go downstairs to grab something to eat.

She remembered Nicholas mentioning at dinner last night that he had planned to leave the hotel early and do some sightseeing. She hoped he had not changed his plans, because he was the last person she wanted to run into. Tonight was the night of Mr. Ming's dinner party, and she would see Nicholas soon enough for that. He was becoming more of a challenge than she had anticipated. Whenever he talked about Chenault Electronics, he was always serious, focused, intense. And when he had kissed her last night, he had been just as serious, focused, and intense. The hands that had held her body snugly against his while the heat of his tongue had devoured hers had scorched her through the material of her clothing, and they had promised a higher degree of pleasure if given the chance to touch her bare skin.

Shayla shook her head to clear her lustful thoughts.

She would not, and could not, go there. Doing so would be a mistake. A very big mistake.

Nicholas was determined to avoid Shayla for most of the day. He had cancelled his plans to go sightseeing. Instead he had ordered room service and remained in his room, reading the report he had been unable to read last night and checking on how things were going at the Jacksonville and Chicago offices.

Thomas Jordache's presence in Hong Kong had not been good news. In his line of business there was nothing wrong with a generous dose of healthy competition, but when someone made it an all-out war, things could get pretty nasty. And basically that was what Thomas Jordache was doing, and had been doing for years—declaring war on Chenault Electronics. The man was determined to destroy the company.

Nicholas knew Jordache's drive to destroy Chenault stemmed from a breach of trust between his father and the man years ago, when both of their companies were first formed. But now that Alan Chenault was no longer living, Nicholas could not understand what still motivated Jordache to indulge in unsavory business tactics against Chenault Electronics. All Nicholas knew was that when it came to Thomas Jordache he had learned to always be on his guard and to watch his back. The man would use anything and everything against him, if given the chance.

Nicholas placed the ink pen he'd been using down. Earlier he had placed a call to his mother and a call to Sterling's home in the North Carolina mountains to see how they were doing. His mother was doing fine, and his sister-in-law, Colby, had told him that Sterling had gone out of town unexpectedly and would be returning in a few days. Nicholas had inquired about his niece, and was glad to know she was doing well. He wasn't used to being around children, but with his niece, Chandler, he was getting the hang of things. He always enjoyed the time he spent with her. She was such a beautiful and happy baby.

He glanced down at his watch. It was two o'clock already. He, Shayla, and Paul were to arrive at Ming's residence around six. He stood. He had time to take a quick nap to make up for the sleep he'd lost last night when thoughts of Shayla had consumed him. Not that she was no longer consuming him, but today he felt more in control. If he could make it through the next few days, he would be okay when he returned to the States.

His problem, he had concluded, was that he had gone a long time without a woman. It had nothing to do with Shayla Kirkland. He would probably feel just as hot and bothered around any beautiful woman. Unfortunately, it was Shayla he was constantly around lately, so logically his body and mind were reacting to her. Once he began dating again, things would be fine. He was certain of it.

Walking into the bedroom, he flopped down on the bed, knowing he was just fooling himself. He had dated other women since Olivia, but none of them had managed to rejuvenate his sexual desires with just their scent, and none had made him ache in places he had forgotten existed with just their glance.

Nicholas stifled a groan and squeezed his eyes tightly shut, willing his mind and body to return to his complete control. Now was not the time to behave like a teenager discovering sex for the first time and hungry for the taste of it.

He opened his eyes and realized that what he was feeling went beyond mere hunger. For the first time in over a year, he was showing some really serious interest in a woman.

Shayla glanced at her profile in the full-length mirror. The black satin dress emphasized every curve of her body and provided a smooth and sleek fit, and the diamond necklace and diamond stud earrings accented her attire without overdoing it. It was important to her that she look her best tonight, especially if everyone assumed she was Nicholas's fiancée. The dress, another purchase from her aunt's shop, was perfect. Luckily, Aunt Callie had talked her into bringing it along just in case she needed a really classy outfit. As far as she was concerned, this one was certainly appropriate. She wondered what Nicholas's reaction would be when he saw her in it.

After taking a full turn in the mirror she took a deep breath and walked out of the room. Anxiety had plagued her most of the day. She had not heard from Nicholas, and the thought that in less than five minutes he would be knocking on her door had her stomach tied in knots.

Moments later, when she heard the knock, she took a deep breath to maintain her composure and walked over to the door. After taking a brief moment to swallow deeply, she opened it. She wished she could let out a sigh of relief when she saw that Paul was with Nicholas. But then she remembered that Paul had been a witness to their torrid embrace. That only made her more uncomfortable around Paul than usual.

"Nicholas. Paul. I'm ready. I just need to grab my purse."

"No hurry, we have plenty of time," Paul said, entering her room and leaving Nicholas standing outside her door. Nicholas had not said anything. He just stood there leaning against the doorjamb, looking at her. Shayla found his stare unnerving. She walked over to the table and picked up her purse, feeling his gaze on her every step.

When Shayla turned back around and saw that Nicholas was still standing in the same spot staring at her, she couldn't stand it any longer. Even at a distance, with Paul in the room with them, she could feel his heat, and it was touching her. "Is something wrong, Nicholas?" She ignored the chuckle Paul tried smothering by placing his hand over his mouth in a fake cough.

Nicholas shook his head and straightened his stance. He knew it wasn't polite to stare, but he couldn't help it. When she'd walked to the desk, he studied the sweeping line of her spine, which extended from her neck all the way down to her curvaceous bottom. The sight of it had almost challenged his sanity.

Eyebrows slightly raised, his gaze still locked on hers, he said, "No, there's nothing wrong." He came into the room and walked over to stand in front of her. "You look beautiful tonight, Shayla."

"Thank you, Nicholas." His compliment floated over Shayla, lifting her spirits and at the same time rallying her fears. How was she going to spend an entire evening in his company pretending to be his fiancée? Especially with all the sexual tension flowing between them.

"And I ditto that," Paul piped in. His words intruded into Shayla's thoughts and reminded her that she and Nicholas were not alone.

"Thanks, Paul," she said, glancing over at him. The smile he gave her was one of kindness, but the one she returned was plastered on. She still felt wary of him.

A few minutes later they were in the elevator riding down to the lobby, where, according to Paul, a limo was waiting. When the elevator stopped, Nicholas's hand moved to the center of Shayla's back and touched her bare skin.

"This way," he said softly as he led her off the elevator and down the same stairs they had taken last night while on their way out to dinner. Just before he opened the door for her to get into the limo, she felt his thumb gently stroke the part of her back left bare by the cut of her dress. Her breath caught in her throat at the sensations his touch evoked.

She slid into the backseat of the limo, and he got in after her. Paul, she noted, got up front with the driver. She scooted over to the far corner of the car. When she did, Nicholas reached out and gently pulled her back to the center of the seat toward him. "I don't bite," he whispered silkily. He was sitting so close to her that his breath caressed her face.

"I—I know you don't," she managed to say. She tried staring straight ahead and not concentrating on the man sitting so close beside her.

"I meant what I said earlier, Shayla. You look beautiful."

She turned and looked at him and stared straight into his gold eyes. "Thank you, and you look nice tonight, too." That, she thought, was an understatement. If not for Paul's presence, she probably would have stood in the doorway and stared at him just as long as he had stared at her. Dressed in a black tux, a crisp white shirt, and cummerbund, he was the epitome of sexiness. The only thing sexier would be him without any clothes on.

That thought made heat settle in the center of her body. She shifted positions in the seat and looked out the window, tightening her thighs together.

"Hong Kong is beautiful at night, isn't it?" Nicholas said. He shifted his position. If they sat any closer they would be in each other's laps. She turned to face him, and immediately wished she hadn't. His face was right there, directly in front of hers, so close she could see the darkening of his gold eyes, so close that if she moved another millimeter their lips would brush. She tried to will her body to stop throbbing, but it wasn't paying any attention to her shaky command. She couldn't utter a response to his question. She could only nod.

"This is a different route than the one the limo took last night. I thought you'd appreciate seeing this part of Hong Kong," he added.

Again, she could only nod. She tugged her gaze away

from his face and tried relaxing against the seat. However, the sensual force of his closeness made relaxing impossible. Her pulse took a giant leap when Nicholas placed his arm across the seat and around her shoulders. A heated sensation shot from her toes to every single strand of hair on her head, forcing her to draw in a deep breath. The last thing she needed was something else to stimulate the sensations that were already sizzling through her. A quick glance toward the front of the vehicle indicated that Paul and the driver were deep in conversation and not paying any attention to what was going on in the backseat. She wondered how much longer it would take for them to reach their destination. She needed to keep all her wits about her if they were to be displayed as a happy engaged couple tonight.

As if he knew she was worrying about something, he took her trembling hands in his, entwining their joined fingers into a tight knot. "If you're worrying about tonight, don't. We'll survive."

His words were whispered in her ear, assuring her and arousing her at the same time. Shayla was tempted to tell him that she wasn't as certain of that as he seemed to be. Because right then, while they were sitting close together, holding hands and surrounded by an invisible sensuous mist, she wasn't quite sure she would make it through the night.

Nicholas had to seriously question exactly what was taking place between him and Shayla. He had not been himself since meeting her, and being on this trip with her was making the situation even more complex.

When she had opened the hotel room door for him and Paul, the sight of her had taken his breath away, literally. He had stood speechless, spellbound by her beauty. It had taken a few minutes to get his bearings. What he had told her earlier was true—she did look absolutely beautiful. The dress she was wearing seemed to have been designed just for her. He couldn't imagine any other woman wearing it. The suggestion of all the nubile curves beneath her dress was staggering. She looked incredibly sexy in it. The outfit placed emphasis on every part of her body that he had been fantasizing about—her firm uptilted breasts, her tapered waist, which flared into graceful curved hips, and those magnificent legs of hers.

Paul, who had been talking to the driver, suddenly shifted positions and turned around in his seat. He showed no surprise at discovering the two of them sitting very close together and holding hands. "So when is the wedding?" he asked, smiling.

Nicholas blinked once, then twice. "What?"

Paul's smile widened. "I asked, when is the wedding. I'm sure that question will come up sometime tonight. Has either of you decided on a date? If not, I suggest you do so. It'll make your engagement more believable, don't you think?"

Nicholas glanced at Shayla. "Do you have a date in mind?"

Shayla shook her head. "No, but since this is all pretend I suggest we make it a rather long engagement. How about a year from now?"

Nicholas's expression showed he was pondering her suggestion. "That's fine. Next March, then?"

Shayla nodded. "Yes, that'll work. What day in March?"

"The first day of the month, to make it easy to remember?"

Shayla nodded her head. "All right. March first."

Paul turned back around in his seat to hide his smile. Silence descended on the occupants in the limo once more.

Chapter 9

From the moment the limo drove past the entrance gates to Shin Ming's home, Shayla was spellbound. The house sat high on a hill, and provided the dazzling effect of an ancient imperial palace. With its elaborate garden and spacious courtyard, it was a prime example of Chinese architecture.

By the time the limo stopped in the circular driveway, the calm suddenly disappeared that had encircled Shayla as she sat beside Nicholas while he held her hands. Butterflies settled in her stomach, and her nervousness returned.

"Just remember, I'll be by your side as much as I can tonight," Nicholas whispered when he felt the tension return to her hands. He tightened his hold on them, liking the feel of her soft skin. During the limo ride he could not resist brushing his fingertips against the sensitive skin of her hands. A couple of times he had felt her shiver when he had touched her that way, and thoughts had dominated his mind of making her shiver in another, more intimate way.

Paul and the driver had already gotten out of the limo, leaving the two of them alone. Nicholas was glad to have the few moments of privacy with Shayla. "Are you okay?"

She looked up at him and nodded. "Yes. I just hope I act appropriately. I've never been engaged before."

Nicholas smiled reassuringly. "Neither have I."

The headlights from a car that had come up behind them illuminated the car's interior, and Nicholas's gaze swept across Shayla's face. He breathed in slowly. She was both beautiful and captivating. No doubt she would garner the attention of a number of men tonight, and the prospect of sharing her company, even for business reasons, bothered him.

Paul's thump on the roof of the limo indicated that it was time for them to make their entrance. Nicholas was shifting positions to get out when Shayla reached over and touched his arm, reclaiming his attention. He turned back to her. "Yes?"

"Thanks for calming my nerves tonight."

His gaze went to her mouth before moving back up to her eyes. He smiled softly. "It was my pleasure, Shayla." And he meant every word. Nicholas took her hand in his as they climbed out of the car.

The structure looming before them looked huge and ancient. He couldn't imagine anyone calling the place home. It seemed more like a museum. Carved into the walls leading to the entrance door were nine dragons in various sizes and positions. The designs evoked images of intrigue, philosophy, and power. Nicholas could tell only the best craftsmanship had gone into the building, which had served as a second home for an emperor centuries ago. This place was grander than any home he'd ever visited in China.

The servant who stood at the door ushered them inside and into a great hallway. While the outside made a statement, the inside made a bigger one. Numerous Chinese paintings and pieces of Asian art decorated the room, and huge, beautifully designed Oriental rugs lined the floors.

Shayla took a deep breath, willing her anxiety away when she saw Mr. Ming and a woman she assumed was his wife approaching them. Surprisingly, by the time introductions were made she felt more relaxed, especially with the feel of Nicholas's arm around her waist. Because of what they had to pull off tonight, she would temporarily forget that Nicholas was her enemy, that despite how much she enjoyed being in his company there was no place in her plans for a personal relationship with him. So, instead of concentrating on what could never be, Shayla would put all of her energy into making things go smoothly that night.

It was soon quite obvious she dazzled Ms. Ming with her fluency in their language as well as her in-depth knowledge of Chinese history and customs. After several minutes of informal chatter, the Mings led them into another room, which Shayla concluded was a ballroom. Nicholas had been right. It was no short-order dinner party the Mings were hosting. The lights were dimmed, but Shayla could tell there were quite a number of people present. All of them, like her and Nicholas, were dressed for the elaborate occasion. With her hand resting in the crook of Nicholas's arm, they entered the huge room, and some of those in attendance turned their gazes toward them.

"Even in a semidark room you can automatically pick out the Americans," Nicholas said, leaning sideways and whispering in Shayla's ear.

She arched a brow at him. "How?"

"The women immediately turned to check you out, just to make sure your outfit isn't a duplicate of theirs. The men are also checking out your outfit, but for a totally different reason. They're straining their eyesight to see how good you look in it," he quipped teasingly.

His statement got the intended effect. Shayla gave him a radiant smile as she looked up into his wickedly teasing eyes. "Are you saying that by nature most Americans are nosy?"

Nicholas chuckled. "What I'm saying is that by nature American women are often envious creatures, and American men, more times than not, are lechers where a beautiful woman is concerned."

Shayla smiled and her gaze searched his. "Are you a lecher, Nicholas?"

He shrugged. "I admit my eyes have checked out a good-looking woman a time or two, but not tonight. The most beautiful woman here tonight is with me, so I don't have to resort to being lecherous." The grin he gave her was a bit rakish, nonetheless, and made every part of her body throb when he added, "But I am feeling somewhat territorial."

Silence ensued between them, and during that lull the sexual tension they always seemed to generate returned. "Do you know what I'm saying, Shayla?" Nicholas rasped softly as he stepped in front of her, completely blocking her view so that her attention was entirely on him.

"No, I—I don't," she admitted shakily, honestly, and truthfully.

On a long heavy sigh that seemed to come from a forced decision, he said huskily, "I'll explain things later tonight, after we return to the hotel."

He then captured her hand in his. "Come on. Let's enjoy ourselves."

After an extraordinary dinner everyone retired once more to the ballroom, where a Chinese musical ensemble was providing the entertainment. A few minutes later, Shayla heard Paul, who had come to join them, release a disturbing sigh. "I can't believe he's here. And not surprisingly, he's conversing with Ho Chin. What does that tell you?"

Without thinking, Shayla automatically asked, "Who's here?"

Paul grunted before he responded. "Chenault Electronics's major competitor, Thomas Jordache."

With a supreme effort at self-control, Shayla forced in a deep breath before allowing her gaze to follow Paul's. She focused all of her attention on the tall older man standing across the room from them, deep in conversation with Ho Chin. As if the man somehow felt her eyes on him, he stopped talking and tilted his head. For an instant, their gazes locked, then Shayla quickly looked away. She knew she had just looked into the face of her biological father—a man she had never seen before, a man she couldn't keep from despising after reading her mother's diary.

She lowered her eyes to get her bearings before turning to Nicholas. "Why do I get the feeling he's bad news?"

Nicholas's face, unlike Paul's, was very calm, but his gaze was penetrating. "Because he usually is. He's determined to keep an old feud between him and my father going. It's nothing that I had anything to do with, but it's something that Thomas Jordache wants to make me pay for, anyway."

Shayla nodded as the full impact of Nicholas's words hit her. She had the same agenda. Wasn't it her plan to do the same thing to him? Make the son pay for the sins of the father?

"Jordache is determined to destroy my company, and I can't let him do that. He's still holding a grudge because of something that happened years ago. He takes every opportunity to try to sabotage my business." Nicholas's voice took on a serious tone. "As an employee of Chenault, you need to know that and be aware of it, as well as cautious."

Shayla swallowed. "There's nothing you can do?"

Nicholas smiled. "I try to ignore him."

Paul snorted. "I prefer beating the hell out of him, if I ever get the chance. When I do finally get hold of him, I plan to make up for the old as well as for the new."

Shayla lifted her gaze and took a good look at Paul's features. His eyes were intense, hard, cold. It was evident that he despised Thomas Jordache as much as she did. When she noticed Paul staring back at her with an odd expression, she lowered her gaze. Had her curiosity about Thomas Jordache concerned Paul? Had he picked up on something she'd said, or her shocked reaction to seeing the man? She made a wholehearted effort to convince herself that she was just imagining things, and that she hadn't given anything away.

"Well, I'll be. Look who just walked in," Nicholas said as his face split into a wide grin. He turned to Shayla. "Excuse me. A good friend just arrived, and I haven't seen him in over three months."

Shayla watched as Nicholas quickly walked over to the man who had just entered. Like Nicholas, he was wearing a black tux and a white shirt. Also like Nicholas, he was tall, broad-shouldered, and extremely handsome. She watched the two men exchange hearty handshakes as well as bear hugs. That was the most affectionate display she had seen Nicholas give anyone, other than the one he had given her when he'd kissed her. She swallowed, not wanting to remember the passionate scene that had taken place outside her hotel room door.

"They must be very good friends," she said to Paul as she watched the two men.

"Yes, they are." Paul let out a chuckle. "Even I can't believe it at times."

Shayla looked up at Paul and lifted a curious brow. "What do you mean?"

Paul met her gaze. "They became friends before they realized they were supposed to be enemies."

Shayla frowned as she mulled over what Paul had just said. "I don't understand."

Paul's face was rich with amusement when he replied. "You will soon. You're about to meet Trent."

The funny feeling that Shayla'd had all evening returned. Her stomach suddenly began to dance with uneasiness. "Trent?"

"Yes, Trenton Jordache. He's Thomas Jordache's son."

Shayla took a sharp intake of breath. She closed her eyes, and a feeling of total shock consumed her, making her feel light-headed and dizzy. She opened her eyes and rubbed her forehead, suddenly feeling a deep pounding there.

"Shayla, are you all right?"

She glanced up to find Paul looking at her with a concerned expression on his face. "For a moment you looked as if you were going to pass out," he added in a worried tone.

She didn't say anything for a scant few seconds as she tried getting a grip, retaining her balance, and reclaiming control of her senses. Doing all three, she found, wasn't easy. "He's Thomas Jordache's son?" she asked in a shaky voice. "But I thought you and Nicholas said that Jordache has been trying to ruin the company, and that—"

"He has. But Trent, thank God, is nothing like his father. He worked with the old man for a while, but couldn't tolerate his father's unscrupulous work ethics. Jordache has been trying for years to bring Trent back into the business. In a way I really wish he would go back. He was good at what he did. Besides, Trent's the only person who can keep the old man in line."

"But how did he and Nicholas become such good friends?"

Paul let out a throaty laugh. "It was nothing Thomas Jordache planned, believe me. As teenagers, Nick and Trent were sent to the same exclusive summer camp in Orlando each year. There weren't many black kids at the camp, and the ones who were summer regulars bonded. Trent and Nick became the best of friends. They were in college before they discovered their fathers were business enemies. Alan and Thomas didn't know their sons even knew each other. Later it was too late for either to do anything about it. The bond between Nick and Trent was set for life."

"How did the fathers handle that?"

"Alan was fine with it, but then he was a fair man. He had wanted the feud between him and Jordache to end long ago, and thought it wouldn't be right to pass it on to their heirs, anyway. Jordache, on the other hand, isn't that gracious in his way of thinking. He despises the fact that Trent and Nicholas are such good friends. He's tried a number of times over the years to destroy that, too, but so far nothing's worked. Their friendship is too solid."

Shayla nodded. She then glanced back at Trent Jordache to study him. He appeared to be the same age as Nicholas, approximately thirty-one or thirty-two. A thought suddenly occurred to her. Had Thomas Jordache been married twenty-seven years ago when he slept with her mother?"

She shook her head to clear it. There was no way she would believe her mother had knowingly gotten involved with a married man.

"Is Thomas Jordache still married to Trent's mother?" she asked Paul quietly, not taking her eyes off the two men, who were still standing across the room deep in conversation.

If Paul found her question odd, he didn't say so. "No, Trent's mother died giving birth to him. For health reasons, she shouldn't have gotten pregnant in the first place. Jordache knew it and got her pregnant anyway, intent on building a dynasty."

Shayla turned her attention to Paul when she heard the

hard cold hatred in his voice. A constricting ache tore through her when she saw the torment in his eyes. She inhaled sharply. Not even knowing the full story, she felt that one thing was crystal clear—at some point in his past, Paul had cared deeply for the woman Thomas Jordache had married. "You knew her?" She whispered the question brokenly, still in shock about the information Paul was sharing with her. She saw the tense muscles along his jaw harden.

He gritted his teeth and drew in a deep breath before he answered her. "Yes. She was my sister."

Shayla blinked several times before asking, "Trent's your nephew?"

"Yes. But during his childhood I couldn't be a part of his life. Jordache forbade it, so we didn't have any kind of relationship. I know that if my sister had lived things would have been different. At least now, since he's become a man who makes his own decisions, Trent and I have established a connection. I'm so terribly proud that, although Jordache raised him, he turned out to be a decent man." Paul shook his head. "But then, it really isn't surprising. Trent's mother was a very decent and loving woman."

Shayla knew she had no right to question Paul further about anything. She could tell by looking into his eyes that—although what happened occurred years ago—his pain was still deep.

Just like hers had been after reading her mother's diary.

She glanced back over to the table where Thomas Jordache was standing. He was no longer indulging in conversation with Ho Chin, but was watching Nicholas and Trent with an unreadable expression on his face.

Her dislike for him intensified. Her mother had not been the only person he had hurt. How many other lives had he ruined? She wondered if he felt any remorse for any of the things he'd done.

"Nick and Trent are headed this way," Paul said, bringing her thoughts back into focus. She looked up to find Nicholas and Trent Jordache less than ten feet from where she and Paul were standing.

Shayla inhaled deeply, silently asking God to give her the strength to handle the introductions she knew Nicholas was about to make.

She was about to meet the brother she hadn't known she had.

Chapter 10

"Uncle Paul, it's good seeing you," the man with Nicholas said to the man at Shayla's side, shaking hands with him. He then turned his undivided attention to Shayla.

"Shayla," Nicholas was saying, "I'd like you to meet a good friend of mine. Trent Jordache, this is Shayla Kirkland."

Shayla accepted Trent's hand in a warm handshake. A flutter of nerves rose up and twisted in the pit of her stomach. She was so tense her body felt like a piece of board. "It's nice meeting you, Trent," she somehow managed to say as she studied him. His black hair was cut low, and his handsome features, if studied closely, would possibly remind someone of a younger Paul. Trent had inherited some of his uncle's features. They had the same straight nose, angular chin, and dimpled smile. His eyes were so dark they appeared black, and his lips, she noticed, were tilted in an outlandishly handsome grin so heartwarming that she couldn't keep from returning it.

"Ahh." Trent sighed after releasing her hand. "If you don't intend to marry her for real, Nick, then maybe I will."

Shayla blinked. Evidently Nicholas had told Trent the truth regarding their fake engagement, and he was flirting with her, not knowing they were related.

"Word of warning, Trent," Nicholas murmured softly. "Don't even let that cross your mind."

Nicholas's gold eyes met Trent's dark ones in an open challenge. Wicked amusement danced across Trent's handsome features. "So that's the way it is?"

Nicholas's mouth twitched in a smile. He knew that his best friend was an incorrigible flirt. "Yeah, man. That's the way it is." He looked over at Shayla before meeting Trent's gaze once more. "And that's the way it's staying."

Shayla looked up and met Nicholas's gaze again. He was looking at her with an intensity that almost took her breath away. She inhaled deeply before turning her gaze back to Trent. She wanted to know everything she could about him.

"Where are you from, Trent?"

Trent smiled. "I was born in Jacksonville, Florida, but I attended private schools in New York. Now I'm what you might call in transit. Recently, I became part owner of a cruise ship that makes frequent trips to the Islands and Africa. So I guess you could say that for the last six months I've been living aboard my ship off and on. But I'm looking into purchasing a second home in the Chicago area."

Shayla's heart rate kicked up. He would be living in Chicago! She took a deep breath to pull her thoughts together. "I have a friend who's a Realtor. I'm sure she'll be glad to assist you any way she can."

Trent gave her a smooth smile. "I'll only deal with her if she's as pretty as you are."

Shayla couldn't help smiling again. Trent Jordache was

quite a charmer. "Thanks. I know you and Tonya will get along just fine."

Trent grinned. He then answered Paul's questions about the cruise business. A few moments later, when the Chinese musical group surprised everyone by playing an American piece, a slow number at that, many people began moving toward the dance floor.

Nicholas moved closer to Shayla, his gaze holding hers intently. "Dance with me?" he requested in a deep husky voice.

Shayla nodded, and Nicholas took her hand in his and led her out to the dance floor, leaving Paul and Trent alone. She swallowed hard as Nicholas pulled her into his arms and they moved to the slow music. Blood rushed to her head at the feel of his hard masculine body so close to hers. Everything about Nicholas oozed sensuality. His smile, his touch, his walk, his talk…and his kiss.

Shayla felt her body tensing up again, and commanded it to relax in his arms. She felt his hands caress her bare back. One of his hands dropped to her waist, and his fingers placed light pressure there, bringing her closer to fit him.

"You're nervous again. Why?" He whispered the words low and deep in her ear.

Heaven help me, I actually wish I could tell him, she thought as she pulled back and met his gaze. How could she form the words to say, *I'm really not who I seem to be. In addition to pretending to be your fiancée, I'm also pretending to be your faithful and loyal employee. But that's just the tip of the iceberg. I'm also the half sister of your best friend, and the daughter of your company's worst enemy.*

"Nicholas, I—I…" She couldn't finish because she wasn't even sure what she would say.

"What is it, Shayla?" he asked as his gaze searched hers intently. "What's bothering you tonight?"

The deep concern in his voice was her undoing—almost. She knew that she could not be completely honest with him. She had a lot to think about, especially now that others had somehow entered the mix in her plot for revenge. She had a brother, for Pete's sake! She needed a clear head to totally think things through, and there was no way that she could have a clear head around Nicholas.

"Shayla?"

Knowing she owed him some sort of an explanation, she came up with one that really wasn't too far from the truth. "It's nothing," she said, smiling a little. "Other than tonight."

He continued to study her. "What about tonight?"

She couldn't handle his gaze, all intense, all serious. "Let's just skip it. It's nothing, really." She leaned her head on his chest, and he continued to hold her close.

"Tell me," he whispered in her ear as his fingertips brushed her cheek. "Talk to me, Shayla. What's bothering you?"

Shayla shivered at his touch and lifted her gaze to his. "I feel like Cinderella at the ball. Right now everyone thinks I'm your fiancée, but when the clock strikes twelve—or better yet, when we get into the limo to return to the hotel—the fantasy is over. Then I go back to being Shayla Kirkland, your employee, and you'll become Mr. Chenault, my boss. Things will become business as usual." She took a deep breath. "I know it. I understand it. I accept it. But for right now, Nicholas, it's all rather depressing."

All around them other couples swirled, lost in their own world as they danced. Suddenly Nicholas stopped dancing. Holding her hand firmly in his, he led her toward the huge double doors leading to the gardens. She didn't say anything as they moved through the cluster of flowers and over the immaculately groomed and beautifully landscaped lawn.

What she hadn't told him was that at the moment her emotions were jumbled up. And there was nothing she could do about it, because she had done the one thing she should never have done. She had let her guard down.

Suddenly they stopped walking. Shayla felt the heat of Nicholas's gaze on her, but she didn't dare look at him. Instead she looked across the lawn at the beautiful lake, and tried to place her concentration there. It didn't work when he lifted her chin with his finger and forced her to lock her gaze with his.

"I thought it would be true, but I had to see it for myself," he whispered softly. "You're even more beautiful out here in the moonlight."

A sigh broke from Shayla with his words—a defeated sigh. She shivered, not from the coolness of the night but from the intensity of Nicholas's gaze and the passionate charges that were skittering through her bloodstream.

Then, without another exchange of words between them, Nicholas pulled her into his arms and slowly lowered his mouth to hers. Shayla was profoundly thankful for the cluster of hedges that blocked them from anyone's view. This, more than likely, would be their last kiss, and she wanted to savor every heartstopping moment of it.

Shayla knew she was totally past gone the moment Nicholas's lips touched hers like a whisper. At first his kiss was slow, thoughtful, and gentle as he moved his mouth over hers, devouring her completely. She tightened her hold on his shoulders when he put his tongue into action, deepening the kiss and tasting her in a very passionate way.

Nicholas forced Shayla to experience the same divine ecstasy that he was experiencing as he stroked the insides of her mouth with all-consuming intensity. He wanted this. For some reason, he needed this, craved this. What he was sharing with her was potent. It was soul-stirring. It was what he'd been lacking in his life for a long time.

It was Shayla.

That thought totally filled his mind as he continued to kiss her with an intimacy that had his mouth burning and still wanting more. A groan of pleasure escaped his lips and mixed with the sound of the wind flowing through the trees. If she could bring him to this point of madness with just a kiss, he didn't want to think of the outcome if he ever made love to her. The force of his climax just might kill him.

But then, if he had to die that way it would be a very pleasurable death.

Out of the necessity to breathe, the kiss ended—somewhat. He continued to shower kisses around her lips and along her jaw. His mouth grazed her earlobe, the tip of her nose, and then brushed against her brow. There wasn't a place on her face that he didn't want to kiss.

"Nicholas."

His name flowed from Shayla's lips in a breathless sigh. He felt a tightening in his groin just from the sensuous sound of it. He needed to hear his name, and only his name, from her lips. He had actually experienced jealousy tonight when she had smiled at Trent. That had never happened to him before with any woman. "Say my name again, Shayla," he coaxed in a whisper, sweeping her lips with the moist tip of his tongue.

A heated shiver ran up her spine, and a soft moan escaped her when she spoke. "Nicholas."

He pulled her closer as the seductive sound of her voice inflamed his desire and sent ripples of wanting through his entire body. "After tonight," he whispered against the warmth of her lips, "it won't be business as usual between us ever again."

Then he lowered his mouth to reclaim hers once more, with an ache he intended to ease. Moments later, when they heard conversation, they broke apart.

Nicholas inhaled sharply. So did Shayla. It took them a few moments to catch their breaths.

"Nicholas, I—"

He placed a finger on her lips to silence her. He looked deeply into her eyes. "No. Let's not try to analyze anything tonight."

Shayla took another deep breath and shivered when Nicholas's hands covered hers. He was right. She didn't want to think hard about anything tonight. Thinking would make her remember everything, and confuse her even more.

"Come on," he said softly. "Let's find Paul and say goodnight to Trent. I'm ready to leave and return to the hotel."

Shayla nodded. So was she.

"Where's Trent?"

Paul eyed the couple speculatively before answering. "He's over there talking to his old man. Why?"

Nicholas's face was calm and controlled when he said, "I wanted to let him know I'm leaving and going back to the hotel."

Paul made a conscious effort to keep his face expressionless when he said, "You're leaving? So soon?"

"We've stayed an appropriate length of time."

Shayla took a deep breath when Nicholas looked at her. The heat of his gaze flooded through her with a force that left her in total awe.

Nicholas returned his gaze to Paul. "If you want to stay longer I can send the limo back for you."

Paul shifted his gaze from Nicholas to Shayla, then back to Nicholas again, assessing them, "Yeah, I think I will. That'll give me the opportunity to visit some more with Trent tonight. And don't worry about sending the limo back for me. I'll just catch a ride back with Trent, since he's also saying at the hotel."

"Won't he be spending time with his father?" Nicholas asked.

"No. Jordache has some sort of business meeting later."

Nicholas nodded and turned his attention to Shayla. "Ready to leave?"

Shayla had to mentally shake herself from the spell Nicholas cast on her whenever he looked at her a certain way with his golden eyes. "Yes. Good night, Paul."

"Good night."

When Nicholas and Shayla turned to leave, Paul said casually, "Oh, Nick. You may want to tell the driver not to take the scenic route back. It'll take longer if he does."

Shayla felt herself flush. Paul's comment, followed by his dimpled smile, caught her off guard.

After saying good-night to the Mings, Nicholas and Shayla were crossing the room to leave when she happened to glance sideways and see Thomas Jordache watching her with a sharp tilt of his head and a rather curious gaze. His look made her shoulders stiffen.

Nicholas pulled her closer, and whispered low and deep in her ear, "You're not having second thoughts about leaving, are you?"

Shayla relaxed her shoulders when she felt Nicholas's touch move down her arm and caress the center of her back. She smiled up at him, forcing her mind to dismiss Thomas Jordache. "No, I'm not. What about you?"

He laughed, a small laugh that indicated her question had amused him. "Not on your life, sweetheart."

Chapter 11

Although the limo driver avoided taking the scenic route as Nicholas had instructed, it seemed to be taking an enormous amount of time for them to return to the hotel. Unlike on the drive to dinner, Nicholas didn't have to ask Shayla to sit close to him. She automatically did so once she had gotten settled in the limo. And this time she was not surprised when he placed his arms around her shoulders.

Whenever she looked at him, he gave her a smile that seemed to come as automatically as a heartbeat. He was seducing her, not putting a whole lot of effort into it. He was just being himself. The one thing she had found out about Nicholas Chenault in the time she'd known him was that he never did things half-measure. Whatever he did, he went all the way. He was meticulous about whatever he was doing, and she had a feeling that that would include making love. There was no doubt in her mind that he was as exceptional a lover as he was a businessman.

Shayla fought the warning signs that began to go off in her head. She knew they had only met two weeks ago, and had spent less than a week together since that time. But something was taking place between them that she was unable to stop. She had never in her twenty-six years wanted a man the way she wanted Nicholas. She hadn't known that such desire and longing, such ardent craving, could exist.

Was it momentary madness? Possibly. At that point she wouldn't rule anything out. Whatever it was, she didn't understand it, but tonight she would accept it. How could she not, when her senses were spinning with wanting him? His masculine scent was stirring her femininity in a way it had never been stirred before. No man had ever pushed as many of her buttons as Nicholas could push, seemingly without even trying.

Shayla's eyes fluttered closed when she felt Nicholas's fingers graze the side of her face with a gentleness that almost robbed her of breath. He tilted her face to him to meet his gaze.

"I want to make love to you," he whispered in a low husky voice.

His bold declaration made heat travel up Shayla's legs, past her thighs, and settle in the very core of her. She knew that the sultry sigh that escaped her lips told him all that he needed to know. He smiled, and the look in his eyes held promises of a night she would never forget.

She inhaled deeply when the limo pulled in front of the hotel. When it came to a stop, Nicholas got out and offered her his hand. Then they walked up the steps and into the lobby to catch the elevator.

There were quite a number of people in the elevator. Nicholas stood very close to her, and it seemed to Shayla that his gaze was honing in on everything about her. He touched her, stroking her arms tenderly up and down, nerves. He leaned over closer to her and whispered seductively in her ear, "Which do you prefer, my room or yours?"

For a long moment she didn't answer. Did it matter which room they used? Then, for some reason, she decided that it did. She didn't want to be just another woman he took to his bed, but she did want him to be the first man she took to hers.

"Mine," she replied softly.

She felt his arms tighten around her waist when the elevator doors swooshed open. Once they reached her door she nervously inserted the key in the lock. Before she opened the door she turned to him, hesitating.

Nicholas gazed down at her with a questioning glint in his golden eyes. "Is this where you tell me you've changed your mind, after all?" he asked in his deep husky voice.

Shayla shook her head. "No. This is where I tell you that I've never done anything like this before. I've never invited a man in after a date for the sole purpose of making love to me," she said quietly, honestly, unashamedly.

Golden eyes met her dark ones. The look in his was intense and thoughtful. "Do you want to tell me why you're doing it now?"

Shayla pursed her lips, wishing she knew. Maybe it was the impact of seeing her biological father for the first time, and the discovery that she had a brother. Maybe she felt the need to lose herself in passion instead of thinking about it. Then, maybe, it wasn't anything as deep as either of those. There was a good chance, a darn good chance, that Nicholas had touched her in a way no other man ever had, although she'd never meant for it to happen. He had somehow found a way to mess with her heart. Now she understood her aunt's warning.

"Shayla?"

He still waited for her response. "Because I want to," she finally answered truthfully, meeting his gaze before opening the door.

Nicholas followed her inside. No sooner had the door closed behind them than he reached out and pulled her into his arms, promptly kissing her. The fierce need to make love to her shocked him. He drew back abruptly, breaking the kiss. His mind was trying to resist, telling him it was too soon for them to make love although it was what they both wanted. But his body was urging him to become lost in her sensuality. He felt helpless under Shayla Kirkland's spell.

Gently pulling her back into his arms, he kissed her with a frenzy that washed away any lingering doubts. His lips seared hers, hot, hungry. He needed her so much, and his need was profound when he felt her melt in his arms. The heat of her burned through to him. An overpowering rush of desire rumbled from deep in his throat. He tried to fight for calm, and discovered that with Shayla there was no such thing.

Shayla felt her senses reel, and she moaned faintly when Nicholas continued to kiss her in such a way that made pure sensual abandonment run through her. He was making her body want something it never had before—intimate contact with a man. She felt lushly wanton, her skin hot and flushed. Something had her in a grip beyond anything she'd ever known, in a tight hold beyond her control. All the torrid dreams she'd had of him came crashing in on her, and she became caught up in a quivering need that was just as strong as his.

Out of control, almost out of his mind, Nicholas pulled Shayla down with him onto the plush carpet. There was no way they could make it to a bedroom. He wanted her, and he wanted her now.

Swept up in a rush to be one with her, he groaned as he continued to kiss her, tangling his hands in her hair, consuming her mouth with an intensity that overwhelmed him.

He suddenly came to his feet, and began removing his

clothes at a frantic pace. All the while his eyes were hot on hers, watching her, absorbing everything about her—the way she was looking up at him through passion-glazed eyes, and the soft "oh," that escaped her lips moments later when she looked at him, every inch of him, standing completely nude before her. He saw her body tremble with desire as she watched him quickly put on a condom.

Then he got on his knees and began removing her clothes, kissing her, making love to her mouth while doing so. When he had removed her dress and she lay before him in a filmy black lace chemise and matching bikini panties, he felt any control he had slip away. And when she rose on her knees, cupped his face in her hands, and covered his lips with her warm moist ones, imitating what he'd done to her mouth moments earlier by sucking on his tongue, he was almost done in.

With a deep guttural groan he eased her back and began removing the last of the clothes from her body. He didn't think he was going to make it when he eased the lace bikini panties down her hips, exposing the very essence of her to his eyes. He struggled desperately for breath, wanting so much what he saw, wanting to become lost in the very essence of that part of her body.

"Shayla…"

Nicholas slid between her thighs, letting his body cover hers. He drew in a deep breath when she bent her knees and wrapped her silky legs around his waist, hooking their bodies together. She captured his mouth again, wrapping her arms around his neck. Her hold was as tight as her legs were around his waistline. She kissed him as she whimpered her need and her desire. She was driving him and his body mad. She had no idea what she was doing to him.

It was time she knew.

Bracing himself with an arm on each side of her, he looked

down at her. Her eyes glowed with total desire for him. No woman had ever made him feel this way, this hot and this ready…this out of control. He couldn't even think straight. He stared at her, stunned, overwhelmed that any woman had the power to bring him to this state. Greedy. Needy.

She whispered something to him, a request—an urgent plea, and he sucked in a deep breath when he comprehended her words. When he didn't act quickly enough to suit her, she repeated them. "I need you inside me, Nicholas. Now!"

Her words made the primitive urge to mate, man to woman, male to female, overpower him. He lifted the lower part of her body and in one swift hard stroke he began to enter her.

He froze when he became confronted with a barrier… which meant…

The shock of his discovery jolted through him. Perspiration sprang onto his forehead, and with a groan he leaned down and buried his face in the crook of her neck, inhaling a sharp breath of air, trying to get control and failing miserably.

"Why didn't you tell me?" he murmured, still struggling for breath when he lifted his face and looked down at her.

She didn't answer. Instead, she reached up and looped her arms around his neck and pulled his mouth down to hers, kissing him in a way that was totally different than before. This kiss was gentle, pleading, probing, and gripping. She was kissing him mindless. And when she arched her body and brought him deeper inside of her, he knew he couldn't pull out then even if he wanted to.

Gritting his teeth, he drove deeper, his mouth absorbing her shock of pain. Seconds later, after her body had adjusted to the invasion of his, she thrust her hips upward, urging him to continue what he had started.

And so he did.

With an instinct as old as mankind, Nicholas made love

to the woman in his arms. His body gave to her in a way it had never given to another woman, freely, uncontrollably. Each thrust he made into her was hard and went deep. Each downstroke made his body shudder with pleasure and shiver with emotions he didn't understand. His throat ached with the effort of trying to be gentle, but he wanted her too much. His need for her was too great, and she was drawing everything out of him with a hunger that was just as fierce as his.

"Nicholas…"

Somewhere in the recesses of his mind, there came a warning—from his heart—but he ignored it. He couldn't think of anything but meeting the upward movements of Shayla's hips, stroke for stroke. And when he felt her inner muscles that surrounded him tighten, when her body arched in a bow that would have been an archer's dream, he threw his head back and a deep loud growl sprang forth from his throat. At the same time, she screamed out his name. He tightened his hold on her to keep her in place as his body exploded inside her, driving him to a shattering release. She continued to cry out his name over and over as her fingernails dug in the center of his back. He felt her shuddering uncontrollably under him, and instinctively covered her mouth as their joined bodies quivered in the aftershocks of a climax that had rocked both their worlds.

Nicholas collapsed on the floor beside Shayla and pulled her into his arms. He turned his head to look at her, not knowing what to say. Never had making love to a woman been that wild and that intense. He had taken her on the floor, for heaven's sake! There was no way he could have made it to the bedroom. His need had been urgent and desperate. She had taken him to a place he had never been before, and had been an absolute sensuous tigress in his arms. Now she lay beside him looking sweet, serene, innocent.

Innocent.

That one word made him remember. "Shayla, why didn't you tell—"

The words he was about to say were cut off when his phone sounded. Forcing enough energy into his body, he reached for his pants, got the mobile phone out of the pocket, and checked it. "It's Paul."

Shayla watched as Nicholas stood nude and answered his phone. Her gaze was mostly on his body, but a quick glance up at his face while he talked to Paul indicated something was wrong. Not sharing his lack of modesty, she put her panties and chemise back on before easing to her feet and crossing the room to him when he hung up the phone. "Nicholas, what is it? What's wrong?"

"Paul just got word that there's been a fire at our Jacksonville laboratory. Our security people seem to think it was set deliberately. I need to leave right away."

Shayla nodded, understanding completely as she watched him begin putting on his clothes. "I'm sorry to hear that. I hope everything's all right."

"Luckily no one was there."

"Was there much damage?"

"I don't know, and Paul didn't know, either. I hope not. That was the lab we were using for our most recent project." The muscles in Nicholas's jaw hardened. "If I thought for one minute that Thomas Jordache had anything to do with this, I'd—"

"But how could he? He's here in Hong Kong."

"Trust me. The man can pay people to do anything he wants to have done."

Shayla swallowed. "Do you actually think he was involved?"

Nicholas inhaled sharply and patted the top of his head. "I don't know. Paul seems to think so. But Paul had to be careful what he said because Trent was with him just now. Although Trent knows how ruthless his father used to be, he wants to believe his old man has changed."

"But Paul doesn't?"

Nicholas nodded. "No. But he doesn't want to damage his relationship with Trent by making accusations that may not be true against Jordache."

Nicholas paused for a brief moment. Then he reached out and lifted Shayla's chin to meet his gaze. "I need to go to my room, change clothes, and pack. Paul's making arrangements for the two of us to fly out of here in an hour." He leaned over and brushed a kiss across her lips. When he saw that would not be enough for him, he sighed heavily before his mouth ascended over hers, feasting hungrily. He could feel his body getting hard, wanting her again. Reluctantly, he ended the kiss. "I have to go," he said softly.

Shayla nodded. "Have a nice flight back home."

"Will you be all right?" he asked when it suddenly occurred to him that he and Paul would be leaving her alone, in Hong Kong. "Your flight doesn't leave until tomorrow afternoon, and—"

"Nicholas, I'll be fine. You have enough on your mind. Don't think about me."

He then leaned over and kissed her soundly on the mouth. "But I am thinking about you, anyway, and I'll continue to think about you, Shayla Kirkland, for quite a while." He looked at her and drew in a deep breath. "About tonight, what we shared and it being your first time. I—"

She reached up a placed a finger on his lips, sealing off any further words. "Don't, Nicholas. No regrets. Everything I did tonight I did because I wanted to," she said. *Because I now know in my heart that I love you,* she thought silently. *That's why I gave my body to you. My heart had already become yours.*

He searched her face, and she felt the deep intensity of his gaze. He bent his head and brushed his lips across hers before her mouth parted under his. He then kissed her with a devastating sweetness that stole the very breath from her body.

Moments later, he raised his head and walked over to the door. Before opening it he turned back around to her. His gaze was on her face, then moved over her near-naked body as if remembering what they had shared moments ago. He returned his gaze to her face. The hot look he gave her heightened her senses and made her body quiver from the sharp rush of emotions it evoked. "I promise to call you," he said huskily.

He opened the door, then closed it behind him.

The phone was picked up on the first ring. "Yes?"

"It's been taken care of."

"Are you sure?"

"Positive. Nicholas Chenault isn't going to be too happy when he returns."

"Be careful. He's bound to figure out it was an inside job."

"Maybe, and maybe not. But if I were you, I'd make sure I covered my tracks. Paul Dunlap isn't a dummy."

A frown touched the man's face. "Believe me, I know that."

Chapter 12

"Need help with those?"

Shayla glanced over her shoulder and blinked twice when she saw Trent Jordache standing beside her in the terminal. She was so surprised at seeing him that she nearly tripped over the luggage sitting in front of her. Transfixed, she stared at him a second before finally asking, "What are you doing here?"

Trent smiled, then glanced around. "This is an airport. I'm here like everyone else—to catch a flight."

Shayla shook her head, realizing how stupid her question must have sounded. "What I meant is that I'm surprised to see you. I didn't know you'd be leaving Hong Kong today."

"I had planned to stay a little longer, then changed my mind. My father's business meetings concluded early. He wanted to stay a while longer, and I didn't."

Shayla nodded. She then remembered something Paul had mentioned to her last night. "I thought that you weren't involved with TJ Electronics."

He glanced down at his wristwatch, then said, "Actually I'm not, but my father makes it a point to include me in certain aspects of the business. Especially if it involves something major."

"And the meeting was about something major?" she asked calmly.

"Ah, I can't tell you that, Shayla," Trent said with a slow grin. "After all, you do work for Chenault Electronics, and everyone knows that TJ and Chenault are big competitors."

Shayla nodded. "Yet you and Nicholas are friends."

He chuckled. "Yes, the very best. We make it a point to not discuss any business when we're together."

"But still, I'd think it would place a strain on your friendship."

He shrugged. "We work very hard at not letting it. There's more to life than money. There's something like true friendship, which has an even greater value. Speaking of Nick, have you heard from him?"

Shayla shook her head. "No, but he should be back in the States by now. I hope he finds everything all right."

"So do I." He glanced at his watch again. "It seems we're on the same flight going back into Chicago. After we get our luggage checked in, how about if we go somewhere and grab a cup of coffee? We have a good hour to kill before our flight takes off."

Shayla smiled. "I'd like that."

Nicholas looked around the laboratory, too stunned to move as he assessed the damage.

"It's not as bad as it could have been, Nick," said Elliott Russell, Jacksonville's fire chief, when he came to stand next to Nicholas. Elliott and Nicholas had been star football players, helping to make the Vikings of William M. Raines

High School state champions for two years straight. Elliott had been captain of the team their senior year.

Nicholas nodded, then knelt in front of a burned-out piece of lab equipment. Shaking his head, he stood up. "Do you think it was an accident?"

Elliott shook his head. "Can't say. I want to do a thorough investigation, not jump to any kind of conclusion."

Nicholas nodded. He glanced over at Paul, who was talking to Fred Bostwick, the security man who'd been on duty. From the young man's grim expression he could tell that Paul was giving him hell for what could be perceived as a breach in security at the lab. From what Elliott had told Nicholas earlier, due to the state-of-the-art smoke alarm system Nicholas had installed, the blaze had been discovered early enough to cause minimal damage, and fortunately no one had gotten hurt. Although the lab had been closed, security guards on duty usually made their rounds in the building periodically.

"How long will the investigation take?"

"A few days, but you can get your insurance people in here as early as tomorrow."

Nicholas nodded. He was glad to hear that. But still, he was under a tight schedule, and in order to stay on it he would have to move this part of the project to the Chicago lab. He hadn't really wanted that. For security purposes it would have been much better to operate things in Jacksonville, but now that wouldn't be possible.

Elliott tipped his head back and looked at Nicholas. He smiled. "I hate to tell you this, but you look like hell. Jet lag combined with a burned lab just don't agree with you, buddy."

Nicholas couldn't keep from chuckling. Leave it to Elliott to find humor even in a bad situation. He'd done that in school whenever they'd lost an important game, especially when they'd worked their butts off to win. Elliott's easy wit and sense of humor had kept the team's spirits high.

"I would imagine they wouldn't agree with me, El. By the way, how's Nina?" Elliott had married a childhood friend of theirs who had attended a rival neighborhood high school.

"Nina's fine. She wants a baby, and is rather insistent about it. My body's being used as a means to an end."

Nicholas shook his head, smiling. "And you really look all torn up about it."

Elliott lifted a brow, returning Nicholas's smile. "I do? Really?"

"No, you don't. You look like a man who likes being used that way."

Elliott laughed. "I admit that it has its advantages."

Nicholas joined him in laughter, realizing just how much he needed it. "You'd have a hard time convincing me that it doesn't."

Shayla placed the magazine she'd been reading in her lap and glanced at the man sitting beside her. Trent's head was tilted back against the headrest, and his fingers were resting across his chest. She could tell from the gentle rise and fall of his chest that he was sleeping. She couldn't keep from smiling at the way he had finagled the seat from an older lady who had been sitting next to her on the plane.

Shayla glanced at her watch. They had six more hours of airtime to endure. She had just finished reading her fourth magazine in its entirety. She adjusted her seat back and closed her eyes, remembering the conversation she and Trent had over coffee. She liked him. If things had been different, he could have been the big brother she had wanted while growing up.

But things had not been different. Even now, after meeting him, she was still glad things had worked out the way they had for her parents. They were meant to be together, and now, knowing the truth about her father's sterility, she was so glad she had been his daughter. Knowing that he had unselfishly accepted and loved another man's child as his own just made that much more love flow in her heart for Glenn Kirkland.

But then, a terrible ache grew in her heart as she realized that she would probably never be able to tell Trent that they were brother and sister. She had made a decision to give up her plan of revenge against Chenault Electronics, since she'd allowed personal feelings to get involved. She could never tell Trent of their true relationship, for fear of Thomas Jordache finding out. Under no circumstances did she ever want the man to know. As far as she was concerned, she was better off if he believed her mother had gotten the abortion that he had suggested.

"Is it too much to hope for that we're about to land?"

Shayla opened her eyes and tilted her head sideways to glance at Trent, who was looking at her with sleepy but hopeful eyes. She gave him a rather rueful amused look. "Sorry, we're still about six to seven hours away. You may want to go back to sleep."

He smiled over at her. "I think I will, Ms. Kirkland." Then he closed his eyes.

Happiness slid through Nicholas when he pulled his car into the driveway and saw his mother, Angeline Chenault, on her knees tending her rose garden. He thanked God every time he saw her. Last year he had come very close to losing her when she had developed a brain tumor. On the same day she had sat him down to tell him about her medical condition she had also told him that he had a brother—a brother he hadn't known existed.

She had been married at seventeen to a man she had thought she loved, only to discover she had made a mistake marrying so young. A pregnancy soon after the marriage had complicated things, and six weeks after the child was born Angeline had asked her husband for a divorce, given him full custody of their child, and left both husband and child behind in North Carolina to pursue her dreams.

She had worked in Atlanta for a couple of years before deciding to move to Miami. While she and a girlfriend made a stop in Jacksonville on their way to Miami she'd been fortunate enough to meet Alan Chenault. They had married, and a couple of years later Nicholas had been born.

Nicholas had not known about his mother's other life before she had met his father, and he sure hadn't known that the world-famous movie actor Sterling Hamilton was the son his mother had turned her back on years ago. But Sterling had known, and he'd grown up bitter that Angeline could so easily replace the life she had shared with him and his father, wiping both of them from her memory, and start a new life that included another husband and son.

After asking Sterling for forgiveness last year—for the actions of a confused young woman who at the age of seventeen had thought that fame and fortune were everything—Angeline and Sterling were working very hard to build the relationship they'd never had. Nicholas was enjoying the fact that he had an older brother. Even more important, Sterling had become a good friend.

When Nicholas got out of the car he saw his mother had stood, and was smiling brilliantly at him. He smiled back. From the time he could remember, he and his parents had had a very close relationship, and he'd thought that he'd known his mother better than anyone. That was why it had been hard for him to believe what she'd told him about turning her back on her first husband and son. The person who had done such a thing could not be the warm, caring, loving woman he knew as his mom. But, as she had explained to him, she'd been young and naive and had believed that money was everything, and she had been willing to sacrifice the love of a good man and her child to search for it.

But all that was in the past, and she had lived regretting her mistakes. His father had known the truth about her past, and had loved her with all his heart, anyway. Since she'd become his wife her values had changed, and she was an exceptional wife to him and a wonderful mother to their only child.

"Welcome home, Nicky," Angeline said, taking off her work gloves and placing them in a basket on the ground.

Nicholas shook his head. His mother was the only one still brave enough to call him by his childhood nickname. He walked over to her and gave her a huge hug. "It's good to be home, Mom."

After the hug Nicholas looked down at her. Even disheveled, dressed in an oversize workshirt and pair of frayed shorts, his mother was a fine-looking woman. She carried her age well, and didn't look a day over fifty. And she sure didn't look like a woman who had two sons in their thirties and a granddaughter a little over a month old.

Angeline took Nicholas's large hand in her smaller one and led him into the house. "Come on in and join me in a cup of coffee. I want to hear all about your trip to China. I also want you to tell me about the fire in the lab last night."

"So you heard about it?"

"It was in this morning's paper. Was there much damage?"

Nicholas sat at the table while his mother went about pulling mugs out of a kitchen cabinet. "It's not as bad as it could have been. I won't know if the fire was deliberately set until the fire department finishes their investigation."

Angeline's expressive face mirrored her doubts. "Do you really think that was the case?"

"I don't know what to think, Mom, but you know Paul. He's willing to let the fire department and the insurance people come up with their own ideas, but he definitely has thoughts of Jordache being involved."

"Do you think he is?"

Nicholas accepted the mug of coffee his mother handed him. It smelled delicious. "I don't want to. Trent really believes his father has changed and intends to keep his promise and not cause Chenault Electronics any more problems. But still—"

"You can't let your guard down, right?"

Nicholas's smile widened. "Right." A frown settled on his face. "I just wish I knew the entire story of what brought on this bad blood between Dad and Jordache in the first place."

Angeline came and sat down at the table across from her son. "It happened a few years before I met your father, and he never divulged the full story to me." Deciding to change the subject, his mother took a sip of her coffee before asking, "So, how was Hong Kong?"

"Hong Kong was fine, and we were able to close out the Ling Deal."

"Oh, Nicky, that's wonderful. I'm glad to hear that. You must be pleased about it."

"Yes, I am. The negotiations were rough going for a while, but then a new employee of mine, Shayla Kirkland, saved the day. She was something else."

Something in Nicholas's tone caught his mother's attention and piqued her interest. "Really? Tell me about her."

Nicholas looked into the coffee mug, thinking of what he could say to his mother about Shayla. There was so much to tell. "She's smart, intelligent, and used to manage the Business Department at Howard University. She came to work for us a week ago. She speaks four languages, and, with an MBA from Harvard, she has a great sense of business. I think she'll be an asset to the company. Even Paul thinks highly of her." He couldn't tell his mother that he also thought highly of her, but for other reasons—she was beautiful, sensuous, and he had enjoyed making love to her. The bottom line was that Shayla Kirkland had gotten to him in a way no other woman had, and truthfully, that scared him. Now that there was distance between them and he had reclaimed his space, he needed to think things through. He had actually slept with one of his employees, something he'd never done. He needed to get his mind back on track and put things between him and Shayla back into perspective.

"Will I get the chance to meet her, Nicky?"

Nicholas shook his head. "I doubt it. She works out of the Chicago office. I see no reason for her to ever visit my office here. Besides, there's no reason why you would ever have to meet her."

Angeline nodded. Her son was saying one thing, but the wistful look in his eyes while he'd been discussing Shayla Kirkland had hinted at something else. Angeline decided to change the subject, for now. "Sterling and Colby have sent more pictures of Chandler. Do you want to see them? She's getting bigger every day."

Nicholas smiled. "Yes, I'd love to."

When his mother left the kitchen to get the pictures, Nicholas stood and walked over to the window and looked out. He was missing Shayla something fierce, and—although he was fighting thinking about her—he was doing so, anyway. Her plane should be arriving in Chicago about now. He had told her he would call her, and he'd intended to, but now he knew that wouldn't be wise. The attraction that had developed between them had been a mistake from the start. He had been thinking more with a certain part of his body—the one below the belt—than with his head, and that was what he had acted on. It had taken something like the fire at the lab to reel him back in. He didn't have time to let his mind wander, to allow his body to start constant cravings. He had gotten caught up in the moment. Chances were that Shayla, like him, was also regretting what had happened in Hong Kong.

Nicholas turned away from the window when his mother returned carrying a large envelope filled with photographs. Somehow he would get Shayla out of his mind, and when he did see her again he would be able to deal with it.

"Are you sure you don't need a ride?"

Shayla smiled up at Trent. "I'm positive. My aunt is picking me up, but thanks for asking, anyway."

"No problem. Nick would have my hide if he thought I'd left you stranded." Trent reached into the pocket of his jacket and pulled out a business card. "Pass this on to that Realtor friend of yours."

Shayla accepted the card. "Thanks, and I will."

"Well, take care, and when you do talk to Nick ask him to call me."

"Okay."

"I hope to see you around."

"Same here."

Trent turned to leave, and Shayla watched him until he got lost in the crowd of people rushing across the terminal.

"Who was that?"

Shayla turned, hearing her aunt's voice. She hadn't heard her approach. She dropped her carry-on and gave her aunt a hug, glad to see her. "That was Trent Jordache… my half brother."

Shayla watched the expression on her aunt's face turn into one of total shock. "Come on, Aunt Callie, let's get out of here. I'll tell you everything in the car."

Chapter 13

"So what do you plan to do now?"

Frowning, Shayla briefly mulled over her aunt's question before finally answering, "There's only one thing I *can* do, and that's to quit. I'll turn in my two weeks' notice when I go into the office on Wednesday."

Callie looked over at her niece, who was sitting across from her on the sofa. Shayla's shoulders were hunched slightly forward, her gaze was pinned to the floor, and the expression on her face was one of abject misery. But it was the sadness she saw in her eyes that bothered Callie more than anything. There was no doubt in her mind that there was more to Nicholas Chenault than Shayla was saying, and that he meant more than she was admitting.

She watched her for a moment, thinking about another young woman who'd once had that same look of sadness in her eyes over a man. A part of Callie didn't want to see Shayla make the same mistake.

"And then there's Paul."

Callie shot her niece a quick look. "Paul?"

"Yes, Paul Dunlap, Nicholas's top security man. He worked for Chenault long before Nicholas was born, so he had to have been there when Mom worked there. A couple of times I saw him looking at me oddly. Do you think he made the connection between me and Mama?"

Callie thought long and hard as she studied Shayla's face, carefully examining her features. She had a resemblance to her mother, but not so much that anyone would easily make a connection. After all, it had been over twenty-seven years. And in Callie's opinion, she looked more like her father. "No, I don't think so."

"Good."

"What about Trent Jordache?"

Shayla lifted her head and held a calm level gaze with her aunt. "A part of me wants to tell him, but then another part of me wants to forget that I've discovered we're related. Trent being my brother makes the fact Thomas Jordache is my biological father that much more real. And I don't want to deal with that man being connected to me in any way."

"People make mistakes, and they do change, Shayla."

"He hasn't changed if he's the one responsible for that fire at Nicholas's lab."

"People are also innocent until proven guilty."

The frown on Shayla's face deepened, and she lifted her chin a notch. "Why are you coming to that man's defense?"

"For the same reason I didn't want you involved with Chenault Electronics in the first place. You don't know the full story of what happened twenty-seven years ago, and you don't know the full story of what's happening now. I think you'll do everyone an injustice if you assume anything."

Shayla nodded. "That's why I'm turning in my resignation. There's no way I can work there now."

"I think you should rethink that decision."

Shayla was startled by her aunt's suggestion. "But why?"

"Because, although you haven't admitted it to me and possibly not even to yourself, I think that you care a great deal for Nicholas Chenault." She stood and crossed the room and sat down next to her niece. "I think I can even go so far as to say you've fallen in love with him."

Callie held up her hand when Shayla started to interrupt her. "Don't bother denying it, especially to me. I don't know what happened between you and Nicholas Chenault in Hong Kong, and maybe it's for the best that I don't know, but what's important is how you feel for him inside, here," she said, placing the same hand over her heart.

Shayla gazed lovingly at her aunt, wondering if she'd ever been in love. For as long as she could remember, her aunt had never been involved in a serious relationship, although she was sure numerous men had been interested. Callie Foster was too good-looking for men not to have been. She did speak like a woman who had experienced love at some point in her life.

The look in Shayla's eyes turned soft, curious. She thought about what her aunt had just said. She didn't have to wonder if she was in love with Nicholas. She knew that she was. "What if everything's one-sided?" she asked her aunt quietly. "What if Nicholas was just caught up in being happy about things working out the way he'd wanted regarding the Ling Deal? What if what he felt was nothing but a case of lust and nothing more, and what if—"

"And what if," Callie interrupted, "he left Hong Kong caring as deeply for you as you care for him? Don't you think you'd want to know the truth?"

"The truth..." Shayla's voice trailed off with those words. A thick lump formed in her throat. "How can I expect the truth when my working at Chenault Electronics has been a lie from the very beginning? I only went to work there to destroy the company."

"Then at some point you'll have to be completely honest with Nicholas, tell him everything. And if he loves you he'll understand."

Shayla rose and walked over to the window and looked out. She knew what her aunt had just said was the truth. At some point in time she would have to tell Nicholas everything, and hope he understood.

Callie came and stood beside her. "I suggest you put everything out of your mind for a while and get some rest. You have too many issues to deal with, and you don't have to tackle everything all at once."

She put her arms around Shayla's shoulders. "Go on and take your shower and get into bed. When you wake up you'll feel better."

Shayla nodded, but she knew it would take more than a shower and a few hours of sleep to make her feel better.

It was close to midnight when Nicholas shut the door behind him, thinking how good it was to be back home. This was his place. His space. And he shared it with no one. He wanted to take a shower, but was too keyed up to do it right then.

After he left his mother's home he had gone back to the office to see if Elliott had any news for him. He had. Just as was suspected—arson. Someone had deliberately set fire to the lab. Traces of kerosene were found in one corner of the room near a window.

Nicholas inhaled deeply, wishing for something stronger to drink than the can of beer in the refrigerator. Better still, he felt the need to slam his fist into a wall. It was a good thing the phone rang right then. He picked it up. "Yeah?"

"Nick? This is Trent. You okay?"

With a heavy sigh Nicholas sat down on the edge of his desk. "I'm just fine and dandy, for someone who discovered that someone tried to burn him out."

There was a pause. "You think my father had something to do with it, don't you?"

Nicholas rubbed his palm against his forehead. "Considering his past track record, I'd be lying to you if I said the thought hadn't crossed my mind, Trent. But I want to be fair."

"You always have, and I appreciate that, Nick."

"Yeah, well, it's not always easy where your old man is concerned."

Nicholas heard a slight chuckle. "I know that."

Nicholas frowned. "There's going to be an investigation. Whatever the outcome, it's out of my hands," he said carefully.

He heard Trent draw in a slow breath. "Yeah, I know." There was another pause, then Trent asked, "Did Shayla give you my message?"

The raw ache Nicholas had been battling all day intensified. "I haven't talked to Shayla since I left Hong Kong."

"Oh?"

"But you have?" Nicholas found himself almost snapping out the question.

"Yes, we were on the same flight returning to the States. I managed to get a seat next to her."

For the second time a feeling of jealousy began to take root inside Nicholas, and that infuriated him as much as the thought of Trent and Shayla spending time together on the long flight. He was tempted to tell him to find a woman of his own, but stopped short. No woman had ever made him feel jealousy toward his best friend. He knew that Trent, like any man, would appreciate a beautiful woman. But he also knew his best friend could be trusted.

"Nick?"

"Yes?"

"Why haven't you talked to Shayla?"

Nicholas's frown deepened. "I've been busy."

"We've been back four days now."

"Yeah. So?" Nicholas found himself feeling irritable because he knew he should have called her, and guilty because he hadn't.

"I'd think you'd have at least picked up the phone to contact her. She indicated that you said you would," Trent said.

"As I told you, I've been busy. Besides, our engagement was fabricated for Ming and the others. I told you that."

"Yeah, but you also gave me the impression—in fact you made it pretty damn clear—that she was off-limits."

Nicholas struggled to keep his hands from tightening around the phone. "I got caught up in the moment, being in the company of a beautiful woman, Trent. Forget anything I said, or insinuated."

There was a long pause. "Are you sure about that, Nicholas?"

Nicholas laughed softly, wanting desperately to believe the words he had spoken to Trent. "Yeah, I'm sure. I have too much going on to get involved. A woman like Shayla can cloud your mind," he said. *She can invade your space,* he thought, *even worse, she could get into your heart.*

There was another pause. "When will you be returning to Chicago, Nick?"

"In another week or so. I have plenty of stuff to do here."

"Give me a call when you get to town so we can get together. There's something I need to talk to you about. There's a favor I need to ask," Trent said.

"Okay."

Nicholas ended the call with Trent, knowing he had just lied through his teeth. As much as he wanted to deny it, he was already involved with Shayla. Sleeping with someone like her constituted some sort of an involvement.

With a disgusted sigh he walked off to the kitchen.

Shayla made it through her first morning in the offices of Chenault Electronics. After her conversation with her aunt on Sunday, she had decided to continue working for the company until she could decide how she would handle giving Nicholas her resignation. His still being at the Jacksonville office made things easier for her. She didn't agree with the saying, "out of sight, out of mind," though—Nicholas was constantly in her thoughts.

It had been five days since she had returned from China, and he hadn't called her. At first she thought he hadn't gotten around to calling because of the fire situation. He'd probably been too busy. But, according to conversations she had overheard among the employees in the break room, damage wasn't all that extensive, and things were now pretty much back to normal. There was also some talk about bringing the big Jacksonville lab project to Chicago while the lab was being repaired.

Leanne, Nicholas's Chicago secretary, had put her in a spacious office down the hall from where Nicholas's office was located. She'd given her a huge stack of reports to read and go over that were related to her training as one of the managers for this particular site. The woman had also informed her that Mr. Chenault was not expected in the Chicago office for another week or so.

Deciding to put Nicholas out of her mind and concentrate on doing a good job, Shayla had begun going through all the papers on her desk. When she looked up, a man she'd never seen before was standing in her doorway.

"I didn't mean to disturb you, Ms. Kirkland."

Shayla put aside the papers she had been reading. She

had been introduced to the office staff earlier that morning, and since she knew how office gossip worked, she wasn't surprised that the man knew her name. "You didn't."

He entered the room. "I'm Carl Stockard, head of security here at Chenault."

Shayla frowned. She thought Paul was head of security. She stood and held out her hand. "Nice meeting you, Mr. Stockard. What happened to Paul?"

The man lifted a dark eyebrow and accepted her hand in a businesslike handshake. "What do you mean?"

"I thought Paul was the head of security here."

The man frowned. "Technically he still is, but more than likely I'll be the one taking his place when he retires next year. Normally, I rotate working out of both offices, but Mr. Chenault felt Paul was needed in Jacksonville because of the fire. So, I'm the one who'll be handling the security in this place for a while."

Shayla nodded. "Oh, I see."

"I might as well inform you that I like running a tight ship as far as security is concerned, Ms. Kirkland. I'd appreciate it if you'd follow all the rules and procedures that are established. You're to wear your name badge at all times, and avoid going to any areas that are marked unauthorized."

The man's curt words fanned Shayla's anger. She didn't too much care for Carl Stockard's brash tone, authoritarian manner, or the untrustworthy way he was looking at her. He was speaking to her as if she were part of Nicholas's clerical staff, and not his management team. "Well, I'm sure all that will change, Mr. Stockard, when Nic—Mr. Chenault—returns to this office. As one of his managers for this site, I'm sure I'll be authorized to go into any area here."

Carl Stockard narrowed his eyes at her. "Maybe you will. Maybe you won't. In the meantime, I'd appreciate it if you'd follow my directions and stay within the boundaries you've been given. It will make my job of keeping this place secure that much more easier."

Shayla nodded.

"Good day, Ms. Kirkland." The man then turned and walked out of Shayla's office.

Chapter 14

Nicholas wasn't listening to a word the speaker was saying. He had flown to D.C. to attend an important meeting of the NSBE, the National Society of Black Engineers. The NSBE's aim was to prepare African-American students for managerial roles in the technical force. Their present project—Technology 2000—targeted junior and senior high school students to encourage them to pursue careers in math and the sciences, stimulating their interest in new technology.

Today's speaker was very informative, and was providing the group with information about methods and resources that could be used to encourage interest in their targeted group.

But still, Nicholas's mind was elsewhere. It was on Shayla Kirkland.

It had been ten days, and still he had not contacted her. He had been busy, true enough, but not so busy that he couldn't have picked up a phone to call her. Instead, he'd called and spoken to Leanne to find out how Shayla had fared her first week on the job. His secretary had provided him with a glowing report. According to her, Shayla was a quick study and had a take-charge attitude, which was something that office needed. Already she had met with two first-level supervisors. She had also represented Chenault at a meeting of regional black businessmen whose focus was to increase African-American awareness of major on-line Internet services designed specifically for and by blacks.

Nicholas was also aware that Shayla was receiving additional job training by videoconferencing with his Jacksonville management team. He had also received another glowing report from Matt Sullivan, the senior operations manager from Jacksonville, about how well Shayla had done her first full week on the job.

The sound of applause brought Nicholas's attention back to the speaker, which meant the meeting was just about over. He would be dropping by Sterling's place in the North Carolina mountains before heading to Chicago. He wasn't looking forward to that meeting, knowing he would be seeing Shayla again. That would be awkward for both of them.

"I bet I can guess what you're thinking about right now," a deep voice said from his right.

I hope not, Nicholas thought as he looked over at Jessup Baron, a businessman in his late fifties from Jacksonville whom he had come to know over the years. Jessup owned a growing computer company that specialized in providing software for corporate users. Although his company had grown in sales and services over the past couple of years, it lagged far behind Chenault and TJ Electronics, preferring to operate as a regional and not a global operation.

"And just what is that, Jess?"

"What's on most young people's minds these days,"

Jessup replied, smiling. "How to go about making more money, and about all those other pleasures in life."

Nicholas nodded. What Jess had said was true—at least, the part about the pleasures in life pretty much equated with his thoughts about Shayla. Nicholas waited for the next question, which he knew was coming. He didn't have to wait long.

"How's your mother, Nicholas?"

Nicholas couldn't keep from smiling. It had become quite obvious that Jess was interested in his mother, and had been since first meeting her when he'd opened his business in Jacksonville two years ago. But so far the man hadn't made any effort to bring that interest out front to Angeline Chenault. Maybe it was time to nudge him in that direction.

"She's fine. You're always asking me about her. You ever thought about calling and talking to her yourself?"

Jess hesitated as he studied Nicholas. When he saw the teasing glint in the younger man's eyes, he grinned. "Actually, I've been thinking about it a lot lately. You don't mind?"

"Why would I mind? My mother's a grown woman. Trust me, she doesn't seek my permission on anything relating to her personal life."

"I wasn't sure how you would feel…considering your father," the man added.

Nicholas met Jess's gaze. "Dad's been gone over three years now. My parents had a good marriage, the best. I want my mother to be happy. She deserves it."

Jess was silent for a moment. "As a young man I always wanted a family, but I got my priorities mixed up and never married. I thought that making money was far more important than settling down with a wife and making babies." There was sadness in his voice when he added, "There was never any time." He met Nicholas's gaze. "Don't make the same mistake I made, son. Capture the moments, and do more than just think about those pleasures in life—pursue them. Then, when you get to be my age, you won't have regrets."

Nicholas nodded as he looked at Jess. "I'll keep that in mind."

Jess released a faint good-natured sigh. "Well, I'll be seeing you. And I will be giving your mother a call."

"Yeah, you do that."

Jess nodded, and then he stood and walked out of the room.

Shayla had seen the memo when she pulled up her e-mail at work on Friday. There would be a management meeting first thing Monday morning, and Nicholas would be attending it. It had been two weeks since she'd seen him.

She took a deep breath to calm her nerves. Her decision had been made. She would be giving him her two weeks' notice when she saw him. She had tried listening to her heart, but facts were facts. And the fact was that Nicholas was deliberately avoiding her. She didn't have to be a rocket scientist to figure that out. Due to Leanne's chatty nature, Shayla was aware of every time he called to get a report on her, but he never bothered calling her. So she went about her daily routine, trying to put Nicholas out of her mind.

That wasn't always easy—not with his employees always singing his praises, or her instant review of documents that contained his signature.

She had once walked into Leanne's office just as she was concluding a conversation with him. He'd been on the speakerphone, and the sound of his voice had been like heat sliding over her skin and seeping into every pore of her body. She had stood in Leanne's doorway with her heart pounding at a rate of two thousand beats a minute, her knees shaky, her fingers trembling. It was totally bizarre, the extent of what she felt for him. She couldn't help wondering how she had let herself fall in love with him. She had come to work at Chenault Electronics looking for revenge, not love.

She had known she was a goner the moment he kissed her. The touch of his mouth on hers had elicited a response that had totally overwhelmed her. All she had been able to do was wrap her arms around his neck, hang on for dear life, and return his kiss, shaking with passion so profound she could have kissed him all night. And when he had made love to her, joining their bodies as one as he stroked hers to a feverish pitch, it had been the ultimate in sexual pleasure. Although he had been her first lover, she couldn't imagine anything better than what she had experienced in Nicholas's arms. He had given her sensations so intense she'd literally felt she had come apart.

"Those must be some thoughts, Ms. Kirkland."

Shayla's gaze snapped up and she met the teasing glint in Trent's dark eyes. He stood in her doorway and watched her for a moment, his arms casually folded across his chest.

"Trent," she began, clearing her throat, glad that he wasn't a mind reader. "What are you doing here?"

Trent gave a bark of laughter. "I've noticed that whenever we see each other you always start by asking me that. Are there certain places you think I shouldn't be?"

"No, I'm just surprised to see you."

He smiled. "But pleasantly surprised, I hope? I just dropped by hoping to see Nick. I thought he would be in Chicago today, but his secretary says that he won't be coming in until Monday."

Shayla shrugged. "Yes, that's what I understand."

Trent saw the flash of hurt that crossed Shayla's face. Evidently Nick still had not called her. "Have lunch with me, Shayla."

"Lunch?"

Trent smiled. "Yeah, you know—that meal most people eat between breakfast and supper? I know a swell restaurant around here. I came to see if I could drag Nick off, but since he's not here I'd love your company. Come to think of it," he said as his smile widened, "I'd prefer it. You are a whole hell of a lot better-looking than your boss, anyway."

Shayla's lips curved upward in a smile. "Are you always this uplifting to one's ego?"

"I try to be. So, how about it?"

Shayla wanted nothing more than to get out of the office for a while. "Lunch sounds wonderful."

As Trent and Shayla left the building, Carl Stockard stood in the doorway of his office and watched as they got on the elevator. Trent was a close friend of Mr. Chenault, and the son of Thomas Jordache. Although Mr. Chenault seemed to trust Trent completely, Carl didn't. He didn't trust anyone. Paul often accused him of taking things to the extreme and having an overly suspicious nature, but he felt the security of Chenault was now actually in his hands. Paul's style of operating was outdated. He was far too trusting, not cautious enough.

Stockard's hands tightened into fists at his sides when his thoughts shifted back to Trent and Shayla. He didn't like the idea of Chenault's new management employee fraternizing with the competition. He would definitely have to watch her more closely.

Nicholas had been in his brother's house less than two minutes, and already his sister-in-law, Colby, had placed his niece in his arms. He wasn't as nervous holding her as he had been. She was nearly two months old now, and he smiled down at her when she smiled up at him, her features a mixture of his brother's and Colby's. He had never been around babies much, but it seemed that Colby enjoyed breaking him in good fashion.

"Doesn't Nicholas look like a natural holding Chandler?" Colby said to Sterling, who had walked into the room.

Sterling smiled and gave his brother a "Here it comes" look. He knew his wife was determined to get his brother married, and with a baby. The fact that he was not, as far as they knew, in a serious relationship with a woman didn't make a bit of difference to Colby. She was happily married, and felt everyone else should be, too. And because she believed in doing things properly, she would expect a wedding to take place before there was a baby.

"Yeah, if you say so," Sterling replied, deciding to do his brother a favor and stay out of his wife's schemes. He decided to do Nicholas an even bigger favor by shifting the conversation slightly. "Speaking of babies, although the media hasn't gotten wind of it yet, Diamond is pregnant."

Nicholas raised an eyebrow as he glanced over at his brother, absolute surprise on his face. "Jake's going to be a father?"

"Yes, isn't it wonderful?" Colby exclaimed excitedly. "I'm so happy for them. Now if I can only get you interested in someone, Nicholas. Chandler needs a cousin. But of course, you'll have to get married first."

Sterling shot his brother an "At least I tried" glance. "I'm sure Nicholas is capable of handling his own love life, sweetheart," he said, walking over to Colby and pulling her into his arms.

"I don't know about that," Colby said, smiling at him. "You weren't capable of handling yours, Sterling."

Sterling shook his head, grinning, remembering that time. What had started off as a business deal between him and Colby had ended up being a lifetime love affair.

As Nicholas looked across the room at them, he could actually feel the love flowing between his brother and his wife. He glanced down at his niece, who was still smiling up at him. He recalled Jess Baron's comment of yesterday: *"Capture the moments, and do more than just think about those pleasures in life—pursue them."*

Nicholas shook his head. That was how he had gotten into trouble in the first place while in China—pursuing pleasures. For him the best thing to do was to stay away from them.

Chapter 15

Shayla drew in a long unsteady breath as she walked into the huge conference room Monday morning and quickly looked around. As soon as she saw Nicholas her heart began to pound.

He stood across the room with his profile to her as he talked to Janet Coleman, his public relations manager. Silhouetted against the morning sunlight shining through the window, he looked smooth and urbane. Dressed in a dark suit that fit his tall frame as if it had been specifically designed for him, he was the epitome of a suave businessman.

Drawing in another deep breath, Shayla decided to take a seat quickly. She didn't want to be standing when their gazes met, for fear her knees would buckle.

"So, what do you think of the boss?" a woman next to Shayla asked. She turned and met Cindy Davenport's gaze. Cindy was manager of the marketing department. She was single, and probably extremely attractive by most men's standards. Shayla had been working at Chenault Electronics for nearly two weeks, and already she had heard that Cindy had a thing for Nicholas. It was further rumored that although she'd been trying for the longest time to get Nicholas's interest, he hadn't shown any. Nicholas, it seemed, had a policy against dating his employees.

Shayla had been surprised when she'd heard that, since he hadn't shown any reservations about getting to her on a personal level. Sleeping with someone definitely constituted something personal.

"Well, what do you think of him?" Cindy asked again, as if desperate for Shayla's opinion.

Shayla's response was a noncommittal shrug. It seemed none of the other employees, other than Leanne and Paul, knew she had spent her first week on the job with Nicholas in China, and she saw no reason to enlighten anyone.

"He seems nice," Shayla answered faintly.

Cindy gave her a smirky smile. "Nice? You need to have your hormones checked out if *nice* is the only thing you can think of to say about him. The man is dripping sensuality. I'd do just about anything to get a piece of that."

Blood pounded in Shayla's temples and heat poured through her veins, knowing she had one up on Cindy. She already had gotten a piece of *that* and, although she wished otherwise, her body actually wanted some more of it.

"The brother is so fine," Cindy added. "Just look at him."

Shayla didn't want to, but couldn't tell Cindy that, so she did as the woman suggested. When she looked at him, as if he felt her intense gaze on him, he turned and looked straight at her.

Nicholas felt the blood rush thickly through his veins when he met Shayla's gaze. Never in his life had he been so completely aware of a woman. The desire he felt for her was stronger than before, stronger than anything he had ever known. He hadn't realized just how much he had missed her, just how much his body craved her, until now.

He took a deep breath, and from somewhere inside of him he reined in some fragment of control and forced a break in eye contact between them. Feeling an unwanted tightening in his groin, he was grateful that he was standing behind the table.

He swallowed a sigh and tried to picture Shayla Kirkland as just another employee, but that didn't work. The only picture he could conjure up was the one of her nude in his arms while he made love to her. That was a memory he had been unable to get rid of, no matter how much he had tried.

He suddenly felt an intense itch in his fingers to go across the room and touch her all over and reacquaint himself with her body; the body he knew so intimately. Knowing the thought was totally insane, he knew he had to find a way to keep his hands busy for a while. He picked up his briefcase and put it on the table and began pulling out printouts, handouts, articles, reports...anything and everything that would take his mind off the captivating woman sitting across the room.

Shayla had to swallow the sudden lump in her throat and gripped her ink pen tightly to stop the immediate trembling in her hands at the unspoken exchange of awareness that had passed between her and Nicholas.

"I don't believe it," Cindy leaned over and whispered. "If I hadn't seen it, I wouldn't have believed it."

Shayla heard Cindy's words and glanced over at her. "What?"

The woman gave Shayla a curious stare, then shook her head and said, "Nothing."

Shayla then watched as Cindy picked up a pair of eyeglasses, slipped them on, then went about scanning the report she had in front of her.

Frowning, Shayla picked up her own report and glanced at it. She couldn't help wondering if Cindy had picked up on the sensual interchange between her and Nicholas. She hoped not. The last thing she needed was to be entangled in any sort of office gossip.

Shayla took a chance and lifted her gaze and let it settle on Nicholas once more. He was now standing at the head of the conference table talking to Leanne. She watched as he glanced down at his watch and cleared his throat to bring the room to order, all the while deliberately avoiding eye contact with her.

"Let's get the meeting started. I have a very important presentation I'd like to make," he started off. "As you know, for the longest time, the MC Project was under extremely close security and secrecy. The reason for such drastic measures was to insure that none of our competitors got wind of what we were doing. Now that we've closed the Ling Deal, it's time to let you know what the project is about. Just keep in mind that there are still major aspects of this project about which I'm telling you in the strictest confidentiality."

He nodded to Leanne, who was operating a computer that sent images onto a big screen behind him. "The MC Project refers to the mangolid chip project." A huge smile covered Nicholas's face. "This is the kind of advanced technology that will take Chenault well into the next century."

For the next full hour or so Shayla and everyone in the room watched, totally captivated, as screen after screen of impressive and magnificent technological design and detail was displayed. They sat entranced as Nicholas explained how the installation of the mangolid chip would immediately upgrade every home to a wireless entity and make the use of electricity almost obsolete.

Even Cindy was attentive and alert as she absorbed all

the information, with her eyes glued to the screens. At least, Shayla thought, the woman had something else to occupy her mind besides getting her hands on Nicholas's body—the body Shayla remembered all too well.

"This is a major accomplishment, and I commend Chenault's team of technical experts who have worked hard on this project for the past two years," Nicholas ended the presentation by saying. He glanced around the room, and again he deliberately avoided eye contact with Shayla. "Are there any questions?"

For the next thirty minutes or so he entertained a number of questions from various departments.

"Once again," Nicholas said, "I must ask that you speak of this to no one. The reason I'm giving you so much detailed information at this stage is that due to the fire at the Jacksonville office, the project will be temporarily worked out of this office for a while. I wanted each of you to understand why we'll have to take even more extensive security measures."

As soon as Nicholas indicated that the meeting was over, Shayla stood, intent on being the first to leave the room. She was headed for the door when Nicholas's deep voice stopped her.

"Ms. Kirkland, if you don't mind remaining for a moment, I'd like to speak with you."

Thinking that everyone's eyes were probably on her, Shayla turned slowly, met Nicholas's gaze, and nodded. She glanced around the room. Everyone seemed engaged in conversation about the information Nicholas had just presented, and not at all interested in Nicholas singling her out.

At least, everyone but Cindy. The woman slowly pushed her chair back and stood. Walking past Shayla, she gave her a very cold look. It was as frosty as the sidewalks had been that morning.

Shayla sucked in her breath. She really didn't need that. The last thing she wanted to have to deal with was a co-worker who had the hots for the boss and a jealous streak.

Leanne was the last person to leave the room, and Nicholas asked that she close the door behind her. When just the two of them were in the closed room, Nicholas's gaze locked with hers. Shayla watched as he came around the table to stand in front of her. His expression was unreadable, but his cloaked features were not what bothered Shayla. It was the unadulterated flow of sexual chemistry passing between them, one that they didn't seem to have the ability to control.

Shayla could barely handle the shiver that worked its way up her spine, the increased pounding of her heart, or the intense heat that settled in her womanly core. Nor could she handle the heady scent of Nicholas's aftershave—masculine, arousing, and virile—that was making the palms of her hands feel damp. A force of desire suddenly slammed into her, and she caught her breath. Memories of them making love totally consumed her.

So far no words had passed between them. They just stood there looking at each other, hearing the sounds of their erratic breathing. After a few moments it became quite obvious their intense sexual attraction was going to turn into something torridly physical if one of them didn't take control of the situation, and fast.

"Mr. Chenault," Shayla finally said breathlessly, forcing a small smile to her lips. "Was there something you wanted to discuss with me?"

Nicholas just continued to stare at her, thinking that she looked very professional dressed in a tailored blazer and a pair of wool slacks. Yet he remembered the night when she'd been anything but professional. She'd been a seductress who had set his body aflame. "I was wondering how you were doing," he finally said.

Shayla couldn't help remembering his promise to call—a promise he had broken. Her smile was stiff when she replied, "I'm doing fine, sir."

Nicholas raised his brow at her astute professionalism. He knew what she was doing—trying to erase any trace of a personal nature between them. She wanted to put their relationship back on a strictly professional footing. Wasn't that the same thing he wanted, even though he knew it was impossible?

At the moment the only thing he wanted was to take her into his arms, cover her mouth with his, and give her one tongue-tasting, mind-boggling kiss. With that thought, Nicholas's expression became dark, and his jaw tightened. "Seeing you again is more difficult than I thought it would be."

Shayla didn't have to ask him what he had meant by that. The little knot of wanton need that had settled in the pit of her stomach was telling her precisely what he meant. She took a deep breath. "And seeing you is just as difficult for me. That's why I think it's best for me to give you this."

She handed him a sealed envelope. When he raised an eyebrow she said, "It's my resignation. I'm giving you my two weeks' notice, Mr. Chenault."

Without saying another word, without giving him the chance to do so, either, Shayla turned and quickly left the room.

Chapter 16

Nicholas stood in the conference room alone and stared blankly at the document Shayla had given him. He drew in a deep breath. Her resignation had certainly caught him off guard.

He walked over to the window and looked out, heaving a frustrated sigh. Shayla leaving the company was probably for the best. If anything, being around her today had proved that things wouldn't work with her as his employee. They had crossed the boundaries of what was appropriate between an employee and boss, and there was no way that things could ever be strictly professional between them again. There would always be that fierce awareness and strong sexual chemistry they didn't seem to have any control over.

Nicholas glanced down at the document he still held in his hand. If her leaving was such a good idea, why was the air surrounding him crackling with tension, and why did he feel such a deep sense of loss?

Squinting from the glare of the midmorning sun, he stared out of the window, remembering their time together in Hong Kong, just as he'd done for the past two weeks. He tried to recall at what moment in time he had fallen under her spell. He smiled knowingly. It had been the day he'd interviewed her. He'd known then it wouldn't work, but he'd made the mistake of listening to Paul and hired her anyway.

A knock on the door made Nicholas turn around. "Come in."

Leanne opened the door a little bit. "I just want to remind you that you have a ten-thirty meeting with Trent Jordache."

Nicholas nodded. He had completely forgotten. "Thanks for reminding me, Leanne. I'll be there in a second."

His secretary nodded, then closed the door, leaving him alone again. He turned back to the window and drummed his fingers lightly against the pane. He remembered the tactic Shayla had used to maneuver the Ling Deal through, literally saving his company in a huge business negotiation. She was the best thing to ever happen to Chenault.

Hell, if he were completely honest with himself, he would admit that she was the best thing to ever happen to him, too. He had enjoyed her company more than that of any woman he could name. Besides, he knew that whether she worked for Chenault or not he would never be able to erase her from his mind. She was too firmly rooted there. Making love to her had guaranteed that.

The bottom line was that he didn't really want her to leave. As much as he wanted her to stay, though, he couldn't ask her to change her mind.

Suddenly, he frowned. Why couldn't he?

Without having a definite plan of action, and without fully

analyzing the extent of what he was about to do, he quickly walked out of the conference room and went directly to Shayla's office. Without bothering to knock, he walked in.

She didn't look up until he had closed the door behind him. His gaze went immediately to her and met hers, locking on to it, daring her to look away.

Then he knew.

There was a lot more going on between him and Shayla than just physical attraction. At that precise moment he knew that Shayla Kirkland, in a very short time, had managed to do something no other woman had done. She had gotten embedded in his skin, deep. And if the vibes coming from her were true, he had gotten embedded in her skin, too. He didn't know what to say, or how to say it. He fought a strong urge to cross the room and take her into his arms. There were a lot of things they had to work out, things they needed to understand. This time he needed to think with his head, and not his body. He had gotten them into this mess, and he was determined to get them out of it.

Taking a deep breath, he crossed the room and placed the resignation letter she had given him earlier on the desk in front of her. "Trust me, Shayla. You don't have to resign. Things will work out, I promise."

"Like you promised to call me," she said softly. Her voice held the pain she couldn't hide.

Nicholas flinched. He had unintentionally hurt her. "I'm sorry. I should have kept my word about that. But…look, we need to talk, to straighten out some things, but not here. Can I stop by your place tonight?"

"Nicholas, I don't think—"

"Just to talk, Shayla."

Shayla bit her lip and blinked. After a few tense seconds, she nodded.

Taking a deep breath, Nicholas turned and walked out of her office.

"I hope the boss didn't chew you out about anything."

Shayla raised her gaze from the document she had been reading and saw Howard Reeves enter her office. Howard was one of the managers of the regional sales department, and a loaner from the Jacksonville office. His first day in Chicago had been her first official day in the office. Since both of them were literally new at the site, they had immediately connected. She liked him. He seemed more down-to-earth than a number of the other management people she had met, some of whom had yet to warm up to her. Howard had told her not to take it personally. Everyone was busy trying to get the Chicago office up and running smoothly.

"No, it wasn't anything like that. I'm the new kid on the block, and he wanted to see how I was doing." Shayla sighed. What she'd just said wasn't a complete lie.

"Good. I was worried about you there for a while. Mr. Chenault can be pretty hard at times."

Shayla raised a brow. This was the first time she'd heard anyone do anything but sing Nicholas's praises. "I guess it goes with the territory of being the boss," she said, coming to Nicholas's defense. "Especially if you have major projects you're responsible to your major stockholders for."

Howard nodded as he came into the room and took the chair across from her desk. "I guess you're right. Speaking of major projects, what do you think of the MC Project? Isn't it awesome? Who would've thought something like that could have been kept quiet for two years?"

Shayla shrugged. She didn't want to tell Howard that she had been concentrating more on Nicholas than his presentation. "I guess it's impressive."

"Impressive? That's all you have to say?"

Shayla shook her head, smiling. "I take it that you thought it was more than impressive."

Howard made a sound that was part snort. "What Chenault is doing is paving the way to the top. I bet by the end of the year we'll be the number one black-owned electronics company in the nation, maybe even the world. I'm sure Thomas Jordache won't be too happy when he hears about this."

Shayla's shoulders tensed. "You know Thomas Jordache?"

Howard shrugged. "Not personally, but everyone in the Jacksonville office is aware of him and his personal vendetta against this company. If you ask me, the man needs to get a life. Or better yet, he needs to turn the running of the company over to his son."

Shayla nodded. "You know Trent?"

Howard shook his head. "I've seen him come into the Jacksonville office to visit the boss a few times." He looked at her speculatively. "Word has it that you know him. In fact, I heard you went out to lunch with him one day last week."

Shayla bristled at that. If everyone around the office was so busy, why were they spending time watching her? "Yes, I did." That was all she was going to say. She didn't owe anyone an explanation as to how she and Trent knew each other.

Howard evidently picked up on her irritation. "Hey, look, I didn't mean anything by what I just said. You know how office gossip is. You'd be surprised how it circulates among the management staff here. Everyone has their own agenda to make it to the top, and they get antsy if they think someone else has some sort of connections."

Shayla nodded. Now that she was working in the private sector she was getting exposed to office politics and how it worked. "Thanks for telling me that."

Howard stood. "I wouldn't be a friend if I didn't, now would I?"

Shayla nodded. "No, I guess you wouldn't." She watched Howard walk out of her office. She couldn't keep from remembering something her mother had once told her. *Beware of those delivering news. They also take news away, as well.*

Trent breathed deeply as his eyes met Nicholas's. "I know I'm asking a lot of you, Nick, considering everything, but there's no one else I can ask. You know how Uncle Paul feels about Dad, so I can't ask him."

Nicholas sat in a leather chair behind his desk and nodded. Trent had paced his office several minutes before he'd finally asked for his favor. "And you think there's something physically wrong with your father that he's not telling you about?"

"Yes, I think there's something about his health that he's keeping from me. I'd feel a lot better while I'm on that cruise to Africa for three weeks if I knew someone was here for Dad, since I won't be. I want to give his housekeeper, Mrs. Green, the name of a contact person just in case something comes up while I'm gone."

Trent tilted his head and looked across the room at his best friend. "I'll understand if you'd rather not, Nick. I know my father hasn't been the easiest man to know and get along with over the years, but he's still my father, and I care for him deeply."

"And you should. Of course you can tell Mrs. Green to contact me if anything comes up."

Nicholas's words helped soothe the look of worry that had lined Trent's forehead. "Thanks, Nick."

"You don't have to thank me. If our places were switched I know you'd do the same for me. Nothing and no one will ever have a bearing on our friendship. No matter what."

Chapter 17

At precisely seven that evening Shayla opened the door for Nicholas. Any misgivings she'd had about his visit faded the moment she saw him. He was wearing a pair of jeans, a black pullover sweater, and a Jacksonville Jaguars leather jacket with colors of teal, black, and gold. This was the first time she'd seen him in jeans, and the sight of him suddenly made her mouth water. He looked *so* good.

"Hi," he said, sending her a smile and staring at her with his intense gold eyes.

"I thought there was a chance you wouldn't be coming," she said softly, almost not recognizing her own voice. Her heart slammed against her chest when the extent of Nicholas's sexuality hit her full force.

He took a step closer. "Why wouldn't I have come?"

Shayla breathed in slowly as she cocked her head, emphasizing the snow that was falling outside behind him. "The weather."

He chuckled, and Shayla found the sound so incredibly sexy that it sent warmth up her spine. "It would have taken a lot more than bad weather to keep me from coming to see you tonight, Shayla."

The sound of her name from his lips made her mouth suddenly go dry. She squelched the temptation to ask him to kiss it until it was wet.

"It's sort of cold standing here. May I come in?" he asked, flashing her a heart-melting smile—as if her heart needed to melt any more than it already had.

"Oh, I'm sorry," she said, quickly stepping aside. When he entered she closed the door behind him. "May I take your jacket?"

When he handed her his jacket she noted it was still warm from his body. She had the urge to smother her face in it to absorb his manly scent. Instead, she tried to keep a tight hold on her impulses. "You may want to come in closer to the heat."

The first thought that crossed Nicholas's mind was that he didn't think he could get any closer to heat than he was now. Just being in the same room with Shayla was generating plenty of heat. Instead of telling her that he said, "Thanks. I'd like that."

She led him into another large room, which had a blazing fire roaring in the fireplace. Nicholas glanced around. "This is a really nice place."

Shayla smiled. "Thanks. It belonged to my parents. It's really too big for me, but I don't have the heart to sell it. It holds too many memories. This is where I lived most of my teenage years. We moved from D.C. when I was fourteen."

Nicholas nodded. He understood. His mother still lived in the house where he had grown up. Although he worried about her living in the huge house alone, he knew that whenever he went to visit her, it was truly like going home. She had even kept his bedroom the same.

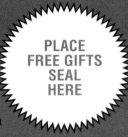

Accepting your 2 free books and 2 free gifts places you under no obligation to buy anything. You may keep the books and gifts and return the shipping statement marked "cancel." If you do not cancel, about a month later we'll send you 4 additional books and bill you just $4.69 each in the U.S., or $5.24 each in Canada, plus 25¢ shipping and handling per book and applicable taxes if any.* You may cancel at any time, but if you choose to continue, every month we'll send you 4 more books, which you may either purchase at the discount price or return to us and cancel your subscription.

*Terms and prices subject to change without notice. Sales tax applicable in N.Y. Canadian residents will be charged applicable provincial taxes and GST. Offer not valid in Quebec. All orders subject to approval. Credit or debit balances in a customer's account(s) may be offset by any other outstanding balance owed by or to the customer. Offer available while quantities last. Books received may vary. Please allow 4 to 6 weeks for delivery.

If offer card is missing write to: The Reader Service, 3010 Walden Ave., P.O. Box 1867, Buffalo, NY 14240-1867

NO POSTAGE
NECESSARY
IF MAILED
IN THE
UNITED STATES

BUSINESS REPLY MAIL

FIRST-CLASS MAIL PERMIT NO. 717 BUFFALO, NY

POSTAGE WILL BE PAID BY ADDRESSEE

THE READER SERVICE
3010 WALDEN AVE
PO BOX 1867
BUFFALO NY 14240-9952

Shayla cleared her throat. "Can I get you something to drink? Coffee, tea, soda, wine, beer…" Shayla stopped midsentence when he came to stand directly in front of her.

"After coming in from outdoors, a cup of hot coffee would be wonderful."

She had to swallow the sudden lump in her throat at his closeness. "All right. I'll be back in a minute."

"Take your time," he said in a throaty whisper, barely audible against the crackling logs in the fireplace. "I'm not going anywhere."

Cheeks flushed, Shayla quickly nodded before escaping to the kitchen. Once there, she leaned against the door to get her bearings and to calm down her racing heart. The strong sexual chemistry was there between them, as always, and just as potent. She could feel it. It was just that intense. If she didn't get herself together she would never last through their talk, and that was the purpose of his visit, for them to discuss things.

Yeah, right, she thought. She couldn't help wondering how much discussion they would get through before their raging hormones kicked in. Taking a deep breath, she walked over to the counter to begin making coffee. A whole pot should do it.

Nicholas stood looking out Shayla's window at the thick and heavy snow that was falling. The weather report had been right. A snowstorm had been headed this way. He was glad he had left his home before the roads were too difficult, or nearly impossible, to drive on. He was always amazed at the differences in the weather between Chicago and Florida. With Easter only a week away, the weather in Jacksonville was in the eighties, with beautiful sunny days, but here in Chicago it was snowing.

He moved away from the window and walked over to the fireplace. Curiosity made him pick up a picture frame to take a closer look at the people standing with Shayla. The man and woman, a nice-looking couple, were probably her parents. Another photo showed her and a very attractive woman in her late thirties or early forties, who he assumed was another family member.

He turned when he heard Shayla approach. She was carrying a tray holding a coffeepot and two cups. He walked over to help her with it. Their fingers brushed when he took the tray from her hands. He heard her intake of breath at the same time he heard his own. He also felt the tiny electrical jolt that passed between them with that touch.

"I'm still trying to thaw out. Do you mind if we sit on the floor in front of the fireplace for a while?" he asked quickly.

"No, I don't mind. I'll grab some pillows off the sofa."

Minutes later, he looked up when he heard her returning with a couple of huge pillows under her arms. "Here you are," she said, dropping a pillow in his lap. Undoubtedly, she had decided not to take a chance on handing the pillow to him for fear of them touching again.

"Thanks."

He watched as she sat across from him, at what she felt was a pretty safe distance. He handed her a cup of coffee he had poured, having no intention of setting it down on the hearth beside her. If she wanted it, she would have to take it from him and risk them touching.

She saw the obvious. Taking a deep breath, she took the cup from him. Once again that tiny jolt passed through them when their fingers touched.

"Don't be bothered by it, Shayla. I'm not." He'd decided to address the issue, which was so blatantly clear, instead of ignoring it.

She nodded and took a sip of her coffee.

For a long moment neither of them said anything. The silence suited Nicholas just fine. As far as he was concerned

Shayla was a woman who deserved a man's complete attention, and he wanted to give it to her tonight. He didn't want to think about the space he'd always craved. He had a strong desire to get as close to this woman as possible.

The flames from the fireplace were reflecting in her hair, highlighting her dark brown strands with reddish streaks. She was wearing what his mother had often called a lounging outfit—pants and a tunic top. Made of silk, it looked comfortable, soft, and feminine.

"You look nice tonight, Shayla."

From studying the coffee in her cup, she lifted her gaze to his. "Thanks. So do you."

"How about some more coffee?"

Shayla shook her head, thinking how easily he had taken on the role of host. "If you're filling me up with coffee because you're worried about me dozing off on you," she said with a little laugh, "then don't be. I usually don't go to bed until late."

"Really? That's good to know," Nicholas said with a blatantly sexy smile. "The time you usually go to bed."

Shayla swallowed, realizing the folly of her statement too late. She cleared her throat. "Uh, you wanted to talk."

Her words reminded Nicholas of the reason for his visit. He placed his cup aside, took the one from Shayla's hands, and did the same. He reached across the distance that separated them and interlaced her fingers with his, trying to ignore the heat automatically passing between them. His voice was seductively low and husky when he spoke. "When I left you in Hong Kong I promised to call you. At the time I had every intention of doing so," he said, looking at her, wanting her to see the truth in his eyes. "But when I got to Jacksonville things got hectic, and I couldn't…at first. Then I made the decision not to."

He felt her hands stiffen under his, and he tightened his

hold. "The reason I made that decision, Shayla, was that the more I thought about it the less I understood what had happened between us in China. I've been sexually attracted to women before, but never the way I was immediately attracted to you. And it didn't just start in Hong Kong. I was fiercely attracted to you that day I interviewed you."

Shayla nodded in understanding. She'd been fiercely attracted to him that day, as well.

Determined to get things out in the open, Nicholas continued. "I had decided not to hire you because of that, but Paul convinced me that I could be a complete professional where you were concerned."

"Paul did?"

"Yes. He picked up on the fact that I was interested in you for more than employment reasons. He knows my rule about not dating my employees."

Shayla nodded. "Oh, I see," she said quietly.

Nicholas shook his head. "No, I don't think that you do. But I believe that Paul did."

Shayla frowned. "I don't understand."

Nicholas took a deep shaky breath. "Paul knows me better than anyone, other than my mother. He knows that since my father's death I've been so caught up in Chenault that everything else, especially my social life, has become nonexistent. My last serious involvement with a woman was more than a year ago. So when Paul saw how attracted I was to you, he figured it was about time something else besides work captured my attention. That's part of why he goaded me into changing my mind about hiring you."

His hand reached out and caressed her chin. "I thought I had everything under control until that night I kissed you. Never in my life have I shared a kiss with a woman that left me so shaken. It only made me want to taste you again and again and again. It also made me want to get to know you intimately, to feel your warm body against mine, and to join my body with yours in the most primitive way."

He inhaled slowly and recaptured her hands in his once more. "That night we made love, I experienced the ultimate in pleasure. You claimed my mind and my body completely. There was nothing about that night that was half-measure. You got into the deep recesses of my soul."

Nicholas shifted, uncomfortable with what he was admitting and even more uncomfortable hearing himself admit it. "After leaving you in Hong Kong and returning to the States," he continued, "I panicked at the realization of just how deeply you had gotten to me. To find an excuse for it, I tried convincing myself that everything between us had merely been physical, that what I had felt for you was lust, nothing more. But today, after seeing you again, I had to honestly admit I was wrong."

He glanced down at the hands he held in his before looking back up and meeting her gaze again. "Oh, don't get me wrong, there's still this physical thing between us. I can feel it even now. It's there every time we come within ten feet of each other. But then there's something else, too, and it's more than just physical," he said in a tremulous whisper. "It's something I've never felt before." He stared at her for a long moment. He'd never been good when it came to saying certain things to a woman. However, this thing with Shayla was different. It was strong. It was unique. And he didn't fully understand it. All he knew was that he needed time to try to understand it, and come to terms with what he was feeling. He didn't want her to walk out of his life while he did that. He needed time with her. "I don't understand what's happening between us, Shayla, but I do want to." He sighed. "And maybe I should regret what we did in Hong Kong, but I don't."

He angled her a look. "The reason I wanted to talk to

you," he continued, "is that I want us to take things slow, get to know each other, spend some time together, and see what happens from there. What do you think of that idea?"

In truth, Shayla didn't know what to think of it. They had already been intimate, and she knew for a fact that she loved him. But she also knew that she had deceived him. Her sole reason for seeking employment with his company had been to destroy it. How would he feel when he discovered that?

She toyed with the idea of being completely honest with him right then and telling him about it, then changed her mind. It was not a good time. He wanted them to take things slowly and get to know each other. Maybe after he'd spent time with her and gotten to know her better, he would understand.

Satisfied with her decision not to tell Nicholas everything until later, the corners of Shayla's mouth lifted into an easy smile. "I think taking things slowly and getting to know each other is a good idea, but what about your rule?"

Nicholas frowned. "What rule?"

"The one about not getting personally involved with your female employees."

"I'll break it."

Shayla pulled her hand from his, shaking her head and letting out a quaint chuckle. "You must have put it in place for some reason," she said. *Probably to deal with aggressive women like Cindy Davenport,* she thought.

He smiled. "There was a time when the rule was definitely needed. I wanted to concentrate on running my office, not on running willing females out of it."

"And now?"

"And now it's standing in the way of me having something I want very much."

"Which is?"

He caught her chin in his hand. His voice was just as intense as his expression when he said, "You."

Unable to speak, Shayla just stared at him. She wanted him very much, too.

"There hasn't been a single night that I haven't lain in my bed thinking of you, remembering our time together, wishing you were there in bed with me—to talk, to make love again, to talk, then make love some more," Nicholas said in his deep husky voice. "I want you, Shayla, but I don't want to hurt you by saying words I don't mean just to make you feel good. I want an honest relationship with you. I won't make idle promises to you."

Shayla's pulse rate increased with Nicholas's words and at the look of raw hunger she saw in his gaze. "I don't need promises, Nicholas, idle or otherwise. I'm willing to take one day at a time with you. I lie awake at night thinking about you, too—wishing you were with me to offer me your warmth when I'm cold, to hold me in your arms whenever I feel lonely, and to want me when I need to feel wanted."

Her gaze remained locked with his when she added, "And to make love to me when I want to be made love to…like right now."

Her bold statement set off an immediate ache within Nicholas. He searched her face for a long probing moment. "I thought we just agreed to take things slowly," he said huskily, dragging in a deep breath.

"And we will," Shayla responded, the words coming from her in a sensuous whisper. She sat staring at him, total desire etched into her features. "I want us to take things really slowly." She loved him, and for her, for now, that was all that mattered. She was willing to risk her heart to be with him, to love him. And one day, when there was complete truth between them, she would tell him everything, including the fact that Thomas Jordache was her biological father.

"Make love to me again, Nicholas. This time, unlike the last, let's take things…slowly."

Nicholas's eyebrows drew together. "Are you sure that's what you want?"

She smiled. "Yes, I'm sure."

Nicholas didn't speak for a moment. He just sat and stared at her with the firelight dancing over her, emphasizing her near-perfect features. His blood was running hot from what she wanted, from what he wanted. He reached out and cupped her nape in his hand and pulled her into his arms. "We *will* take things slowly this time," he whispered mere seconds before settling his mouth firmly on hers. Her lips parted in welcome, and he felt a satisfying sigh escape her mouth, to be captured by his. He was determined to make his kiss gentle as he thoroughly reacquainted his mouth with the texture and taste of hers. He soothingly nipped her lips lightly, bathing them in moisture with the tip of his tongue. He stroked her mouth with heated kisses, making the very air surrounding them sizzle with fierce sexual awareness and overpowering need.

"Nicholas…" Shayla could barely breathe out his name with the lips he was tormenting in a slow seductive way. Then, ever so slowly, ever so intently, he angled his mouth purposefully on hers, easing his tongue inside and coaxing hers to mate with his, possessing her stroke after tantalizing stroke.

They sat there kissing for the longest time before she felt his hand come up between their bodies and begin loosening the buttons on her top. She moaned deep within her throat when she felt the heat of his hand on the lace of her bra moments later. And when he undid the front hook and she felt the warmth of his hand touching her bare breast, a jolt of pure unadulterated pleasure swept through her.

He broke off the kiss. The breath of him was warm against her mouth when he murmured, "I want to remove your top, Shayla." The last time they had made love, he hadn't given a lot of time to her breasts, because he'd been in such a rush to get inside her body. But tonight they would be taking things slowly, and he planned to give them a lot of attention.

She shivered when he completely removed her top and bra. When he stood up and pulled her up on wobbly knees, she went willingly into his arms, moaning slightly when he covered her mouth with his once again.

This is what I need, Nicholas thought as he greedily feasted on Shayla's mouth. *This is what I want.* He wanted her. He wanted it all. It was as if he could not get enough of her—her mouth, her taste, and even her alluring scent. Her perfume was doing a number on him again. He deepened the kiss, wanting to taste all of her, wanting his tongue to mate with hers in all the ways he had ever dreamed about.

His hand reached down and cupped her bottom, bringing her closer to the fit of him, wanting her to feel his hard aching flesh, which symbolized his intense need. She made a small whimpering sound when she felt the hardness of him pressed against her. "I want to make love to you in a bed this time," he whispered moistly against her lips. "Where's your bedroom?"

His question only intensified the need within Shayla, and when Nicholas picked her up in his arms she wrapped her arms around his neck and gazed into his eyes. They were filled with the same desire she knew was in her own. "Upstairs. The first room on your right," she answered, after releasing a long breath.

Nicholas's strong arms held her securely as he took the stairs. He quickly glanced at the interior of her bedroom, his mind barely registering the minor details until he saw the bed, warm and inviting. Driven by a need he had never known, but operating on a promise to take things slowly, he walked straight to the bed, not stopping until he placed her on it. A shudder passed through him when he looked down at her, nude from the waist up, her breasts firm and tilted and sensuously inviting.

Shayla's eyes rounded slightly when she saw that Nicholas's gaze was locked on her breasts. And when he moistened his lips with a quick sweep of his tongue, a direct heat flared within the pit of her stomach.

Every vein in her body sizzled when he leaned down and captured her nipple in his mouth, giving it the same torment he had given her mouth just moments earlier.

"Oh, my," she murmured before sucking in a deep hollow breath and then letting it out slowly. He took his time, cherishing her breasts, tasting them, loving them, slanting the fullness of his mouth over them, gently possessing, stroking, time and time again, going from one breast to the other, delivering slow delicious torment. She became a fiery ball of passion in his arms, cupping the sides of his face, holding him to her as he lavished her breasts in warm, wet, consuming heat.

And he continued to take it slowly.

"Nicholas." His name poured forth from her lips in a deep and ragged breath.

"Tell me, Shayla. What do you want?" he whispered when his lips moved from her breasts to an area just below her ear. "Tell me what you want from me, sweetheart."

His lips then moved from her ear to kiss her cheek and then the corner of her mouth. "Tell me."

Shayla knew what she wanted more than anything, and it was the one thing she could never ask him for. From him it would have to come freely. More than anything, she wanted his love. She wanted him to fall in love with her as deeply as she had fallen in love with him. But instead of telling him her innermost thoughts and desires, she met his gaze, saw the gold of his eyes, felt the need pooling hot in the center of her, and whispered in a soft, seductive voice, "I want you, Nicholas, inside me."

Nicholas's gaze locked steadily with hers. Then he reached out and captured her chin in his hand and leaned closer to her mouth and whispered breathlessly against her lips. "That's where I want to be, too, Shayla."

She watched as he backed away from the bed and began removing all of his clothes. Seeing him remove his sweater and watching him pull off his jeans made her draw in a deep breath. She couldn't help but study each and every inch of his body, remembering the pleasure it had given her before. Then she watched as he prepared to protect her by putting on a condom. His body was strong, well-built, and massive. His gaze never left hers when he returned to the bed. "Now I take yours off," he said throatily as he reached out and began removing the rest of her clothes.

When he had finished he looked down at her. "Remember, we're going to take it slowly tonight," he said, sinking down on the bed and drawing her into his arms and moving his body over hers.

She looked up at him and held his gaze as her body accepted the heated invasion of his when he entered her.

All sense of time was lost. Seconds turned into minutes as Nicholas made slow, thorough love to her. Need clawed within them as they became lost in their fierce lovemaking, recapturing everything they had shared in Hong Kong, in total awe that things could be even better with them a second time, totally uninhibited.

When Nicholas felt her body shudder violently under him with the force of her climax, he allowed his body to do the same. Satisfied that what they had shared had been slow yet totally fulfilling, he uttered a harsh cry and then released a deep growl as his body slammed into an explosion of excruciating pleasure.

Chapter 18

It was a good sound, Nicholas thought, and instinctively moved his body closer to it. It was a sound he was not used to hearing—one of a woman sleeping in his arms.

He lay on his side while he held Shayla, watching her sleep, listening to the sound of her soft even breathing, and thinking that once again he had broken another rule with her. He had made it a point never to spend the night at a woman's place. He preferred sleeping in his own bed. That had been Olivia's one pet peeve about their relationship. Even after a year of them dating exclusively, he had not spent the night at her place, nor she at his. He had tried explaining to her over and over again that he detested the feeling of being crowded. He needed his space.

Yet, with a beam of daylight coming through Shayla's bedroom window indicating that it was morning, he realized he hadn't thought about leaving her bed. He doubted he could have, even if he had wanted to. The slow lovemaking they'd shared had literally drained him. He had felt content just to wrap his sated body next to hers and hold her in his arms through the night while they slept.

When she shifted her body in sleep he reached out and once again cradled her in his arms. He spread his fingers wide over her hip, feeling a moment of intense possessiveness. At the same time he felt the hardness of him stir from her body being so close to his. He moved his hand from her hip all the way to her breasts. He gently massaged them with his hands, thinking they must be tender from all the attention he had lavished upon them.

Last night he had been too busy getting Shayla into bed to take a really good look at the decor of her room. Like her, the room was bright, feminine, and beautiful. Her bed covering, a floral design, and the coordinating arrangements that hung from the high ceiling added an air of spring to the room.

He glanced outside the window and saw it was still snowing. In fact, it seemed to be snowing even harder than it had last night when he'd arrived. When Shayla shifted in sleep again, curling her body around his, he tightened his hold on her and closed his eyes, deciding that sleep was what they both needed.

Shayla woke up alone. She noticed Nicholas's absence the moment she opened her eyes. She didn't move while she tried to remember when he had left her bed. His scent still lingered, so it must not have been too long ago.

She reached out and grabbed the pillow where his head had lain. Clutching it to her, she savored the masculine essence of him and felt the heated intimacy of their lovemaking. He had kept his promise. They had taken things slowly. Almost too slowly. By the time he had given her what she had wanted she'd become a mass of withering need beneath him.

A shiver ran down the length of her spine as she remembered everything about the night in explicit detail. She remembered every kiss on her lips and her breasts, and the feel of him inside of her that had taken her over the edge into passionate oblivion.

She was about to drift back off to sleep with those thoughts when she smelled coffee. Was Nicholas still there? A quick glance outside her bedroom window showed it was still snowing. *That must have been a doozy of a snowstorm that hit last night,* she thought. And just think, she and Nicholas had made love all through it.

"Good morning."

Nicholas turned from looking out of the window when he heard the sound of Shayla's voice. *No woman,* he thought, *should look this refreshed and desirable in the morning.* He smiled and walked over to her and pulled her into his arms for a good-morning kiss, softly at first, enjoying her minty-fresh taste. "Good morning to you, too," he said, releasing her mouth. "I took the liberty of opening a new toothbrush I saw on the vanity in your bathroom. I hope you don't mind."

Shayla shook her head. "No, I don't. It's a consolation prize from my recent visit to the dentist."

Nicholas nodded. "It's still snowing."

She smiled up at him. "So I see. What's the weather update?"

"A severe snowstorm that they don't anticipate going away for at least another day," he murmured against her hair, wondering what there was about her that made him want to hold her in his arms forever. "For the moment we're snowbound. Schools and businesses are closed, since the streets are not safe."

She nodded. "Have you tried calling Chenault?"

"Yes, and I got the twenty-four-hour security crew. They

said other than a few calls there wasn't any activity over there. I'm glad my employees had the good sense not to try to make it in."

"And I'm glad you care enough for your employees not to want them to. You'd be surprised how many businesses would expect their people to come in anyway." She glanced around the kitchen. "Do I smell coffee?"

"Yeah, want some?"

"Sure. You tried mine last night. Now it's time I tried yours."

He smiled as he lifted his hand to brush a curl back from her face. "Yeah, and I want to try something else of yours again," he said, leaning down and slanting his mouth across hers.

Shayla wrapped her arms around his neck and gave in to the sensations his kiss was evoking.

"Still want that coffee?" Nicholas whispered moments later against her moist lips.

"I need something hot," she answered. "You think you might have something hotter?"

"Yeah, I think I do."

"Umm, what is it?"

"It's something I have to show you."

She stepped back mere inches, and looked up into his eyes. "Then show me."

Nicholas swept her into his arms and carried her back upstairs to the bedroom.

"I guess it was just meant for me to feel like a lazybones this morning," Nicholas said when he glanced at the clock on the nightstand next to Shayla's bed. "It's almost noon, and I have no desire to get out of this bed."

Shayla shifted closer to him. "It's the weather. It'll do it to you."

Nicholas shook his head and ran a finger down the side of her face. "No, it's not the weather. It's you. You do it to me."

The smile she gave him made his heart pick up a beat. "No, Nicholas, you do it to me…and quite gloriously, I might add."

Nicholas grinned at that. "You think so?"

"I know so."

He captured her face in his hands. "You're pretty good for my ego, Ms. Kirkland."

Then he kissed her, and Shayla forgot everything. All she could think about was Nicholas's mouth on hers, nibbling at her lips, and his tongue slipping inside her mouth, tasting her.

When he finally lifted his mouth, his gaze locked with hers. "I think we need to get out of here and declare your bedroom off-limits for the rest of the day."

"That's not a bad idea, but first we need to talk."

"I thought we did that last night…among other things," he said, smiling at the memory.

"We did, but we didn't discuss how we would handle our situation at work."

"There's nothing to handle. It was a rule I made to govern my own life, and if I choose to break it, it's nobody's business."

Shayla shifted positions to look at Nicholas. "But how will it look if word gets out that we're involved?"

He shrugged, giving her a masculine smile. "It will look as if I have extremely great taste."

Shayla shook her head and released a sigh filled with exasperation. "Nicholas, be serious."

"I am. I see no reason why we have to hide anything. It's not as if I plan to jump your bones in the office." A thoughtful expression crossed his face. "Umm, on second thought, that doesn't sound all that bad. Have you ever done it on a desk?"

"Of course not!"

Nicholas laughed at the indignation in her voice. "Ahh, that's right, you're new at this. I forgot. But then, I've never done it on a desk, either. Maybe we ought to give it a try one day after the office closes."

Shayla frowned. "You're not taking me seriously about this, are you?"

"No," Nicholas admitted as he caught her chin in his hand. "I don't like the idea of us sneaking around. What's the big deal with bringing it out in the open that we're seeing each other?"

"My credibility. I just started working for Chenault three weeks ago—two, if you don't count that week in Hong Kong, which no one knows about, thank goodness. I don't want to be the center of office gossip. That can ruin my credibility."

"Trust me, Shayla, the only person you should worry about for credibility's sake is me, and you proved your worth to Chenault when you came through with the Ling Deal."

"Yes, but I want the respect of my peers, as well as the people who work under me. I don't want anyone to think I got this job on my back."

Nicholas's eyes narrowed. "No one would think that."

"Yes, they would. Any woman at Chenault who may have come on to you and you deliberately ignored would possibly think that." Shayla couldn't help remembering the look Cindy Davenport had given her after yesterday's meeting.

Nicholas dragged his hand over his face. "You're serious about all of this, aren't you?"

"Yes."

"All right. What do you suggest?"

"That we be very discreet."

"How do you expect that, Shayla, when just being around you drives me to distraction?"

She wound her arms around his neck and grinned at

the pout on his face. "That's something you'll have to work on, Boss."

"Discreet, huh?"

"Yes."

Without warning Nicholas rolled her beneath him. "In that case, if I have to act as if you're invisible in the office, I need to load up on loving you," he said, taking control of her mouth, mind, and body once again.

Chapter 19

There was a break-in at Chenault Electronics.

Nicholas was called that afternoon, and left Shayla's house immediately. Luckily it had stopped snowing, and the roads were somewhat clear. This time he didn't make a promise to call her. Instead, to her surprise, he promised to come back later.

Shayla sat on the floor in front of the fireplace and watched the flames, wondering who was behind the string of incidents at Chenault. First there had been the fire in Jacksonville, and now the break-in in Chicago. From the muttered curses that had flowed from Nicholas's mouth while he'd hurriedly put on his clothes, it was quite obvious that he thought Thomas Jordache was behind everything. If that were true, she couldn't help but wonder what sort of strain that would place on Nicholas and Trent's friendship.

After Nicholas left she called her aunt to see how she had fared during the snowstorm. Callie told her she had enjoyed the day by staying in bed curled up with a good book. Shayla had seen no reason to tell her aunt she had curled up in bed, too—with Nicholas.

It was nearly nine that night when Shayla heard the knock on her door. She had just taken a shower and come downstairs to get a cup of coffee. She pulled her robe together when she heard the second knock and walked over to the door. "Who is it?"

"It's me. Nicholas."

Shayla opened the door immediately, to a blast of freezing cold air. Although it had stopped snowing, the temperature was ten below zero. When Nicholas had left earlier, all he'd worn to ward off the cold had been his short leather jacket. Most southerners, she'd discovered, were not used to the harsh, cold Chicago weather.

"I hope it's not too late, but I promised I'd come back."

Shayla caught Nicholas's arm and quickly pulled him inside, shivering as she closed the door. "Of course it's not." She watched as he removed his jacket and noticed how hard he was shaking. "You might think about investing in a full-length coat."

He tried smiling at her comment, but couldn't. It seemed his features were frozen into place. He was just that cold. "Go on in near the fire. I'll bring you something hot to drink," she said, looking at him with concern. Her father had always referred to this type of cold as pneumonia weather.

Once in the kitchen, Shayla decided to fix Nicholas a bowl of vegetable soup and a sandwich instead of a cup of coffee. He looked weak, but he was wearing a change of clothes, so it appeared he had gone home to shower before coming back. Chances were he hadn't taken the time to eat anything since he'd left.

When she returned to the family room moments later carrying the soup and sandwich on a tray, she discovered

Nicholas had taken the pillows off her sofa and had stretched out on the floor in front of the fireplace with his eyes closed. She could tell he was trying to control his shivering. When he heard her approach, he opened his eyes and smiled at her. "Something smells good."

"Soup and sandwich. I made the soup earlier."

"Homemade? Umm, I'm impressed," he said as he struggled into a sitting position.

Shayla placed the tray across his lap. She sat opposite him and watched him eat.

"How did you know that ham and cheese is my favorite sandwich?" he asked after taking a big bite.

Shayla grinned. "I didn't. It's all I had available. I'm glad you're enjoying it."

Shayla remained silent as Nicholas completed the rest of his meal. When he had finished she took the tray and soup bowl back into the kitchen. When she returned he had stretched back out in front of the fireplace. He glanced up when he heard her and smiled when he saw the blanket she carried under her arms. "Come here, baby," he said, reaching his hand out to her.

She walked over to him and felt his hands. They were still cold. She stretched out on the floor beside him and covered them both in the warmth of the blanket. She snuggled up next to him to share her body's heat.

"How were things at Chenault when you got there?"

His arms tightened around her, and he took a deep measured breath before answering. "Although the person got away, things weren't as bad as they could have been. Luckily, the silent alarm went off, and Stockard surprised the person before he could do whatever it was he'd come there to do."

Shayla frowned. "You think Thomas Jordache is behind this incident, as well?"

"To be honest, I don't know what to think. If he's not behind it, I'd like to know who is."

"Why not talk to Trent? Surely he would question his father about it."

"Trent left a few days ago, for a cruise to Africa. He won't be back for three weeks." Nicholas shifted slightly and turned to face Shayla. "I don't want to talk about Jordache any longer," he said, and he buried his face against her neck. Then he lifted his gaze to hers moments before capturing her mouth with his. A few minutes later the flames roaring in the fireplace were nothing compared to the flames that flared up between them.

Trent Jordache stood in the grand ballroom aboard the cruise ship *Majestic,* feeling the same sense of accomplishment he'd felt for the first time after becoming one of the ship's three owners. He couldn't help thinking how different his life was now that he was pursuing a dream that was his, and not his father's.

He had gone to college and majored in engineering because it was what his father had wanted. After college he had worked in the family business—again because it was what his father had wanted. Working beside his father for more than three solid years had shown him firsthand what a manipulating and tyrannical force his father could be. Thomas Jordache had mended his ways only after realizing that he could lose his son forever unless he made some necessary and positive changes in his life. It was a good feeling to know his father had taken his threat seriously, and was now doing everything he could to become a better person. That's why Trent refused to believe his father had anything to do with the fire at Chenault in Jacksonville. Trent knew the old Thomas Jordache could have been involved in such a thing. But his father had given him his word that the grudge he'd had against Chenault was over, and until it was proven otherwise he would not believe his father had lied to him.

Trent glanced around the huge room again before stepping out on the wide deck. He leaned against the metal railing and looked down. Many passengers were moving to and fro along the decks, enjoying themselves. After operating six months, the *Majestic* had garnered a reputation for providing excellent food and service. He and his two partners intended to keep it that way. The crew members knew to pamper the passengers, and to take care of their every need. Travel agencies were booking them solid for every cruise.

The last time he'd been on board for three months there had been paperwork to do, details to follow up on, shows to book, and a number of other things he and his two partners had to take care of. But this time, on the ship's second voyage to the shores of Africa, he was determined to squeeze in time for a little rest and relaxation.

Trent's attention was suddenly captured when he noticed a sleek and sexy feminine body moving gracefully along one of the wide decks below. Behind the golden lenses of the sunglasses he was wearing, his dark gaze followed the woman's every movement, appreciating the sensuous glide of her hips as she walked like a model on a runway. She was wearing an ankle-length sundress that fit her body very nicely in all the right places. He couldn't help wondering if she was on the *Majestic* alone. She was probably with someone. He couldn't imagine a woman who looked that good doing much of anything alone.

Trent's lips curved in a determined smile. He was intent on finding out who she was. If she was unattached, he was going to make it a point to get to know her better.

* * *

Brenna St. James was enjoying her walk along the deck, taking in the beauty of the ship. She had been on cruise ships before, but this one was different. It wasn't as large as most, and to her that was a good thing. As coordinator of the Ebony Fashion Fair, she spent 70 percent of her time traveling from city to city. It was a refreshing change not to have to deal with a crowd. It was so easy aboard the *Majestic* to find a quiet comer just to sit and absorb the beauty of the ocean, read a book, or just to count her blessings.

And she needed to count her blessings. She needed to give thanks for having been shown just what kind of man Matthew Davis was before she had gotten too involved with him. The man hadn't wanted to develop a relationship with her. All he'd wanted was a lush body that he could jump into. That was evident after he had wined and dined her for three weeks and then had expected her to sleep with him. When she'd refused his offer to become his bed partner, he had dropped her like a hot potato. Although she believed there were men out there who appreciated a woman for her heart and brains, the majority of them placed too much emphasis on a woman's other body parts.

So here she was on the *Majestic* as a result of a birthday gift from her best friend, Corinthians, and her husband, Trevor. She was determined to enjoy herself on the three-week cruise to Africa. When she returned to the States it would be pretty close to the time for Corinthians to give birth. She had left with a warning for her to not have her baby without her.

Brenna smiled as she walked through the double doors leading into the dining room. Thinking of calories on board this ship wouldn't do her any good. The food served continuously throughout the day was much too pleasing to the palate.

There was a purposeful glint in Brenna's eyes as she walked toward the buffet table.

With the snowstorm over, it was business as usual the next day at Chenault Electronics. Shayla had gone into the office earlier than usual to catch up on the full day she had missed. Nicholas had spent the night again, and had gotten up at dawn to go back to his place to get dressed for work.

It was noon, and she had only seen him once. They had passed in the hall and he hadn't stopped to converse with her. Instead, he had flashed her one of his heartmelting smiles and politely said hello. She had rushed into her office, closed her eyes, taken a deep breath, and tried to get control of the rapid pounding of her heart. After that incident she had found it safer to remain in her office, throw herself into her work, and avoid the risk of running into him again.

"Busy, Shayla?"

Shayla glanced up and saw Cindy Davenport in her doorway, giving her a withering stare. "Not really. I was just going over the Argentina sales report. What can I do for you?"

"Some of the other managers and I are going out after work for drinks. I thought I'd invite you to join us."

Once Shayla would have taken the invitation as a friendly gesture, but it had come too late. She could only assume that Cindy had an ulterior motive for inviting her now. What was Cindy hoping for? To get her stoned so she would tell all and confirm whatever suspicions Cindy had about her and Nicholas?

"Thanks, but I've made other plans already."

"Oh, too bad. Maybe next time." Without waiting for a reply Cindy turned and left her office.

Shayla shook her head at the woman's abrupt departure, and then the phone on her desk began ringing. "Shayla Kirkland."

"Ms. Kirkland, this is Leanne. Mr. Chenault would like to see you in his office, and he wants you to bring the South America report with you."

"Of course. Tell him I'm on my way." She hung up the phone and pulled the South America report from her file drawer and quickly left her office.

"Just go on in, Ms. Kirkland. Mr. Chenault is expecting you," Leanne said when Shayla arrived at Nicholas's office.

When she entered she was surprised to find Paul sitting across from Nicholas's desk. She had not seen him since the night of the Mings' dinner party in Hong Kong. He looked up at her and nodded.

Nicholas was on the phone, talking nonstop. "I understand what you're saying, Phil, but I don't buy it. There's something else behind those rumors, and I want to know what," Nicholas was saying to the person on the other end of the line. Tearing his gaze away from the phone, he smiled when he saw her. He motioned for her to come closer and sit in the chair opposite Paul.

"All right, Phil, Shayla Kirkland just walked in. I'm putting the three of us on the speakerphone. Just give me a second to glance over the report." Nicholas reached out, took the report Shayla handed him, and quickly began reading it. After a few minutes he said to the caller, "It's just the way it's supposed to be. Nothing has changed." He then pushed a button and said, "Okay, ask Ms. Kirkland any questions you'd like."

The conference call lasted thirty minutes. Shayla was glad she had become knowledgeable about the South American projects and was able to answer all of Philip Turner's questions. When the call was finally over she leaned back against her chair and sighed deeply, pleased with how well she had done.

"You did an outstanding job, Ms. Kirkland."

Shayla glanced up and met Nicholas's gaze. "Thank you, Mr. Chenault," she said, her voice calmly professional. She then turned to Paul, who had remained in the room during the call. He was now standing and leaning on the edge of Nicholas's desk. "Mr. Dunlap, it's good seeing you again," she said, standing and extending her hand to the older man.

"You, too, Ms. Kirkland," he said. She noted he was studying her intently as he took her hand in a brief but formal handshake. "Nick tells me you're a hard worker, and that you're doing a great job. You just proved that by the way you handled that conference call just now, and on such short notice."

"Thank you." She turned her attention back to Nicholas. "Is there anything else, Mr. Chenault?"

Nicholas rose from his chair and let his gaze travel down the entire length of Shayla's body, enjoying the way she looked in her two-piece business suit. "No, Ms. Kirkland, that's all for now. However, I will see you later tonight at my place for dinner."

At her frown Nicholas said, "We don't have to be discreet around Paul. He knows." Nicholas laughed. "He probably knows more about what's going on with us than we do. As a kid I used to think he had psychic powers. You couldn't put anything over on him."

Shayla glanced uneasily at Paul, who was staring at her with an unreadable expression. That was the last thing she wanted to hear.

"Your secret's safe with me, Ms. Kirkland." He kept staring at her intently. "I still think that you remind me of someone. I just can't figure out who."

Shayla forced herself to stay composed. "When you do, please enlighten me."

Paul's chuckle filled the air. "Trust me. You'll be the first to know."

Shayla nodded and walked out of Nicholas's office.

Shayla took a deep breath when she returned to her office. She closed her door behind her and immediately went to sit at her desk to get her bearings. Nicholas's comment that you couldn't put anything over on Paul Dunlap had her imagination running wild.

She tried calming her overactive nerves by convincing herself that there was no way he could connect her to her mother. She didn't resemble her mother much. Did that mean she had inherited a lot of Thomas Jordache's features? When Paul looked at her did he see a female version of his archenemy?

Shayla glanced at her watch. It was thirty minutes before the time she normally left work each day, and she felt the need to leave early. Nicholas was preparing dinner for her tonight at his place, and she didn't want to eat anything heavy before then. As she reached down to pick up her briefcase, she noticed it wasn't in the same place she had left it. She frowned. Maybe she had moved it earlier, and just didn't remember. Since passing Nicholas in the hall earlier that day, when he'd given her his megawatt smile, her activities seemed kind of blurry. She was surprised she had handled the conference call as well as she had with him sitting across from her. A few times she had looked up and caught him staring directly at her instead of paying attention to what she and Philip were saying.

Shayla closed her briefcase and was about to snap it locked when her phone rang. She immediately picked it up. "Shayla Kirkland."

"Ms. Kirkland, there's a call for you on line three."

"Thanks, Leanne."

Shayla disconnected Leanne and pushed the button on her phone for line three. "Shayla Kirkland. How may I help you?"

"Meet me in an hour at the Reef Bar and Grill and I'll tell you just what you can do to help me."

Shayla frowned, not recognizing the deep rough voice. "Excuse me. Who is this?"

After a pause the caller answered. "This is Thomas Jordache, Ms. Kirkland."

Jordache? Shayla's body was suddenly overtaken with a combination of shock, astonishment, and anger. What could be his reason for calling her? "Mr. Jordache, there must be some mistake. Maybe the person you really want to speak with is my boss, Nicholas Chenault. I'm sure he'll be glad to help you," she said crisply.

"If you want to transfer my call to Nicholas, then by all means do so. However, if I do talk to Nicholas I'll tell him everything, Shayla," Thomas Jordache said in a warning voice.

His words shattered Shayla's control. There was no way this man could know she was his daughter…was there? If so, how? According to Aunt Callie, he had assumed her mother had gotten an abortion. How had he put two and two together and come up with her?

"I figured right. You haven't told Nicholas anything, have you?" Thomas Jordache said when she didn't respond.

Shayla inhaled deeply. She pushed her briefcase aside and dropped down in her chair. "Anything like what, Mr. Jordache?" she asked in a shaky voice.

"I'd rather not discuss it over the phone. Meet me at the Reef in an hour." He hung up.

It took Shayla a few moments after the call to recover. She was mortified, faced with the horror that he knew.

Somehow Thomas Jordache had found out that she was his biological daughter.

Chapter 20

With anger seeping through every pore of her body, Shayla crammed the car key into the ignition and started the motor, ignoring her father's rule of always letting the engine warm up before taking off. She didn't have time to wait. She was on her way to see a man who was as close to a monster as he could get, who evidently thought he could use her in the same manner he had used her mother twenty-seven years ago.

It took Shayla less than twenty minutes to reach the restaurant, which was on the other side of town. She would tell Thomas Jordache what she thought of him, and then when she saw Nicholas tonight she would tell him the truth and take her chances.

She'd barely had time to pull into the parking lot when another vehicle, a limousine, came and parked directly beside her. The back window was rolled down, and Thomas Jordache's face appeared. "Please get in, Ms. Kirkland. We can talk while Martin takes us for a ride around the block. That will afford us more privacy."

Shayla nodded. She needed a lot of privacy for what she wanted to say to him. When his chauffeur got out and opened the car door, she flopped onto the passenger seat and turned furious eyes at the man next to her.

"You're even more beautiful close up, Shayla. I can call you Shayla, can't I? I apologize if my telephone call appeared somewhat threatening, but I knew of no other way to get you to meet with me."

Shayla ground her teeth, wondering what sort of game he was playing. "Let's get one thing straight, Mr. Jordache, and let's get it straight right now. I am not my mother, and I don't know how you figured things out, but—"

"I saw her."

The man's words made Shayla stop talking abruptly. She looked over at him. He was no longer looking at her. His eyes were glued to the scenery out of the window. "What do you mean, you saw her?" She saw his shoulders hunch slightly when he turned toward her. His eyes appeared defeated, and his expression seemed pained.

"When I opened my business here I saw her—I saw both of your pictures in the newspaper. It was not too long after Dr. Glenn Kirkland had died, and a wing of the hospital was being named in his honor. For over twenty years I'd had no idea where Evangeline had run off to."

Shayla drew herself up straight. "Run off? Just what did you expect her to do after you used her and left her pregnant, with orders to get an abortion? You're a vile man, Mr. Jordache."

"Yes, I know," he admitted quietly. "I've done some pretty low-down terrible things in my life, but causing Evangeline such pain and humiliation was probably the lowest." His expression and his soft-spoken words were sad. His tone was regretful, and repentant. But Shayla wasn't quite ready to buy into it.

Thomas Jordache moved his gaze back to the window and stared out. He began coughing. It was a few long moments before he had gotten his coughing under control and spoke again. "Besides being vile, Shayla, I'm also dying of lung cancer. I have less than a year to live."

His words were not what Shayla had expected. She rubbed her temples, not knowing what to say, not even sure she believed him. She decided it was better not to believe him. "And just what do you want me to do about it? Donate one of my lungs so you can live a little longer, to continue to be the vile person you are."

For a moment they stared at each other across the space of the backseat. "I guess I deserve that."

Suddenly Shayla remembered the words her mother had written in her diary about the humiliation that this man had caused her. "That's not the tip of the iceberg of what you deserve, Mr. Jordache. If it's pity you want from me, you won't get it. All my pity goes to my mother, for your treatment of her twenty-seven years ago."

Shayla saw a muscle twitch in Thomas Jordache's cheek. "I didn't know she was still in love with someone else until that one night we made love. She called out his name instead of mine."

"So you decided to pay her back and set her up with Chenault Electronics by making it seem she was disloyal to them?"

"I felt used, and lashed out to hurt her out of anger. It was my way of getting back at her. I was sorry afterward."

Shayla shook her head in disgust at the man's admission of what he had done. "You were sorry? Too bad she never knew that."

"You're wrong, Shayla. Evangeline knew it before she died. I told her."

Shayla looked at him. "What do you mean?"

Thomas Jordache rested his back against the car seat. "After seeing the two of you in the paper I figured that she hadn't gotten the abortion, so I went over to the hospital one day when I knew she would be there, doing her volunteer work. We talked, and I told her then. And she forgave me."

"Big deal," Shayla said curtly. "She forgave you, but that doesn't mean that I will. Mom was loving and forgiving. I'm not."

Shayla watched as Thomas Jordache rubbed his hand over his nearly bald head several times. "Why did you want me to meet with you, Mr. Jordache? I'm sure it wasn't to rehash old times, since we don't have a history."

He looked at her and was silent for a long moment before saying, "No, we don't. But you've met Trent, and I know you're fond of him. At least, I know he's fond of you. He speaks highly of you."

Shayla's expression was wary. "What does Trent have to do with this?"

"I love my son. I love him more than life, and if this person succeeds in doing what's he's trying to do then I'll—"

"Wait a minute. Back up. What are you saying? What on earth are you talking about?" She eyed him, trying to make sense of his words.

"Someone, I don't know who, is trying to make it seem that I'm behind all those things that are happening at Chenault Electronics."

"Aren't you?"

"No, I'm not. I promised Trent that I wouldn't have any dealings with Chenault, and I haven't. But because of what's happening, Trent's going to believe I'm involved. I don't want that. I have less than a year left to spend with my son.

I don't want that time spent with mistrust and anger between us. I want his last memories of me to be good ones."

An uncomfortable silence filled the car, and a lump formed in Shayla's throat from the look of heartache on Thomas Jordache's face. It was an emotion he wasn't trying to hide.

Was it an act? Maybe she was the world's biggest fool, but she honestly didn't think so. Across from her sat a man who had wrestled with life and lost. It took several seconds for all of it to finally sink in. Thomas Jordache *was* dying.

She urged her gaze away from him, telling herself she didn't care. She didn't know this man. This was the longest amount of time she'd ever spent with him, so why should the fact that he wouldn't live long bother her? She hadn't even known he'd existed until she read her mother's diary. Glenn Kirkland was her father, not this man who wanted to die on good terms with his son…and who had not yet acknowledged her as his biological daughter. Did she care? She shouldn't care for him, or about the situation that had created her twenty-seven years ago.

But still…in spite of all that, she knew that she did. Her parents had raised her to care about others. Her father had been a doctor, and he'd loved his profession, the vocation of healing and caring. And her mother had worked by his side. She had been involved in a number of worthwhile charities whose main focus was caring for others, too.

So, Shayla thought, as much as she didn't want to care, she did. And at that moment something inside of her yielded. "If you really believe someone is trying to frame you as you claim, Mr. Jordache, why don't you tell Trent or Nicholas?"

Thomas Jordache's eyebrows drew together. "I don't think either of them would believe me. I've tried too often to destroy their friendship for that. Trent might want to believe me, but he'll still have his doubts. That's why I need your help."

His last statement surprised Shayla. "My help? What do you expect me to do?"

"I want you to keep your ears and eyes open. Those two incidents were inside jobs. Nicholas needs to watch his back. Someone inside his operation is trying to ruin him, and is making it seem that I'm the one responsible. I can't confront Trent and Nicholas with that until I have solid proof."

"Why don't you go to Paul? The two of you know each other."

"I'm sad to say that Paul and I have barely tolerated each other over the years. He's never forgiven me for marrying Dawn, and for keeping Trent away from him all that time. If anyone won't believe me, it's Paul. He wouldn't buy my story."

"But you expect me to?"

"Yes. I'm hoping that you will."

Shayla didn't say anything for the longest time. Then she noticed that the car had stopped moving and they had returned to the restaurant. "I need time to think about this."

Thomas Jordache nodded. "I understand. In the meantime, be careful. I don't know who's behind this, or how desperate he may be to get whatever it is he wants." His expression then became solemn, bleak. "Some people will do just about anything to be successful. Trust me. I know," he said quietly, regretfully.

Shayla nodded before getting out of the car. Without saying goodbye she closed the door behind her.

Initially Nicholas was stunned by the information Paul had just given him, but the more he thought about it, the more it made perfect sense. Someone on the inside of his organization was working with Thomas Jordache. "And you're sure Jordache is involved?"

"I don't have concrete proof, if that's what you're

asking," Paul said, looking directly into Nicholas's eyes. "But this morning Harris was able to pick up on several attempts of someone trying to infiltrate our network."

"How?" Nicholas turned and directed his question to Silas Harris, the manager of his Technical Department.

"By password guessing and data diddling, looking for vulnerabilities. I was able to trace it for a few seconds, and the snoop was identified as coming from one of Jordache's based modems."

Nicholas sighed as he tightened his fist at his side. That the snoop had been identified as coming from one of Jordache's modems didn't mean anything. It could have been a system he had sold to someone. "If Jordache is involved, what do you think he's trying to do?" Nicholas asked, knowing that whatever it took he needed to protect his software and systems. The importance of the MC Project dictated that every precaution be taken, especially at this stage of the chip's design.

Harris glanced down at the report in his hand before meeting Nicholas's gaze again. "Someone is trying to introduce a virus into your system, one that'll render the mangolid chip so ineffective that it will take another two to three years to get it back right." He sighed deeply. "And I agree with Paul. Whoever is doing it may have inside help."

Nicholas's entire body shook with a murderous rage. Someone with malicious intentions could render what had taken his company two years to develop and perfect totally useless with the infiltration of a virus. And it made him even angrier to know that someone from inside his company might be involved.

"If this is an inside job, I want to know the person involved. Do whatever you have to to beef up security. I want you to use hidden cameras throughout the buildings here and in Jacksonville—especially here, since the mangolid project will be worked out of this office starting Monday."

He took a deep breath before continuing. His next statement was directed at Harris. "I want hour-by-hour checks of the logs, and audit trails to monitor any further attempts. I want a list of the names of any employee who's been on vacation within the past six weeks, or who has left the company, for whatever reason—on my desk in an hour."

He looked at Paul. "Where's Stockard? I haven't seen him all day."

Paul leaned back in his chair. "I ran into him over an hour ago. He was rushing out of the building like he was on his way to a fire." Paul shifted in his seat to find a more comfortable position. "Maybe he was chasing down a lead or something. He's taking these incidents personally, and won't stop until he brings the culprit to justice."

"I appreciate his eagerness," Nicholas said, "but tell him not to be so obvious. I don't want any of my employees to know they're under suspicion."

Paul nodded.

Nicholas turned and glanced out of the window. "I meant what I said. I want the name of the person who's working with Jordache."

The decks aboard the *Majestic* were clean as a whistle, Trent noticed as he made his way along them. Although he appreciated his crew for such outstanding work, at the moment the main thing on his mind was getting to know a certain woman better. Being one of the owners of the ship had its advantages. The ship's computer had given him a name: Brenna St. James. The ship's steward in charge of Ms. St. James's deck had confirmed that she was traveling alone. As far as he was concerned, the coast was clear for him to make his move. Now if he could only locate her.

More information supplied by the computer indicated that

Ms. St. James had a last dinner call. That meant she should be in the dining room, and that's where he was headed.

Once he walked through the double doors it didn't take long for him to find her. She was sitting alone. The lights were dim but captured her stunning beauty, nonetheless. Unhesitatingly, he walked over to her.

"May I join you?" he asked simply.

Brenna raised her head from studying her menu to lock gazes with the man who had suddenly appeared at her table. He had asked so casually that she had to fully concentrate on just what the question was. It wasn't easy to concentrate on anything other than how good-looking he was.

She then remembered that she'd had her fill of dealing with good-looking men, who were usually as hot-blooded as they were good-looking. The only thing they wanted was to charm their way into her bed.

"Why?" she demanded just as simply as he'd asked the question.

From the expression on his face, she could see that her question had evidently taken him by surprise and left him baffled. "Why what?"

"Why do you want to join me?" she asked as dispassionately as she could.

"Because you're dining alone."

"So. Did it occur to you that maybe I want it that way?"

Trent lifted a brow. "If that's the case, when I asked if I could join you all you had to say was no," he answered easily. "In a nice way," he added.

"Do you really expect me to think it would have been that easy, Mr.—"

"Jordache. Trent Jordache."

"Do you really expect me to think it would have been that easy, Mr. Jordache?"

"Yes. I don't know why not. I've never forced my company on any woman, and I have no intention of starting now. Please enjoy your meal."

Trent walked away, thinking it was a shame that with all Brenna St. James's outside beauty she definitely lacked charm and manners.

Brenna watched as the man walked away. She didn't need anyone to tell her that she'd behaved rudely. Before his approach there had been two others who had cornered her right outside the dining room, also asking to join her for dinner. Neither of the men had been nice. In fact, one of them had acted as if he would be doing her a favor to dine with her. The second man had all but asked to sleep with her, as well. That was the reason she'd asked for a table by herself.

She had come on the cruise to have a good time, not to get picked up. She wrinkled her nose in frustration. Why did some men assume a single woman traveling alone was an open invitation to be hit on?

As she resumed looking at the menu, she thought she could easily forget all of them. *Not so,* her mind quickly countered. *Trent Jordache isn't a man you can easily forget. He's handsome. Incredibly handsome.* Unfortunately, his timing had been lousy when he had approached her just now, since she hadn't had time to recover from the two jerks. What she'd said to him and the tone she'd used had been uncalled for, and totally unlike her. In all fairness she owed him an apology, and when she saw him again she would make sure that he got it.

Chapter 21

Shayla's meeting with Thomas Jordache completely filled her mind as she drove away from the restaurant. She had thought about going straight to Nicholas's place, but figured he would still be at work. She wasn't supposed to join him for dinner at his condo for another three hours.

She needed someone to talk to. Aunt Callie was in New York on a buying trip, and would not be returning for a few days. She could have called her at the hotel, but immediately decided against it. Her aunt would not want her to get any more involved than she was already. But for some reason Shayla felt she had to find out if Jordache's allegations were true, if one of Nicholas's employees was working with someone to ruin his company.

She shook her head, thinking how ironic it was that in the beginning, ruining Chenault Electronics had been what she herself had planned to do. Now, less than a month later, after falling head over heels in love with Nicholas, she was willing to do whatever was in her power to save it.

After she parked her car in the driveway and opened the car door, an abundant amount of icy air hit Shayla full in the face. Although it wasn't snowing, the weather was freezing cold. She entered her home wondering what, if anything, she would tell Nicholas when she saw him later.

Approximately three hours later, Shayla, her features flushed from the frosty temperature, knocked on Nicholas's door. It opened immediately.

She took a step back and made a conscious effort to pump air steadily in and out of her lungs. Every cell in her body felt numb, but not from the cold. Standing in the doorway dressed in a pair of well-worn jeans and an Orlando Magic T-shirt and with no shoes on his feet, Nicholas Chenault looked like anything but a successful businessman. He was the most magnificent looking male animal she had ever seen. His body was taut and firm in all the right places, and his eyes were a sharp gold as he looked at her.

"You're right on time," Nicholas said huskily, stepping aside to let Shayla in and then closing the door. He reached out for her, bringing her into his arms. The scent of her, he thought, was pure seduction, as usual, just like the name of the perfume she was wearing. Everything about his day that he wanted to forget evaporated from his mind as he held her. He wondered how such a thing was possible, and at the same time he realized just how unfair he had been to Olivia during the year they had been together, because he'd never felt this awesome need, this magnified possessiveness, this being filled with such inner fire for her. His parting with Olivia had been best for both of them, especially for her. She deserved someone who could give her the degree of emotional attachment that she needed and he'd been unable to give her. But with Shayla it was another story. He'd only known her for a month, but she affected him deeply, and not by slow degrees. Around her he felt something vital and fierce take over, every time.

"I need this," he said as those feelings automatically came over him and something stirred deep within him. He cupped her chin in his hand and brought her mouth to his. At the same time he slipped the coat from her shoulders. He had thought about kissing her all day. When she'd attended that impromptu meeting in his office, he had watched her mouth move while she talked on the phone, wishing his tongue inside her mouth, tasting her, kissing her mindless.

As he was doing now.

He hadn't meant to come on so strong so soon, but his hormones were raging out of control. There were too many things on his mind that he wanted to forget. He wanted all his thoughts to be concentrated on her and the desire rearing up from deep within.

Nicholas would have been surprised to know that Shayla desperately needed to forget some things, as well. On the drive over she'd had time to think, and had decided not to mention anything to Nicholas until she could somehow check out Jordache's story. But for tonight, she didn't want to think about it. She only wanted to think about the man who held her in his arms and was kissing her with an intensity that she returned tenfold.

He dragged his lips from hers. "My bedroom."

Without waiting for her response, he picked her up in his arms in one fluid movement and began walking in what Shayla could only assume was that direction.

It was, she found out when he placed her gently on his huge bed moments later.

"This is crazy," Nicholas said as he quickly began removing his clothes, feeling out of control with a need to make love to her. He'd had her both ways—fast and hot, and slow and easy. Now he wanted a mixture of both, and hoped he'd survive the experience. His eyes stayed on her after removing his T-shirt. He then began pulling down the zipper of his jeans.

"Yes, absolutely ludicrous," Shayla finally said, watching him inch the zipper down and then peel the tight jeans down his hips and kick them aside. His briefs quickly followed and then he took the time needed to put on a condom. She felt the breath catch in her throat when he reached out and dragged her sweater over her head and tossed it aside.

Then she watched his lips curve in a delicious hungry grin when he saw that she wasn't wearing a bra. She released a trembling sigh when he reached out and filled his palms with her breasts, kneading her flesh with measured caresses. She tilted her head back to look at him and saw the strain of desire, the tension of keeping control bunching his forehead.

He moved in closer, leaving her breasts and concentrating on removing her boots and socks and then her jeans. Shayla swallowed the sound she made at the back of her throat with the same ease with which he pulled her jeans down her hips.

The air surrounding them seemed to thicken. The temperature in the room seemed to simmer. Shayla felt as if she were about to go up in flames when he tossed her jeans aside and turned his full attention to her flimsy, lacy, bikini panties.

They were too flimsy, she thought. Then, with a flick of his wrist he ripped them from her body with strong accomplished hands. He then tossed what was left of them aside.

"I'll buy you another pair," he promised hoarsely, coming closer, looming his body over hers to cover her.

"Yes, you do that," she murmured mindlessly as sensations spiraled throughout her and took firm root dead center, between her legs, where the heat of Nicholas gently probed just seconds before he entered her, gripping her hips to hold her still.

"This is what I want. This is what I need," he whispered as he pushed himself deeper into her.

"This is what I want. This is what I need," she repeated, savoring the feel of him inside her. He was holding her body in place, not yet establishing their rhythm, and not yet feeding the fire between them that was raging out of control. His warmth and scent alone were driving her insane. When she thought she couldn't stand the torture of not moving another minute, her body went into action. With a smooth gracefulness that was the result of endless hours of dance lessons as a child, she arched her body and pushed upward against the cradle of his thighs, demanding that he move.

"Shayla…" Her name was spoken barely above a whisper when, his hungry mouth hovering over hers, he slipped his tongue through and began moving with the same rhythm his body had begun inside her.

Shayla didn't think anything could be better than the last two times they'd made love, but immediately decided she'd thought wrong. Everything about this had her keyed up in earth-shattering ecstasy. Each long strong stroke was possessive, needy, desperate. The sounds coming from deep within his throat with every thrust were raw and urgent.

Her mouth protested when moments later his mouth left hers. His eyes, open and starkly aroused, stayed on her, staring deeply into hers, daring her to close hers or look away.

"Come."

He uttered that single command at the same time he drove into her with incredible force. She knew at that moment that somehow, someway, without him even realizing it, he was staking his claim on her forever. And, as if her body had to obey his order, she came, and a turbulent climax slammed into her at the same time she felt it slam into him.

They trembled in each other's arms. He gave. She took. She gave. He took. The only thoughts consuming their minds were of each other and the timeless essence of their mating. The connection between them was as breathtaking and as powerful as the sensuous rapture that totally consumed them.

And just as binding.

"Well, what do you think?"

When Nicholas asked that question, Shayla picked up another piece of meat with her fork, closed her eyes, tasted, savored, and moaned. She slowly opened her eyes and looked at him. "It's simply delicious. Who taught you how to cook such mouthwatering steaks?"

"My mother," Nicholas replied, smiling, as he sat across the kitchen table from Shayla. With her hair tossed about her face she looked wild, fulfilled, and contented. She resembled someone who had been thoroughly made love to in a most passionate and satisfying way. He knew the feeling. At the moment he felt the same way. Instead of putting her clothes back on she had opted to wear his bathrobe. He thought for the umpteenth time that his robe looked a hell of a lot better on her than it did on him. And it certainly didn't help matters knowing that she didn't have a stitch of clothing on underneath it.

"You and your mother are close, aren't you?"

Shayla's question drew his mind back into the conversation. "Yes, extremely close."

"What about your brother, Sterling Hamilton? Are you close to him, as well?"

Nicholas took a sip of his coffee as he thought about her question. "We're getting there. I'm sure you've read it in all the newspapers like everyone else—the intimate details of my mother's past, how she abandoned Sterling as a child. It's something he's now forgiven her for."

Shayla nodded. "How did finding out about your mother's past affect you, Nicholas?"

Nicholas stared at Shayla for what felt like an eternity as he tussled with deciding just how open he could be with her. He knew she meant more to him than great sex. At that precise moment, he knew that he cared a lot for her.

"I'm sorry, Nicholas. I didn't mean to pry."

Her softly spoken words of apology reeled him back into their conversation. "You're not prying. You can ask me anything you want." He reached across the table and captured her hand in his. "Maybe it's time I talked to someone about it. At the time it was hard to express my innermost thoughts and feelings to anyone, even to Paul."

He stared at her for several seconds before speaking again. "My mother didn't tell me about Sterling until after she'd discovered she had a brain tumor, until she thought it was necessary. She and my father had been all the family I'd had, and she didn't want me to be alone if anything happened to her. It was only then that she told me I had a brother."

Nicholas released her hand and stood. He walked over to the window and looked out, swamped with emotions and feelings he'd never shared with his mother. It was a few moments later when he turned around. "It was a heavy blow to me, Shayla. A part of me initially felt betrayed and disillusioned when I discovered the truth. As a child, I thought I had the perfect mother. She was loving to me, loving to my father, and loving to all who knew her. I had put her on a pedestal. In my eyes, she could do no wrong, and definitely not something as appalling as abandoning a child, giving up full claims and rights to him."

He released a deep long sigh and came back to the table and sat down. "But she had, and once I realized my mother was not Saint Angeline, as I'd always assumed, a part of me resented her for it. To this day she doesn't know about how I felt the day she told me, and the emotions I had to deal with."

"How did you handle your feelings of resentment?" Shayla asked, needing to know because of the resentment she felt toward Thomas Jordache.

"True love overlooks a multitude of faults, and none of us is perfect. At one time or another we've all done something we wish we hadn't. Something else that helped curtail my resentment was the fact she was dying. I loved her deeply, and wanted our last days together to be filled with all the love a child and parent could possibly share."

Which is the same thing Thomas Jordache wants for Trent, Shayla thought after hearing Nicholas's words. "But she lived," she felt it necessary to point out. "How do you feel about it now?"

"I feel blessed that Angeline Chenault is my mother, and that things happened the way they did. There was a reason Sterling was raised by his father, and not by my mother. He and his father shared a deep relationship and a very unique bond, just as I did with my own father. Besides, I can't and I won't hold my mother responsible for what she did as an immature seventeen-year-old girl. That was then. I appreciate her for being the woman she is now."

"And you say Sterling has forgiven her, too?"

"Yes, which I'm sure wasn't an easy thing for him to do. He was on his honeymoon when I got word to him that a blood clot on our mother's brain had burst. When I sent word to him, I didn't know if he'd even want to know, but I felt that he had a right. I certainly didn't expect him to come see her."

"But he did?"

"Yes. Within twenty-four hours of getting my message he flew into Jacksonville. The first time I set eyes on my brother—except on a movie screen—was when he appeared at the hospital. The connection between us that day was automatic and absolute. We knew, even without speaking, that it might be too late to capture that special bond that exists between brothers. But it would be a start if we could at least become friends. And we have. And I want to believe that the brother thing is slowly developing, as well."

Shayla nodded. After listening to Nicholas it seemed that more people than she imagined had some sort of skeleton in their closet. She couldn't help remembering what she had discovered about her own mother and wanted to share that with Nicholas, but she knew that now wasn't a good time.

Getting up from the table, she walked around to him. He automatically pushed his chair back and pulled her down into his lap, holding her tightly. For long moments neither of them said anything, and she placed her head against his chest.

"Do you have any plans for Easter weekend?" Nicholas asked her, breaking into the silence.

"No. My aunt and I haven't made any plans, and I doubt we will. She arranged a trip sometime last year to journey to the Holy Land with a group of friends. After Mama died she was going to cancel it, but I wouldn't let her."

Nicholas nodded. "Is your aunt your only relative?"

Shayla immediately thought of Thomas Jordache and Trent. "Why do you ask?"

He looked down at her and regarded her with an intensity that made her pulse rate increase. "My mother and I have been invited to Sterling's place in the mountains for Easter weekend. I know it's kind of short notice, since Easter is this coming weekend, but I'd like you to come."

Shayla looked up at him, her gaze just as intense. "You want me to spend Easter with you?"

Nicholas smiled. "Yes, with me, my mother, and anyone else Sterling and his wife, Colby, may be inviting." He smiled down at her enticingly. "So what about it, Shayla? Will you?"

Shayla took a deep shaky breath to control the emotions she was feeling. He wanted to take her with him, to meet the people who mattered to him. Could that mean that she mattered greatly to him, too? "Oh, Nicholas," she whispered, loving him so much. "I'd love to go. You've made me feel special just by inviting me."

To prove her sincerity, she smoothed her soft fingers across his sensuous mouth and leaned in closer to kiss him, displaying all the love she felt for him in her heart.

Nicholas fumbled with the belt at Shayla's waist and untied it as she continued to lavish his mouth with smoldering kisses potent enough to make his insides turn to jelly. Deciding that two could participate, he opened the robe and let his fingers trail down the curve of her breast, then move lower, and then lower still.

"Want more?" he asked in a forced whisper after she broke off the kiss and collapsed weakly against him. He felt her entire body shudder from the impact of his caresses. He stood with her in his arms.

"More?" he asked again as he stared down into her flushed features.

"Yes, more," she answered with a long sigh that caught in her throat. She wrapped her arms around his neck as he carried her back into his bedroom.

The last thing Brenna St. James expected to see when she walked into the dining room for breakfast the next morning was Trent Jordache eating alone. Her lips curved into a smile as she tipped her sunglasses, thinking that the brother was pretty good on the eyes.

She sighed deeply, knowing she needed to get the apology out of the way, and began walking toward him. Before she got halfway, he lifted his gaze and met hers, as if he'd sensed her approach. Sheer panic invaded her, but intense feminine pride kept her walking. The eyes looking at her were dark and all-consuming, and for a brief moment their intensity made her knees go wobbly and a tightness settle in the pit of her stomach.

Go on, she thought. *He's just a man. But, oh, what a man he is,* she couldn't help but add when he stood. The closer she got to him the more all five of her senses came alive. And then a sixth sense suddenly came out of nowhere when his mouth curled into a mirthless smile—a sense that warned her that he wasn't going to make her apology an easy one.

She came to a halt next to his table. "Mr. Jordache."

"Ms. St. James."

Brenna lifted an eyebrow, wondering how he knew her name. She had not given it to him last night.

"Was there something you wanted, Ms. St. James?"

Brenna's head whirled with his question. She hadn't noticed last night just how deep, rich, and sexy his voice was. She took a deep breath before saying, "Mr. Jordache, I want to apologize for my behavior last night. I was rude."

"Yes, you were."

She frowned. He didn't have to be so quick to agree with her, and she told him so.

"Why shouldn't I agree? I didn't deserve getting sliced into a zillion pieces with your razor-sharp tongue."

When he said the word *tongue,* Brenna's gaze latched on to his as he casually moistened his top lip with the tip of it. She swallowed, feeling hopelessly ill at ease under the intense dark gaze. "I'm apologizing. That's the best I can do," she finally said.

Trent cocked his brow. "I don't think so. What you can do is make it up to me by joining me for breakfast."

Brenna's gaze dropped to his plate. "You're almost finished."

He chuckled. "Yes, with the first round. I was about to go for seconds." He looked at her intently. "So what about it, Ms. St. James? Will you join me for breakfast, or do you prefer eating alone again?"

Brenna couldn't help smiling. Trent Jordache was smooth, but in a tolerant sort of way. "Yes, I'll join you, but only if you call me Brenna."

He extended his hand to her, returning her smile. "And I'm Trenton, but I prefer being called Trent."

"Care to tell me what had you on the defensive last night?"

Brenna lifted her head and stared at Trent for a moment before answering. They had finished a rather quiet breakfast and now sat drinking coffee and enjoying the ocean and its breeze.

After she told him, Trent frowned. As one of the owners of the ship, he didn't like the idea that one of his passengers had been harassed. Further, he didn't like it that the passenger had been Brenna. But he could see how any man would want to hit on her. She was a beautiful woman. "Do you think you would recognize those two men if you saw them again?"

Brenna shrugged. "It doesn't matter now. Really, it's no big deal. It just annoys me how some men react whenever they see a woman alone. Even while modeling—"

"You're a model?"

"I used to be."

Trent nodded, really not surprised. He'd noticed her walk that first day and thought that about her when she'd been walking along the deck. "Are you no longer in the business?"

"Only as a coordinator. I travel most of the time, going from city to city, putting on shows."

"When you were a model men used to hit on you a lot?"

"Yes. Some men think models are all body and no brains, and that's not true. I have a bachelor's degree in history from Grambling and a master's in African studies from Clark University in Atlanta." She sighed disgustedly. "It annoys me that sex is the number one thing on most men's minds."

Trent tilted his head and studied her. He smiled. "You have something against sex?" he asked teasingly.

Brenna's brows knitted, wondering how they had gotten on this subject, which was a pet peeve of hers. "Yes, I have something against it, if it's the only thing holding a relationship together. There should be more."

Trent's eyes stayed on hers. "Like marriage?"

"Or a firm commitment."

"Like an engagement?"

Brenna nodded. "That'll work."

Maybe for you, but not for me, Trent thought. He'd been there, done that, and didn't plan to ever go that way again. Luckily he had discovered his fiancée's true colors before the wedding. She had liked the idea of getting her hands on his money more than she had liked the idea of him getting his hands on her. At first he just assumed she'd had old-fashioned ideas, not wanting to sleep with a man before marriage, and he'd accepted her holding out until the wedding. But he'd soon discovered she'd only been manipulative and had used withholding sex as a means to get him to the altar. In the end, when push came to shove, he decided he wasn't that hard up and could do without sex—at least from her. After that folly he had made himself a promise never to take the plunge without first testing the waters. In other words, he did not intend to commit himself to a woman he hadn't slept with first.

"Most men don't like ultimatums," he finally said.

Brenna arched an elegant brow. "Then it's a good thing most women aren't willing to settle on most men. They want that special man, a one-of-a-kind man who will love, honor, and cherish them. With that type of man, a commitment comes easily."

Trent lifted the cup of coffee to his lips and took a sip, deciding it would be best to change the subject. "How about if we take a stroll around the ship to walk off breakfast?"

Brenna smiled. "I think that's a good idea."

"So, what brought you on this cruise?" Brenna asked as she slipped her sunglasses back on, needing protection against the brilliant sun as they walked along the deck.

"A bit of relaxation, and business." Trent decided he didn't know her well enough to tell her that he was one of the owners of the ship. That kind of information would put dollar signs in some women's eyes. "What about you?"

"The cruise was a birthday present from my best friend and her husband. They'll become parents later this month, and I'll be a godmother. Imagine that."

Trent shrugged. He couldn't imagine it. Growing up with just his father, he'd reached fourteen before he had discovered that his mother, who had died at his birth, had had a brother. His father had never told him about his uncle, Paul, because of the animosity between the two men. As a child he'd been sent to private schools up north, to keep them separated.

"So which birthday was this?"

Brenna frowned slightly. "The big three-o."

Trent chuckled. "That's not so bad. I turned thirty-two a few months ago."

They stopped walking, and she leaned on the rail and watched the ocean. They seemed to be right smack in the middle of it. She thought it was a beautiful sight, all aqua blue and billowy white foam. Then she thought about the route the ship was taking—the same one the slave ships had used, coming and going.

Trent studied her intently. He could see that she could easily bring some man to the altar if he thought doing so would make her his woman forever. Some man would gladly place a ring on her finger if he knew she would be the one he woke up to in the morning, and the one he would come home to at night.

Trent inhaled a deep breath of ocean air, forcing his thoughts not to go there. He had decided after his botched engagement never to let any woman try wrapping him around her finger. As he continued to watch Brenna he saw a lone tear flow down her cheek. "What is it? What's wrong?"

She turned, and despite the sunglasses she wore he could see her misty eyes. "I was just thinking how it must have been for them—the slaves—being forced from the only land they knew, getting packed like sardines on a ship. A number of them jumped overboard whenever they could, preferring a watery grave to enduring the life awaiting them in America. How awful it had to be for them."

Trent nodded. He understood how she felt. He had felt the very same thing—grief, anger, their pain—the first time he had taken a cruise to Africa. Sometimes, in his cabin at night, he'd imagined hearing their tortured cries and the sounds of their shackles as they jumped ship, embracing imminent death.

Without thinking twice about it, he gently pulled Brenna into his arms, ignoring the feeling of pleasure he felt having her there. A gentle ocean breeze flitted over them as they stood on deck with his arms wrapped around her shoulders and her body leaning against his.

At that time and at that moment, Trent grudgingly admitted that holding her in his arms felt right.

Chapter 22

Shayla sat back in the chair at her desk, sipped a cup of coffee, and gazed lovingly at the flowers that had been delivered to her at work.

They were from Nicholas, and just in case someone had wanted to sneak a peek at the card, she had immediately slipped it in her purse after reading it. His message—Thanks for a wonderful weekend—was something she didn't want to share with anyone.

She sighed, thinking about their time together on Sterling Hamilton's mountain, and how much she had enjoyed herself. They had flown into Raleigh, North Carolina, late Friday night and then had taken a chartered helicopter to the mountains. Sterling's other guests—the Garwoods, the Madarises, and the Wingates—were already there when they arrived. Nicholas and Sterling's mother didn't arrive until early Saturday morning.

Over breakfast that morning Nicholas had teased his

mother about a date she'd had with someone named Jessup Baron. From the smiles that had appeared on Angeline Chenault's face it was apparent that she had enjoyed Mr. Baron's company.

Shayla had felt overwhelmed that Friday night when Nicholas had introduced her to everyone. These were not everyday people. Sterling Hamilton and his wife, Colby, were the perfect host and hostess. Well-known movie actress Diamond Swain-Madaris and her husband, a wealthy rancher from Texas named Jake, had been all smiles when they announced that they would be parents by Christmas. Just last month it had made national news that an obsessed fan of Diamond's who happened to be a news reporter, had been arrested for plotting to kill Jake.

The Wingates consisted of Colby's brother James, his wife, Cynthia, and their seven-month-old son, James Jr. James Sr. was the CEO of Wingate Cosmetics, a company that Shayla knew was doing extremely well with its newest masculine cologne called Awesome. A national advertisement that cast Sterling as the Awesome Man had proved highly successful. It seemed women all across the country wanted to purchase the cologne for the man in their life, no doubt thinking that if their man couldn't look like Sterling, the next best thing was for him to smell like him.

Then there had been Kyle and Kimara Garwood and their six kids. It amused Shayla that like their parents, all six of the Garwood children had names that began with the letter *K*. It amused her even more that Kyle and Kimara were actually considering having a seventh child.

Everyone, including Nicholas's mother, was extremely nice to her, and in no time at all Shayla'd felt completely at ease. It was uncanny how much of Angeline's looks Nicholas had inherited, while Sterling didn't resemble her at all...except when he smiled. Both sons had their mother's heartwarming smile.

Shayla was amazed at how much love clearly shone in Sterling's, Jake's, Kyle's, and James's eyes for their wives. It was there whenever they looked at them, touched them, or spoke to them. Colby, Diamond, Kimara, and Cynthia were special women, and their husbands treated them as such.

By the time she left Sterling's mountain Sunday night, she had felt she had somehow established a special relationship with everyone she had met that weekend. She also felt she had fallen even more hopelessly in love with Nicholas.

Shayla let out a deep breath as her thoughts returned to the present. Her life right then would be just about perfect if not for her relationship with Thomas Jordache. What he'd told her last week was very much on her mind. She had tried being more observant at work, and had even resorted to asking a few innocent questions of her coworkers, making it seem she was interested in the mangolid project. But for some reason everyone viewed her interest cautiously, and wasn't saying much.

Everyone except Howard.

As usual, he had a lot to say, and most of the time what he said wasn't flattering. In his opinion, Nicholas was beginning to place too much importance on the mangolid chip project, while some other projects were being placed on the back burner.

Shayla tried summarizing in her mind everything she knew about Howard. He had been employed with Chenault for less than a year, and had mainly worked out of the Jacksonville office. He was handsome and single, but never talked about having a social life. In fact, they never had any contact outside of the office. What really stuck in her mind was that on several occasions when she'd walked into his office he'd ended phone conversations abruptly.

Shayla sighed. She'd never paid attention to any of that before, but ever since her meeting with Thomas Jordache she had been seeing everyone in a whole new light—a very suspicious light. It bothered her that she was beginning to act no better than Carl Stockard, who looked at everyone as untrustworthy.

The ringing of the phone interrupted Shayla's thoughts. She picked it up immediately. "Shayla Kirkland."

"Yes, Ms. Kirkland. This is Leanne. Mr. Chenault would like to meet with you in his office. He's asked that you bring the Africa sales report with you."

"All right. I'm on my way."

"You wanted to see me, Mr. Chenault?" Shayla asked, entering Nicholas's office and finding him standing across the room looking out of the window.

"Yes, Ms. Kirkland, I did." He walked over to his desk and picked up his phone. "Leanne, Ms. Kirkland and I will be in a very important meeting for the next twenty minutes or so. Please hold all my calls." He then replaced the receiver.

Slowly, he walked around his desk toward her, his eyes never leaving hers as he took the report from her hands and tossed it on his desk. He pulled her into his arms.

"I have an unexpected trip to Bolivia, and I'll be gone for a week."

Shayla nodded as a lump formed in her throat. She began to miss him already. "How soon do you have to leave?"

"In an hour. I wanted to see you before I left. There was no way I could leave without doing this." He hooked his knuckles under her chin and lifted her face to his and kissed her—gently at first, then with an intensity that took Shayla's breath away.

Moments later, he reluctantly released her. He looked deeply into her eyes. "You and I will have a long talk when

I get back, Shayla. The first thing on my agenda will be the discussion of this *discreet* thing. I still don't like it, and want it to end when I return. Understand?"

Shayla nodded. She didn't want to be discreet anymore, either. She was in love with Nicholas Chenault, and didn't care who knew it. She also knew she would have to be completely honest with him and tell him everything. She would do so as soon as he got back.

"How will your evenings be without me?" he asked as he placed kisses along her earlobe and eyelids, then moved to her jaw and neck.

"Lonely," she whispered throatily when his lips moved to the corner of her mouth and began nibbling there.

He lifted his gaze to hers and watched her lashes flutter when he reached up and brushed his thumbs over the hardened tips of her nipples, which were straining against her silk blouse. "How lonely?"

"Extremely lonely," she managed to get out before her breath caught on indrawn gasps.

Nicholas's lips curved in a slow smile. "Good. Now I have a favor I'd like to ask of you."

"What?"

Nicholas stepped back and walked around to his desk, opened the drawer, and took out a flat black box. He walked back and handed it to her. "This is for you. Open it."

Shayla pulled her gaze from Nicholas, and with shaky fingers she opened the box, which was embossed with the name of a well-known Chicago jeweler. Her breath caught. She could barely breathe. On a bed of white velvet was a beautiful heart-shaped pendant surrounded by dazzling diamonds.

Speechless, breathless, Shayla looked up and met his gaze.

"The favor I want to ask is that while I'm gone," Nicholas said, not taking his eyes from her and speaking in a hoarse thick voice, "I want you to wear my heart. Will you do that for me, Shayla?"

Still unable to speak, Shayla nodded as love and happiness flowed through every bone in her body. Nicholas's gift and the words he had spoken had touched her deeply.

"Turn around, please."

She did what he asked, and he took his time placing the beautiful necklace around her neck and tucking it inside her blouse so that it wouldn't be seen.

Nicholas turned Shayla back around to face him. Nearly blinded by the beauty of her face, he was deeply touched by the tears he saw shimmering in her eyes. "You and I will definitely have a long talk when I return, Ms. Kirkland. Count on it."

He then pulled her into his arms and kissed her once more.

Shayla was on cloud nine as she walked back to her office, and was surprised when she nearly collided with Cindy coming out of it. A vague uneasiness stirred in Shayla when she saw her. "Were you looking for me, Cindy?"

As if taken aback, Cindy stared at her. "What makes you think I was looking for you?"

"Because you were coming out of my office."

Cindy flicked a nervous glance in the direction of Shayla's office. "I was inside for just a minute, admiring your flowers. They're beautiful."

"Thank you." *And no doubt you were trying to find out who sent them,* Shayla thought.

"Well I'll see you later. I have over a million things I need to do," Cindy said in a rush.

Shayla raised a curious eyebrow as the woman hurriedly walked away.

* * *

"You wanted to see me, Nick?"

Nicholas looked up from putting papers into his briefcase. "Yes, Paul, come in."

Paul came into Nick's office and closed the door behind him.

"Any new developments?"

Paul shook his head. "No, but we're on top of it." He lifted a brow. "Going somewhere?"

Nicholas nodded as he continued to stuff items into his briefcase. "Yes, and that's the other reason I wanted to see you. I got a call from Franklin this morning, and I'm needed in Bolivia right away for a special meeting. I'll be gone a week." Nicholas snapped his briefcase closed and looked up at Paul. "There's a favor I have to ask of you. It's something Trent asked me to do for him while he's away on that cruise to Africa, and now, with this unexpected trip, I'm asking you to cover for me while I'm gone."

Paul nodded. "Sure, what is it?"

Nicholas came around the desk and sat on the edge of it. He knew Paul wouldn't be so quick to volunteer if he knew what the favor was. "Trent has a feeling his father's ill, and I promised to be the contact person if anything unusual happens. Jordache's housekeeper was to call me if it did."

Paul's features hardened. "You would do that, knowing Jordache may be behind everything that's been happening here lately?"

Nicholas stiffened at the words Paul flung at him. "Yes, because Trent asked me to. I'd do anything for Trent, and you know that. And I know you would, too." Nicholas watched as Paul fought for acceptance of what he'd just said to him. Paul might detest his ex-brother-in-law, but he loved his nephew.

"You're asking a lot of me, Nick."

"I'm not asking you to go hold Jordache's hand, Paul.

Chances are you won't have to have any contact with him. All I'm asking is that you be the contact person while I'm away. If something happens that I need to know, all you have to do is reach me immediately."

"Why can't the housekeeper just call Trent?"

"She can, and she will. In the meantime, he wants someone available to take care of any immediate action that might be necessary."

Paul frowned. "There's nothing wrong with Jordache. He's too evil to die. People like him hang around a long time just to torment others."

"Maybe, maybe not. All I care about is the fact that Trent was concerned enough to come to me. Now, with this unexpected trip, I'm coming to you. Will you do it?"

Paul walked over to the window and looked out. When he didn't say anything for the longest time, Nicholas asked, "The bad feelings between you and Jordache go deeper than him marrying your sister, don't they, Paul?"

Paul turned around to Nicholas. "Yes, although that's what started it all. There was a woman I cared very deeply about, and because of Jordache I accused her of doing some things she didn't do."

Nicholas nodded. A part of him had always known there had been more to Paul's intense dislike of Jordache. "You loved her?"

Paul met his gaze. "More than life itself."

Nicholas's gaze was concentrated on Paul when there was a knock on the door and Leanne stuck her head in. "It's time for you to leave if you want to make it to the airport and avoid heavy traffic, Mr. Chenault."

"Thanks, Leanne."

When the woman had closed the door Nicholas turned his attention back to Paul. He stood. "I have to go, Paul. Forget the favor. I'll just let Mrs. Green know that—"

"No, I'm fine with it," Paul said, taking a deep breath. "I'll do it for Trent. As you said earlier, I'd do anything for him. Even that."

"You sure?"

Paul stuck his hands in his pants pockets. "Yes, I'm sure." He walked over to the door. Before opening it he turned back to Nicholas. "Have a safe trip, Nick, and don't worry about things here."

Later that evening Paul Dunlap was pacing the confines of his office. He had noticed Shayla Kirkland's wary expression when he had passed her in the hall after leaving Nicholas's office.

She had tried avoiding all eye contact with him, and a flush had covered her delicately molded cheekbones. He'd gotten the same gut instinct he always got whenever he saw her, the same weird feeling that he'd seen her before…or that he knew someone she resembled. There was just something about her that he couldn't put his finger on.

A moment later he picked up the phone and dialed Leanne's extension. "Leanne, this is Paul. Bring me Shayla Kirkland's personnel file."

Brenna stood on deck as the *Majestic* pulled into port at Cape Town. She was held spellbound by the town's beauty, surrounded by spectacular mountains, lush vineyards and shimmering seas. She couldn't remember seeing a place so inviting and welcoming.

She turned when she heard her name and saw Trent make his way through the crowd toward her. They had spent the last five days together, strolling around deck, going swimming, and sharing lunches and dinners. And when he walked her to her cabin each night, he'd been the perfect gentleman, only kissing her on the cheek before leaving.

"Ready for a full day of fun?" he asked, smiling when he reached her side.

"Yes." Like her, he was dressed in a pair of shorts, a festive and colorful T-shirt—compliments of the ship—and a pair of good walking shoes. She gave him a thorough once-over, liking what she saw. If the way he returned her look was any indication, he liked what he saw, too.

"Are you sure you want to spend your time with me again today, Trent?"

He smiled at her as his dark eyes held her gaze. "I'm positive." Taking her hand in his, he led her off the ship.

After taking a tour of Cape Town they caught an air-conditioned motorcoach to tour the Cape of Good Hope Nature Reserve. By the time they had reached their destination, Brenna had taken several rolls of film. Now she understood what Trent had meant when he'd told her that the Cape of Good Hope was one of Africa's best-kept secrets. Clifton, a picturesque and scenic town they had passed through, was enough to guarantee that she would retain memories of Africa forever.

Trent and Brenna enjoyed lunch at a seaside restaurant in Seaforth, and later had dinner at a restaurant along the coast as they watched the union of two oceans. It was close to midnight before they returned to the ship.

"I'm going to be sore tomorrow from so much walking," Brenna said as Trent walked her to her cabin.

"That's very likely," he said, smiling. They had taken in a lot, but the most enjoyable part of his day had been her company. She had been fun, and expressive of emotions at certain times, when her deep love of African history had shone through.

"What are your plans for tomorrow?" he asked when they reached her cabin door.

"Since tomorrow is our last day before heading back to the States, I plan to do some shopping in Cape Town."

Trent nodded. "Mind if I tag along?"

"Are you sure you want to? It might get boring."

Trent smiled. "I'll take my chances."

"All right, if you're sure."

"I'm sure."

Brenna was sinking in a warm sea of pleasure at the thought that he still wanted to spend time with her though there was nothing sexual going on between them. "Good night, Trent."

She wasn't surprised when he took a step forward. Nor was she surprised when he leaned down and touched his lips to hers. From the looks he'd been giving her all day, she'd had an idea that tonight his kiss would be different, less chaste, more passionate. She shuddered in response as tiny electrical shocks escalated up her spine, intensifying her nerve end feelings. She could actually feel the blood race through her veins, making her heart pound and her breathing unsteady.

"Trent…"

Somehow his name escaped her lips, barely, just seconds before he deepened the kiss. The only thing she could do was hold on by placing her arms around his neck, feeling the strong corded muscles there. With very little urging she opened her mouth beneath his, giving him the taste he sought. His breathing was thick and rough in her ear, his lips warm and hungry. The tongue that slipped into her mouth was hot and searing, stroking her into participation. Her arms left his neck and clutched his shoulders to hold on, to enjoy, to receive.

Only the sound of someone coming down the hall broke them apart.

"I knew it would be like that," Trent said heatedly, thickly, feeling something he'd never felt before after kissing a woman—aftershocks of pleasure. He drew in a deep breath, still reveling in Brenna's heat and lingering passion.

Her deep intake of breath matched his, and as he looked into her eyes he saw a mass of confusion there. He wanted to reach out and take her back into his arms and tell her that he was just as confused. But tonight he didn't want to dwell on that confusion. He didn't even want to think about it. He needed to go somewhere and relive the moments when he had held her in his arms and kissed her to sweet oblivion.

"Good night, Brenna."

He then watched as she opened her cabin door, went inside, and closed it behind her.

"Corinth? Did I catch you at a bad time?"

Corinthians Avery Grant eased her pregnant body into the nearest chair. She smiled. "Brenna, of course you didn't. Trevor and I just finished eating lunch. You're calling from the ship?"

"Yes."

"What time is it there?"

"Around two in the morning."

"Two in the morning? Are you still up enjoying the nightlife?"

Brenna grinned into the phone. "Among other things." She took a deep breath as she stretched out on the bed. She and Corinthians were best friends, and had been since preschool. There were no secrets between them. "Corinth, I met someone."

"You did? Who?"

Immediately, visions of Trent infiltrated Brenna's mind. "His name is Trent Jordache."

"Umm, sounds sexy. Is he good-looking?"

Brenna smiled. "Girl, good-looking ain't the word. The brother is everything a brother should be. He's all that, and a bag of chips. Besides good-looking he's thoughtful, considerate, fun to be around—"

"Umm. Can he kiss?"

Brenna closed her eyes while she became lost in a dreamy haze of sensual memories. "Can he *ever!* I've never been kissed like that before—that thorough, that complete, that intense."

"Wow!"

"Yeah, I know." Brenna's smile widened. "My thoughts, exactly." Then, after a few silent seconds, she said, "Corinth, I've fallen in love."

There was a sharp intake of breath on the other end and then silence…but only momentarily. "Brenna…" Corinthians's voice took on a serious tone when she gathered her wits after her best friend's admission. "What do you know about him other than he's good-looking, thoughtful, considerate, fun to be around, and a wow-me kisser? What personal info do you have on him? Why is he on the ship alone? What does he do for a living? Does he believe in God?"

Brenna's forehead bunched in confusion. She'd spent a good week and a half with Trent, and didn't know any of those things. The only thing she knew for certain was that she had fallen in love with him. "He doesn't talk about himself much. He enjoys hearing about me, my travels, my family and friends, basically anything I have to say." Brenna took a deep breath. "That's what's so different about him. He acts as if he sees me as an interesting person, minus the body parts. Oh, don't get me wrong, I know he's attracted to me and everything, but he doesn't act as if getting me into his bed is the only thing that interests him. He acts as if *I* interest him, and that's so refreshing."

Corinthians nodded. "But still, don't rush into anything. Find out everything you need to know about him, Brenna. I don't care how good he kisses. I want you to be sure he's the one you've been waiting for. I don't want you to get hurt. You and I both know that even with all your talk, you're a forever-kind-of-girl who needs a forever-kind-of-man. You owe it to yourself to make sure he's all that before getting too involved."

Brenna took a deep breath, knowing her best friend's advice had come a little too late. Falling in love with someone constituted an involvement in her book. Needing to change the subject and quickly, she asked, "And how are you feeling?"

Corinthians rubbed her overly large stomach. "Fat. I'm ready for everything to be over. Trevor is a nervous wreck these days," she said, thinking of the husband she totally loved and adored.

"Well, you just have to stay fat until I get back. Don't you dare have my godchild without me."

Corinthians laughed. "I won't."

Trevor Grant walked into the room just as Corinthians was hanging up the phone. He couldn't help noticing the frown on his wife's face. "You're okay?" he asked with deep concern in his voice.

Corinthians looked up and saw the worried expression on his face. Smiling, she said, "Yes, I'm fine, and so is Baby Grant." They had decided they didn't want to know the sex of their child before it was born. All they wanted was a healthy baby, regardless of whether it was a boy or girl. "That was Brenna calling from the ship."

Trevor nodded. "She's enjoying herself?"

Corinthians's smile sagged. "Yes. She may be enjoying herself a little too much. She's met someone."

Trevor leaned against the closed door and looked at his wife thoughtfully. "So? I thought that was the reason you sent her on the cruise alone—so that she could meet someone."

Corinthians shook her head, smiling. She should have

known she wasn't putting anything over on Trevor. She had no secrets from the man. "So, you figured it out, huh?"

"It was obvious. I'm sure even Brenna caught on to what you were up to."

Corinthians tried swallowing back the laughter that formed in her throat. Knowing Brenna, she probably had. "All I wanted was for her to have a good time, not fall in love."

Trevor lifted an eyebrow. "She's fallen in love?"

"So she thinks."

"And you don't think she has?"

Corinthians rolled her eyes. "Trevor, Brenna is too rational to fall in love with someone she's known less than two weeks." The frown returned to Corinthians's features as she remembered the excitement in Brenna's voice.

"She's a big girl who can take care of herself. I think you're worrying for nothing. For all we know, this guy may be just who she needs."

"And maybe he's someone she doesn't need."

"She'll have to be the one to make that determination, Corinthians."

Corinthians nodded, knowing her husband was right. She lifted an eyebrow at him. "What are you doing back so soon?"

Trevor smiled. "I got all the way to the corner. Then I realized that since you were on the phone when I left, I didn't get this." He leaned toward her, pulled her into his arms, and captured her lips in his.

Chapter 23

Callie Foster stood at the kitchen window, listening to what Shayla was saying. A troubled expression covered her face as she turned around. "Are you saying Thomas Jordache actually knew who you were?"

Shayla nodded. "Yes. He'd seen a picture of Mama and me together in the newspaper not long after Dad's death, and put two and two together. He figured out that she didn't get an abortion and confronted her, and she told him the truth."

Callie crossed the room and sat down at the table. "She did?"

Shayla glanced up when she heard the disbelief in her aunt's voice. "That's what he claims." She reached over and captured her aunt's hand. "I know the facts surrounding my birth were supposed to remain a secret between you, Mom, and Dad, but I guess she *had* to tell him. He had figured it out, anyway."

Although Callie nodded, she wasn't too sure about that. "What else did he say?"

Thirty minutes later, Shayla had told her aunt everything regarding her meeting with Thomas Jordache. "So what do you think, Aunt Callie? Should I believe him?"

"It seems you already do."

Shayla nodded. "It's hard to believe he's actually dying. More than anything my heart goes out to Trent. His father loves him very much."

Callie studied her niece. "Are you sure Jordache really wasn't just trying to milk you for information?"

"Yes. He knew something. In fact, I think he knew more than he was saying."

"Shayla, I—"

"No, Aunt Callie. I know what you're about to say, and it's too late. I'm already into this too deep. I love Nicholas too much to look away when he could lose everything."

"But you don't know that for sure."

"No, all I have are gut feelings. Just like my gut feeling that Thomas Jordache wasn't behind the fire and the break-in at Chenault Electronics. But I have no way of proving it." Shayla released a deep sigh and rubbed a hand over her face. "Boy, what a mess."

Callie took a sip of her tea and looked at Shayla for the longest time before saying, "Yeah, what a mess."

Carl Stockard leaned back in the chair at his desk and gazed out the window with a huge smile on his face. Everything was falling nicely into place. Who would have thought that Shayla Kirkland had her own agenda, and was working behind the scenes with Thomas Jordache?

Carl had followed her that day when she had hurried out of the building, and had watched her get into Jordache's limousine. He'd known there was something suspicious about her from the start. He couldn't wait until the boss returned from his trip to Bolivia. Solving this case would look good, and that's what he was counting on, to look good in Mr. Chenault's eyes. He would finally show Paul Dunlap once and for all what he could do. It was time for the man to retire. There was no sense in him hanging around any longer. He hoped this would show Dunlap that he was losing his touch, and wasn't needed. And once he was out of the way, there was no doubt in Carl's mind that he would be Nicholas Chenault's top pick as his number one security man. That would mean living on easy street, running things his way as Chenault's top security person.

Carl shook his head, and his smile widened. Ms. Kirkland was certainly making things easy for him. Unfortunately, the news about her would come as a hard blow to the boss, since the two of them were having an affair. He grinned. Yeah, he had figured that out, too, which was an added bonus. Mr. Chenault would definitely be grateful he'd been saved from the clutches of a deceitful woman. In Carl's book there was nothing worse than a woman who betrayed a man.

Carl whirled around in his chair when he heard someone enter his office. A frown covered his face when he saw who his visitor was. He quickly got up and closed the door. "What the hell are you doing here? You know better than to—"

"I can't do it, Stockard. I can't lie to Mr. Chenault any longer. His daddy was a good man. Alan Chenault would turn over in his grave if he knew what I'm allowing you to do."

Annoyed, Carl released a long sigh. He had no intention of letting anyone ruin his carefully laid plans. "I don't care how good a man Alan Chenault was, Harris. You and I have an agreement. If you don't want your wife and kids to find out about that little affair you carried on with Cindy Davenport, I suggest you continue to do what I say."

Silas Harris, who was normally a soft-spoken, easygoing person, suddenly reached out and grabbed Carl by the collar, shocking him with the force of his actions and the look of steel in his eyes. "I won't let you blackmail me any longer, Stockard. I'll go to Paul Dunlap and tell him everything."

Carl flashed a grin, and the look on his face was pure ice. "Yeah, you do that, and I'll make sure you pay. I'm sure your wife, your son and daughter in college, your pastor, a few of your neighbors, and one or two others will enjoy receiving an unmarked videotape in the mail, one that shows what you really do after-hours. You know, the one I captured on tape of you screwing Cindy Davenport's brains out in her apartment."

Carl felt Harris's hold on his collar loosen. He saw the look in his eyes as they began to clear. "Get your hands off me, Harris, and I mean now."

When Harris released him Carl stepped back with a thin superior grin on his face. He straightened his collar and tie. "I suggest you pull yourself together. When all this is over I recommend that you take a nice long vacation with the wife. You seem a little distraught and overworked."

"There's nothing going on between me and Cindy. She used me that one night."

Carl shrugged. "Yeah, whatever."

"No, I mean it. It was just that one time. She came on to me, tempting me with—"

"Spare me the details, Harris. All I know is what I caught on the hidden camera. And as far as your being used goes, no one forced you to go to her apartment, so you'll never convince me or anyone else that you didn't get what you went looking for. That tape shows you were enjoying mounting her."

"The two of you set me up," Harris said with a hard edge to his voice. "What was I to do when I got there and she began taking off her clothes?"

"Maybe you should have acted like a gentleman and asked her to keep them on." Carl sneered. "No matter what you think about it being a setup, Harris, after watching that video no one is going to believe you weren't enjoying yourself. Think about it. Then think about all you have to lose—your job, twenty-five years of marriage, the respect of your children, your friends, and your community. I'm not asking you to do anything illegal. All I'm asking is that you use your expertise to stretch things a bit. I want Mr. Chenault to realize just how valuable I am to him. Trust me, things will work out. And if you're worried he'll figure things out, then don't be. I have everything under control."

"But it's all a lie. You orchestrated everything—the fire, the break-in, the virus."

A sneer curved Carl's lips. "Yeah, I did, didn't I? And I went to a lot of trouble doing it, and I won't let you or anyone else ruin my plans. So think twice before running to Dunlap. You have as much to lose as I do. Maybe more. Now get out of my office."

Nicholas's meeting ended one day ahead of schedule. He spent nearly half an hour on the phone in his hotel suite trying to get a flight out of Bolivia. When he hung up, he was satisfied. He would be able to return to the States a full day earlier than planned.

With nothing else that he wanted to do at that moment, he stretched out on the bed, and thoughts of Shayla immediately consumed his mind. All through the four-day meeting it had been difficult for him to concentrate on business. His thoughts had been on her. In the time since he had met her, he had come to care deeply about her, emotionally and physically.

Physically he could understand and easily accept. Emotionally, he could not.

His heart moved against his ribs. He knew that whether he understood it or not, and accepted it or not, Shayla Kirkland had touched a part of him no other woman had.

And that was what really bothered him.

The necklace he had given her had been more than a piece of jewelry. The only woman he'd ever purchased expensive jewelry for had been his mother. But the moment he had seen the pendant behind the glass case in that exclusive jewelry store, he'd known he had to get it for her.

Just as he knew she was the main reason he was chafing at the bit to return to Chicago.

Still, the very thought that a woman could consume his thoughts and his mind so deeply was a hard one to swallow. He never thought about needing space when with her, and had proved that on a couple of occasions when she'd spent the night at his place, something that was a first for any woman.

So what was bothering him? When he really thought things through and stopped looking for complications that weren't there, he saw that in truth Shayla Kirkland was the best thing to happen to him in a long time.

Cindy Davenport was nearly wild with excitement when she opened the door to Carl Stockard late that afternoon. "So what's the latest? When will we have Shayla Kirkland out of the picture?"

Carl laughed as he entered Cindy's home. He, of all people, knew of her obsession with Nicholas Chenault. The boss was a challenge to her, since he'd never shown her any interest. Carl also knew Cindy. They had worked together at another company some years ago, a company she had gotten fired from when someone had walked in on her and another employee making out in her office. Neither of them had had enough sense to lock the door.

Carl had known getting Cindy to go along with his plan

to set Harris up would be easy. She had come to Chenault a year ago, looking for a fresh start and a fresh group of men to seduce. Unfortunately, the men at Chenault hadn't been willing to cooperate, bruising Cindy's ego. And then, with Nicholas Chenault's total lack of interest, she'd been more than hungry for someone's attention, even someone dull and boring as Silas Harris.

Carl liked Cindy. He thought she was daring, a woman who could hold her own. She had a backbone. She also had a good-looking body—a body he had gotten a piece of a time or two. As he watched her standing across the room dressed in a short silk bathrobe, he wondered if perhaps she would be accommodating tonight.

"Harris dropped by my office today," he finally said, sitting down on her sofa. "He's getting scared, and he threatened to go tell Dunlap everything."

Cindy's eyes widened. "What did you say to him?"

"I reminded him of everything he could lose if he talked."

Cindy nodded. She wasn't worried about Silas Harris. She knew that Stockard would keep the man under control. "What about Shayla? You promised to get her out of the picture."

"And I will. Just be patient. Things are falling into place, and without very much effort on my part I'll have what I want—Paul Dunlap's job when he leaves. And you'll have what you want—another chance to seduce Chenault."

Carl watched Cindy's eyes light up, and knew her body was probably getting stimulated at the thought. Getting Nicholas into her bed was an obsession, and had been since the first day she'd laid eyes on him. When she'd discovered he was messing around with Shayla Kirkland, she'd been furious and had been willing to do just about anything to get Ms. Kirkland out of the picture. She didn't take too kindly to competition.

"I want him," Cindy said in a tone so absolute that Carl

got turned on from the intensity of it. He slowly got up from his seat and crossed the room to her. He flashed her a smooth smile. He'd discovered that when it came to Cindy he couldn't help himself. She was the only person who could make him lose control. He never cared what other men she was intimate with, or what man she wanted, as long as he could have her whenever he got ready.

And tonight he was good and ready.

Cindy's pulse was slowly increasing its rate and hurling through every part of her body when she saw the raw look of sexual hunger in Carl's eyes. He wasn't Nicholas Chenault by any means, but he would do in a pinch. He always had. Besides, she enjoyed working that cool control out of his body. He was always a challenge she couldn't resist.

She returned his smile. "You brought condoms with you?" she asked. With not much of an effort she kept her voice cool, impersonal.

The look on Carl's face was objective, and just as cool and impersonal. "Yeah, I brought a bunch."

Cindy's fingers began untying the belt at her waist. Her eyes never left Carl's. "Good."

"Are you sure Harris said he traced the virus from one of Jordache's modems?"

Paul looked at the man sitting across from his desk who had asked the question. He was someone Nicholas had brought in six months ago to work undercover for security purposes. They were the only two people who knew his identity and the true purpose of his being there. "Yes, that's what he said. Why?"

"Because I didn't find anything, and I literally took the networking system apart going through it. By using that special code you gave me, I was able to enter Chenault Electronics's network through all the ports in their systems.

I'm positive I didn't miss any points of entry. There was nothing there."

Paul gave the man a quizzical look. "What are you saying?"

The man leaned over and handed Paul a folder. "What I'm about to say is all in that report. There was no importation of a virus of any kind in any of Chenault's computers."

"Are you saying Harris made a mistake in saying someone was trying to get into Chenault's system through a remote dial-in?"

The man's gaze never left Paul when he said, "He either made a mistake, or he deliberately lied about it. The only remote dial-ins that Chenault Electronics has received in the past three weeks were those that I tried to infiltrate from my system at the hotel. And I couldn't have penetrated Chenault's network without the password that you and Nicholas gave me. The system is just that tight. There's not an unauthorized person who can gain access to it, which makes me wonder why Harris is claiming otherwise."

Paul opened the folder and glanced at the documents. A few moments later he raised his head again and met the man's gaze. "You think Harris is involved in something?"

"After reading those inconsistencies, don't you?"

"I never would have suspected it. He's been working here for over twenty years. He's a model employee, and good family man. It's hard to believe he would betray the company. I don't want to believe that."

The man nodded. "He may be doing it because he's desperate for money. But who would pay him to fake a virus in Chenault's networking system?"

Thomas Jordache immediately came to Paul's mind. "Possibly someone who wants word to get out that the mangolid chip is defective when it isn't," he said.

"Possibly, but I don't think so. I ran a check on Harris. The strange thing is that he hasn't deposited any large sums of money in any bank accounts. He's a conservative spender who's sending his son and daughter to college, but—according to what I've been able to dig up—his kids have scholarships, so there's no real hardship there. Unless I've missed something, he doesn't seem to be reaping any type of monetary gain from what he's doing."

Paul shook his head. It was hard to believe Harris was the inside person who could be working with Thomas Jordache. "What about Jordache? Have you made a connection with him and Harris? Do you think Jordache is withholding Harris's payoff until he does something else?"

The man leaned back in his chair. "Now that's another mystery. I know you think Jordache is involved, but personally I don't. So far I haven't found anything to link Jordache to the fire or the break-in. I think someone's trying to make it seem that Jordache is involved when he's not."

Paul raised a dark brow. "Who would gain by doing that? And how is Harris involved?"

The man stood. "That's what I'm working on finding out. I'll check back with you when I have something else to report."

Paul watched as Howard Reeves headed for the door. "Wait. I want to ask your opinion about someone, another employee. Shayla Kirkland."

The man smiled smoothly. "Ahh, yes, Ms. Kirkland. Nick's Ms. Kirkland."

Paul frowned. "Then you know?"

"That the two of them are having an affair? Yes. But Nick didn't mention it. It wasn't hard to figure out. His entire face lights up whenever she enters a room, and as much as he tries not to, he only has eyes for her."

"It's that obvious?"

"Only to those who really know Nick."

Paul nodded. "What do you think of her?"

The man lifted his brow. “Besides being a hell of a good-looking woman, I think she’s fiercely loyal to Nick. The last few times I tried to engage her in negative conversations about him, I got her pretty pissed off with me.”

“It could have been an act.”

“No, I don’t think so.” Howard eyed Paul curiously. “Is there a reason you don’t trust her?”

“It’s not that.” Paul rubbed his hand across his face, then sighed heavily. “Hell, I don’t know what it is, but there’s something. The first time I met her I felt as if there was something about her I should know. That’s the reason I’m in the process of reviewing her personnel file again.”

Howard studied Paul for a few moments before saying, “Before I think about accusing her of anything, I’d make sure I had all my ducks in a row. Nick’s hooked on her pretty bad. He won’t take too kindly to false accusations about her without damn good proof from anyone. He’s in love.”

Paul nodded. He, too, had recognized the signs, although he doubted it was obvious to Nick just yet. “Yeah, he is,” he agreed. “And that’s what’s beginning to worry me. That’s why I’m going to make sure that Ms. Kirkland is as squeaky clean as she seems.”

“You’re quiet today,” Trent pointed out to Brenna as he helped himself to one of the French fries from her plate.

Brenna gazed up at him, her eyes warm and thoughtful. “I was just thinking how much you know about me, and how little I know about you. You don’t share yourself much.”

Trent leaned back in his chair. With that one statement Brenna had put everything in perspective about him. She was right. He didn’t share himself much with others. Although he considered himself very friendly and outgoing, he was a private person, nonetheless. The only person who knew him, really knew him, was Nick. But for some reason a part of him wanted Brenna to know him, too.

"Have dinner with me tonight, and I'll tell you all you want to know," he said in a low husky voice.

Brenna picked up her napkin and blotted her lips while she lifted an arched eyebrow. "That tactic won't work, Trent," she said, smiling. "I'm already having dinner with you tonight, remember?"

He picked up his drink and took a slow sip, his eyes never leaving hers as he did. Then he placed his glass back on the table. "I want you to join me for dinner tonight in my cabin, Brenna. Will you?"

Trent's question had caught her off guard, and she sat studying him for a long moment. Could she trust herself alone with him in his cabin? Was she prepared for the possible consequences if she did?

They had been spending a lot of time together, usually around others, never completely alone. But she knew, just from picking up on the vibes, that at times he had wanted her alone with him, away from others. At those times she'd seen a heated look in his eyes when he gazed at her, and she'd felt the gentleness of his hand whenever he found reason to touch her. His good-night kisses were no longer chaste pecks on the cheek. Now, when he walked her to her cabin she prepared herself to be kissed senseless. Yet, no matter how hot and heavy things got during their kiss, he'd held himself in check. He hadn't applied any type of pressure on her, and had not tried to break down her resolve.

Then why did she have the feeling that all was about to change? Why did she feel that tonight, being alone with him in his cabin could lead to a seduction she might not have the strength to walk away from?

The silence stretched between them. Other passengers by the pool were having fun, noisily romping in and out of the water, enjoying themselves. But at the table where Trent and Brenna sat alone, waiting, thinking, deciding, there was a swirl of sensuality surrounding them, heightening the heated tension around them.

"Yes," Brenna finally answered. "I'll join you for dinner in your cabin."

A worried frown lined Trent's features when he opened the door to Brenna late that evening. "I thought perhaps you had changed your mind," he said as he stepped aside to let her enter.

"Sorry I'm late. I got lost. I didn't know you were on a private deck."

Trent closed the door behind her after she had entered. "I apologize. I forgot to mention it. Did you have problems getting up here?"

"Not really. I just told the steward that you were expecting me for dinner. Luckily he believed me." She glanced around. "I didn't know they had cabins this large. This is the size of a penthouse," she said, noting how extra roomy the cabin was with its private balcony. She looked back at Trent, knowing he was probably paying a lot of money for this sort of accommodation. Now, more than ever, she couldn't help wondering just what he did for a living. He'd told her he was a businessman. Now she wondered just what type of business he was in.

Trent smiled, seeing the questions in her eyes. He invited her to take a seat on the sofa that provided a panoramic view of the ocean. The sun was just setting over it. "There aren't many of these large rooms on board. And you're right. This is a penthouse. I own it."

Brenna raised a brow. "You own a penthouse aboard this ship?"

"Yes."

"Why? You enjoy cruising that much?"

Trent shook his head, grinning. "Yes, in a way. But cruising is my business. I'm part owner of this ship."

Whatever Brenna had expected him to say, that wasn't it. She looked at him, surprised, nearly at a loss for words. "You own the *Majestic?*"

"Yes, with two other guys. It's the first black-owned luxury liner that sails exclusively to the Caribbean Islands and Africa."

Brenna nodded. "I'm impressed."

"I'd hoped you would be."

Brenna met his gaze as he sat down beside her on the sofa. "Why?"

Trent's eyes sparkled. "First we eat. Then you can ask me anything you want."

Brenna lifted an arched brow. "Anything?"

His lips curved into a sensuous smile. "Within reason."

"Anything else you want to know?"

Brenna smiled. After she and Trent finished dinner, her questions had begun, and he had told her everything she wanted to know. He lived in Jacksonville, Florida, most of the time, but was looking into buying a second home in Chicago, the other location of his family business. He had tried working with his father, but when he'd seen that wouldn't work he had gone out on his own. A year ago he and two business associates had pooled their resources and had purchased the *Majestic.* With its current success they were looking into the purchase of another cruise liner, one that would sail out of Florida instead of New York. She also learned that his only other living relative was an uncle named Paul, and that his best friend was a man named Nicholas Chenault. He had even gone so far as to share with her his fear that his father was ill, and wasn't telling him about it.

And most importantly, he did believe in God, although he had admitted he didn't make it to church every Sunday.

"Yes, there is something else," she finally answered. "It's the question I asked earlier. Why did you want to impress me?"

There was a moment of silence while Trent wondered just how he should answer her question. During the two and a half weeks he'd spent with her he had succumbed to every sensual thing about her. However, the one thing that stood between them was her belief that two people had to be totally committed to each other before they shared a bed. Since he had no intention of committing himself to any woman anytime soon, he found the thought of celibacy difficult, nearly impossible to live with. Single people engaged in safe sex all the time, if for nothing more than to ease their raging hormones—nothing personal, nothing serious, and definitely not anything of the magnitude that would require a commitment.

"Trent, why did you want to impress me tonight?" Brenna repeated.

Trent took a deep breath and decided to be completely honest with her. "Because I want you."

Brenna laced her fingers on the table in front of her. He wasn't the first man who had told her that he wanted her, but none of the others had mattered. "Oh, I see," she said softly, looking at him.

"No, I don't think you do." He chuckled, and she became taken with the husky sexy sound of it. She wondered if there was anything about him that she wasn't taken with.

"I want you to understand, Brenna, that my wanting you doesn't mean I only think of you as a bunch of body parts. What it means is that I want all of you, your mind *and* your body. When it comes to you I can't separate the two, and I pity any men who've tried. You're a very intelligent woman, but you're just as sexy as you are intelligent. The plain simple truth is that I like every single thing about you. But I'm a man, and the man in me desperately wants you as a woman."

Brenna took a deep breath. She'd noted that he'd said he desperately wanted her. He hadn't mentioned love.

She watched as he got out of his chair and came around the table. He offered his hand to her. "Want to go out on the balcony for a while?"

"Yes, I'd love to." She placed her hand in his, wondering if he was about to take his seduction of her to the next level and just how she would handle it if he did. She certainly wasn't indifferent to him. It only took a smile from him to make her feel all hot and bothered, or just his touch to make her heart race. If the truth were known, she probably wanted him just as much as he wanted her. But the major difference was that she loved him, as well.

The ocean at night was still, quiet, peaceful. Brenna leaned into Trent's masculine side as he wrapped his arms around her, protecting her against the evening chill. Then slowly, deliberately, he turned her around in his arms and kissed her. The intensity of his kiss made her realize how true his words had been when he'd said he had wanted her. And now he was showing her just how much with his kiss. That emotion she felt whenever he kissed her returned, sending a comfortable feeling from the top of her head all the way through to her heart, the heart that was singing her love for him. She returned his kiss in the same hungry heated way, deciding that if she could not have all of him she would have to settle for this…for now.

So she gloried in the feel of his mouth on hers, and the feel of being held in his arms.

The need to breathe broke them apart sometime later.

Trent's breath caught in his throat when an emotion he had never felt before hit him full force. Not understanding it, not accepting it, he took a step back. "It's been a long day, Brenna. I think we should go to bed, don't you?" The sound of his voice was throaty, sensuous, and persuasive.

Brenna could only nod, knowing the moment had arrived and not knowing how she felt about it. She knew that she loved him, and if this time on the cruise was to be all she had with him, then she would accept that. Corinthians was right—she was a forever-kind-of-girl—but for once she would trade in forever for just this one time with him. Her pulse quickened as Trent led her back into the cabin, still holding her hand.

"Come on, I'll walk you back to your cabin," he said in a soft voice.

Brenna stopped walking and pulled her hands from his. She wondered if she had misunderstood him. "To my cabin?"

"Yes."

"But I thought…" She didn't finish what she had been about to say, and she glanced across the room at the huge king-size bed.

Trent's hands came up to her shoulders and caressed her there. "You thought I invited you here to seduce you," he finished for her.

"Didn't you?"

He smiled. "Yes. But the crazy thing, Brenna, is that now I can't go through with it."

"Why?"

He breathed in deeply. He'd had it all planned. His idea of an end to a perfect evening was getting her into his bed and taking them both up in flames. But somehow Brenna St. James had gotten to him on a level he hadn't counted on. "Because," he finally said, "from the first you set the ground rules. You want commitment. You want forever."

Tension twisted inside Brenna. Yes, she wanted those things. What woman didn't? But she was realistic enough to know that while most women wanted those things, most men didn't. They saw commitment as a shackle around their necks. "And you don't want those things?"

His hands moved from her shoulders to the small of her waist. Right now he wasn't sure what he wanted, other than her. "Maybe I will one day, but not now. And I won't lie and say I do want them to take advantage of you."

He pulled her closer to him, feeling the need to explain further. "Four years ago I was engaged to a woman who declared she wouldn't sleep with me until after we were married. I didn't find out until a few weeks before the wedding that that was her game plan. She knew how much I wanted her, and held herself from me to assure that I'd marry her. I walked in on her bragging about it to her friends."

Brenna frowned. "And you think that's what I'm doing, Trent? You think I'm holding myself from you just to get you to commit yourself to me?"

Trent shook his head. "No. I don't believe you'd try using sex that way. I genuinely believe that you want more from a relationship than merely sharing a bed with a man. And there's nothing wrong with that. In fact, I find it commendable that you feel you're worth more than a toss between the sheets."

He placed a tender kiss on her lips before continuing. "What you said a few days ago has stuck with me. You're right. There has to be more to a relationship than sex. But right now that's all I want. I'm not ready for a commitment of any kind. I don't want anything serious, nothing forever, just good safe sex."

"What about love?"

"Love has nothing to do with it."

Brenna nodded slowly, hearing and understanding just what he was saying. He had pretty much put it bluntly. She was a forever-kind-of girl, but he wasn't a forever-kind-of-guy. She took a deep calming breath, then said, "I'm ready to go back to my cabin now."

Chapter 24

Shayla just didn't quite know how to figure it. She had met with Thomas Jordache that afternoon with no news to tell him, yet he was still convinced someone working for Nicholas was trying to cause ill feelings between Chenault and Jordache Electronics.

A part of her wished she could talk to Paul about Jordache's allegations, but she didn't feel comfortable about doing so. Paul Dunlap still made her uncomfortable. The only time she'd felt totally at ease around him had been that night at the Mings' dinner party, when he had told her that his sister had been married to Jordache and that Trent was his nephew. That night she had felt an affinity with Paul. The only reason she could find for having felt that way was because Thomas Jordache had had a negative effect on both of their lives.

Shayla set down the bottle of lotion on her dresser after rubbing the smooth liquid over her body. She had taken her shower and was about to get ready for bed, although it wasn't quite eight o'clock. Picking up a bottle of cologne, she opened and sniffed, enjoying the fragrance of Seduction. She smiled warmly as she dabbed some across her breasts, near where the diamond heart pendant Nicholas had given her rested against her body. She hadn't removed it since he'd placed it there.

She sighed deeply. She was missing him something fierce, although he called her every night. She had just slipped into her nightgown when she heard the doorbell. She quickly grabbed her robe, thinking Aunt Callie was probably her unexpected visitor. Making her way down the stairs, she absentmindedly opened the door before first checking to see who it was.

"Nicholas!"

Nicholas had not been sure what had driven him to make a mad dash from the airport without going home first, breaking speed limits as he rushed across town to Shayla's house. He was still operating under a state of uncertainty when he'd knocked on her door. However, the moment she opened it and he saw her, everything shifted into focus and became crystal clear.

He had fallen in love with her.

A shiver rippled through him with that realization. He pulled in a long-drawn-out breath as a multitude of emotions engulfed him. Tense muscles eased as his eyes feasted on her face—the face of the woman who wore his heart. He saw the pendant that hung around her throat, visible above the low cut of her robe and nightgown. He felt the irregular beating of his heart as he watched her smile blossom beautifully on her face.

Exhaling slowly, he crossed the threshold when she stepped aside for him to enter. He was vaguely aware of her closing the door behind him. The only thing he was distinctly sure of doing was pulling her into his arms and capturing his name from her lips when she repeated it.

Instantly. Automatically. Fulfillingly. He drank in her taste as his mouth absorbed her moan, his hand felt her softness, and his heart consumed all the emotions any mortal man could stand.

He felt her hands at his back, pressing him closer. He could feel her breasts through the thin material of her nightgown and robe as they brushed against his chest. He could smell her scent. It was just as potent as the last time she'd worn it.

The tone of their kiss changed as the mating of their mouths became urgent, more intimate, more needy. An instant later, he swept her into his arms and began carrying her up the stairs. He had to break the kiss to catch his breath, to see where he was going, and to watch his steps. When he looked down at her, the fever in him grew fast, furious, out of control. He wanted her. He loved her. He needed her.

Shayla couldn't stop the quivering in her limbs when Nicholas placed her on the bed. She watched him step back and begin removing his clothes. She found acute pleasure in watching him, wondering about his thoughts, knowing her own, and hoping they were on the same wavelength.

Eyes wide, she watched as he removed his pants, then his briefs, revealing himself in all his masculine glory, in all his unleashed desire. A shaft of pure need streaked through every part of her body, making her shiver as she watched him put on a condom. Moments later she struggled to draw in a deep breath as her gaze moved from the middle part of his body and up past his hairy chest to his eyes…and held. She shivered again. The desire that glowed within the golden depths of his eyes was hot, enticing, hungry.

Shayla drew up on her knees in the bed, raised her hand out to him.

Offering.

The sensual line of a smile formed on Nicholas's lips when he walked back to the bed and took her hand.

Accepting.

He sighed her name as he removed her robe and her nightgown, leaving her completely bare except for the pendant she wore around her neck.

Shayla's breath caught when she felt the heat of Nicholas's gaze roam her naked body and then felt the bed dip from his weight when he joined her. She willingly went into his arms. The very air in the room seemed to become responsive, heated, charged.

He kissed her again, and she opened her mouth to him in urgent need as he staked his claim, greedily explored, savored his fill, bringing her taste back to his memory.

Suddenly, Shayla broke off the kiss, her breathing heavy, deep, forced. She drew in a shaky breath when he reached down and touched her intimately.

"Every time you wear the perfume you have on, I want this," he said in a raspy voice as his hand caressed the very essence of her sensuality. "I'm becoming addicted to your scent."

He bent his head and kissed her again, impelling with his deed what he couldn't explain in words. She answered his kiss as hot fiery passion took over. They both surrendered to it until the need to breathe prevailed.

Laying her gently on her back, he covered her body with his, the need to become one with her an affirmation he wanted, had to have. He reached down and grasped her soft hips, lifting them slightly. Shayla shifted in need, shuddering at his touch, almost losing her breath when she felt him, his throbbing flesh, at the entry of her womanly core.

Ready…waiting.

She stared up at him questioningly. The gold eyes that met her gaze were soft, compelling, and requested patience. He was not moving. The air surrounding them was still. The hands on her hips held her steady, immobile. All was calm, still, quiescent, as his eyes continued to hold hers. Then, when she thought she couldn't handle the delay any longer, he whispered, "I love you, Shayla," before sinking himself deep into her softness, claiming her body and her soul with words of his love.

True words. True love.

Shayla knew it. She felt it as he made love to her, differently than any other time yet just as effective, just as satisfying. "I love you, too, Nicholas," she whispered.

He then took her mouth voraciously in the same manner he took her body, giving just as much as he took, sharing, flaming a passion already blazing out of control. She released a strangled gasp every time he entered, then withdrew, over and over again, making the inferno inside her swell as she matched his rhythm, clasping each thrust he made deep into her body. He seemed to be making up for all the years he had not known her, had not loved her. Her body responded, somehow understanding and giving him his due.

"Now," he whispered hoarsely against her ear. "Let's come. Together."

Her body complied. On one, powerful, downward thrust that met the perfect arching of her hips, their senses whirled, their bodies pulsed, constricted, and exploded. Shayla instinctively tightened her legs around him when she heard his guttural groan as the ripple that swept through him passed to her, making her scream into his mouth as sensation after sensation tore into her. Rocked her. Enthralled her. Swept away the very last of her breath. She broke off their kiss to cry out his name, her love, her fulfillment.

The power of love, true love, swirled around them. It engulfed them. It drenched them in pleasure so profound, so deep, that their bodies quaked from the force of it. And when she felt him explode inside of her, her body's inner muscles tightened around him to absorb his release, prolonging the intimacy, the pleasure.

Something inside Nicholas shattered. He wasn't certain what. All he knew was that at that very moment he had to have her closer, he had to go deeper. Nothing else mattered but total completion, total penetration, and total fulfillment. He wanted her for his wife, the mother of his children. He wanted her for always. The thoughts were powerful, emotional, and when the last shudder left his body—and hers—he couldn't pull away.

He wanted to stay joined with her forever. Then, as if his wish had been granted, he felt his body get hard once more as it replenished itself. Only after pausing for a mere second to take a much-needed breath and to capture her gaze in his once more, he began moving again within her body, wanting more, needing more, knowing he loved her and would never get enough of her, on this or any level.

"Come again," he whispered hotly in her ear, demanding her body to seek pleasure in his once more.

"Oh, Nicholas." Shayla sighed, biting her bottom lip and arching forward on a moan as he began his steady movements of entering and withdrawing within her body again and again.

Locked together, they mated for a second time, soaring even higher than before and giving in to their bodies' needs and their love.

Paul was about to leave the building when he noticed the light was still on in Silas Harris's office. He decided to knock.

"Come in."

He opened the door and stepped inside. "You're still here?"

Harris glanced up, and Paul read some things he'd never seen in the man's eyes before—nervousness and guilt.

"Yes. There are a few things I need to take care of before I leave."

Paul nodded. "How are Yvette and the kids?" He watched as a faint smile touched the man's lips.

"They're fine. Thanks for asking."

Paul nodded. He then tilted his head toward a recent family picture that sat on the man's desk. "It's hard to believe your kids are in college already. Time sure flies, doesn't it?"

Harris looked over at the framed photo and nodded. "Yeah, it sure does."

For a moment there was silence, then Harris returned his gaze to Paul. "Paul?"

"Yes?"

Harris opened his mouth to say something, then changed his mind. "Nothing."

Paul nodded. He reached into his pocket and pulled out his business card. He handed it to Harris. "If there's something on your mind and you need to talk, call me. There are three numbers on that card. You should be able to reach me at any time of the day or night. Or better yet, you can drop by the condo I'm leasing while I'm here. No matter how late it is."

Without saying anything else, Paul walked out of the office.

Shayla was the first one to wake. Evidently Nicholas was suffering from jet lag, she thought as she shifted, studying his face. His sleep seemed calm, restful. She sighed deeply, lifted her arms, and stretched them above her head, feeling totally elated. He had told her he loved her.

His words had warmed her heart, letting her know he returned her affection. She closed her eyes at the memory of their lovemaking. Torrid. Electrifying. Almost endless. Everything about Nicholas was a turn-on. His kiss had the ability to make her forget her name, the mere touch of his hand could render her speechless, and one look into those incredible golden eyes of his made heat course through every part of her body. She knew that by the time sleep had overtaken them, her skin had been flushed with pleasure and her eyes had been heavy with desire.

The only thing overshadowing her complete happiness was knowing that she had not been completely honest with Nicholas. She needed to tell him about her relationship to Thomas Jordache. Only when she was able to put that behind them could they think about a future together.

She cuddled closer to him, and then a feeling of panic settled in her stomach. Would he be upset with her for not telling him sooner? It took every ounce of strength she had to remain positive and believe that no matter what she told him he would still love her.

She knew she had to tell him the truth when he woke up. She hoped that after she explained why she had kept it from him, he would understand.

With that belief in her heart, she wrapped her arms around his middle and drifted back to sleep.

Paul tensed as he took another sip of coffee. Then he continued to read the information in Shayla's folder and scan information he had pulled up on his computer screen. Adrenaline pumped through his system. He wondered if it was from the coffee, or the connection he had just made. Along with his discovery came memories. He'd been right. There had been something about Shayla Kirkland that was familiar.

When his department had first done the background check nothing appeared amiss. She was, after all, the daughter of a well-known Chicago pediatrician, a man for whom a wing at the hospital had been named, and her credentials were intact, above reproach. There had been no reason to dwell on the information they'd had about her mother. The report had merely noted the name Eva Kirkland. Only after he had begun digging further was it revealed that Eva Kirkland had once been Evangeline Foster, a former employee of Chenault Electronics.

He didn't have to pull up Evangeline's file from the archives to remember the incident relating to her dismissal. He remembered it clearly, because he had headed up the investigation. Only years later had he discovered that the company had made a grave mistake. She had been an innocent pawn in Jordache's game of deceit.

He looked at Shayla's date of birth again. The date was less than nine months from Evangeline's last day of employment with Chenault, which meant chances were she'd been pregnant when she left. If she had been intimately involved with Jordache, that meant…

Paul shook himself, not wanting to jump to conclusions. But he knew someone who could provide him with answers. His gaze zeroed in on the line on Shayla's application that listed her next of kin as an aunt, C. Foster. He knew the C stood for Callie.

He sighed deeply, remembering that summer he'd met her, when she'd visited her sister in Jacksonville. He had fallen in love with her, only to lose her when he'd later accused her of aiding Evangeline by trying to distract him from his in-house investigation. He had wished so often over the past years that he could see her again, to take back the cruel words he had spoken that had separated them forever.

He checked his watch. It was a little past nine. What he needed to know couldn't wait, even if seeing Callie again after all these years would have one hell of an impact on him.

He closed the file after copying down Callie's current

address, then shut down the computer. He stood, and was about to slip into his jacket when the doorbell sounded. Walking over to the door he glanced out of the peephole before opening the door.

His gaze lingered on the man who stood on his doorstep under the porch light. "Harris. I'm glad you decided to pay me a visit."

It was morning, and the sun was just beginning to rise and bathe the ship's decks with its sunny warmth. Trent had gotten up earlier than usual so he could enjoy the view.

And so he could think.

For the last two days Brenna had pretty much avoided him, and he felt the sting of her absence. He had gotten used to their spending time together. The brightest part of his morning had been sharing breakfast with her on deck, looking at the ocean and knowing that he would be spending the remainder of the day with her, as well. But what he'd said to her that night had put an end to all that.

So much for honesty.

Would she have preferred him to lie, then use her without any consideration for her feelings? There was no way he could have done that. He cared too much for her to even think of treating her so shabbily.

Trent inhaled, deeply. What had she expected from him? Some sort of commitment? A declaration of love? Was she no different than Michele, thinking she could wrap him around her finger and make him heed her wants by withholding her favors? He shook his head, refusing to think that way. He knew in his heart that Brenna and Michele were nothing alike.

He looked out over the ocean. All was peaceful and still, but inside him a turbulent storm was brewing. In less than two days the ship would be docking in New York. He couldn't help wondering what Brenna's plans were. Would she return home to Texas, or would she join the group of models she coordinated and begin traveling from city to city on tour? Would she erase him from her mind completely, no matter where she went? What if she met someone else? Someone who would give her the love and commitment she wanted, that she deserved?

Trent's hands tightened into fists at his sides. Before the cruise he hadn't known her, hadn't known she even existed, and now he didn't think he would ever be able to forget her. And to think he'd originally thought she didn't have any charm or manners. The woman had more worth in her little finger than some of the women he'd dated had in their entire bodies. Just the thought of that and the calm sensuality that flowed between them made unwanted emotions spiral deep within his chest, swelling his heart. They were the same emotions he had tried ignoring three nights ago, when they'd had dinner in his cabin.

Now, today, he was forced to acknowledge them.

He had fallen in love with Brenna St. James.

Chapter 25

Shayla got the note Nicholas had left on the nightstand next to the bed when she woke up the next morning. It said he was going to his place to unpack and would return to her place by noon. It also said for her not to think about going to work. He was giving her the day off to spend with him.

She shifted her thoughts to last night. They had awakened in the middle of the night and made love several times. She had finally gotten to sleep a little before dawn completely exhausted.

She slipped out of bed and smiled. She would be spending the day with Nicholas, and couldn't help feeling giddy at the idea. A little while later she entered the shower stall. Closing her eyes, she let the water flow over her body while last night's memories flooded her mind.

She remembered the feel of Nicholas trailing his lips from her mouth down to her throat, where he kissed the pulse that was beating there. She remembered the feel of his hand as it caressed her intimately, making sure she was warm, wet, and welcoming each time he got ready to make love to her.

A rising passion spread through her like flames at the memories, and the feel of the water drenching her skin helped soothe the fire. With trembling hands she cut off the shower faucet, took a deep breath, and stepped out of the shower to dry off.

She had a feeling that today would be like no other she had ever known.

Paul leaned against the refrigerator and drank the last of the milk right out of the carton as he remembered last night's visit from Silas Harris. Harris hadn't left until way past midnight, and by then it had been too late to visit with Callie Foster.

Paul took another swallow of milk. Harris had told him everything—about the episode with Cindy Davenport in her apartment, and how she had taped the whole thing, and how Stockard was using that tape to blackmail him into convincing Nick that a virus was invading Chenault's software. It had taken all of Paul's control not to go into the office this morning and have Stockard fired. But he knew that without adequate proof, it would be Stockard's word against Harris's. He had to let Stockard play what he thought was a winning hand and then nail him just when he thought his plan had succeeded. It was a good thing Nick wasn't due back in the office until Monday. That would give him a chance to brief him on what was going on over the weekend after he returned from Bolivia.

Paul checked his watch. It was a little past 8:00 a.m. It would take him a good thirty minutes to drive across town to where Callie Foster lived. He threw the empty milk carton into the trashcan before slipping into his jacket.

He didn't want to dwell on the fact that Callie had consumed his mind all through the night. He wouldn't be surprised if she refused to see him. The last time he had seen her he had said a lot of mean and hateful things, words he had later regretted. At the time he had believed she had used him and betrayed him, and in anger he had reacted badly.

Her last name hadn't changed, and he couldn't help wondering if that meant she had never married…like him.

He checked his watch again. He would have all his questions about Shayla Kirkland answered. "Soon," he said to himself as he walked across the room to the door. "Real soon."

Thinking that it was Shayla, Nicholas answered the phone before the second ring. No one else knew he had returned a day early. "Miss me already, sweetheart?"

"Uhh, Mr. Chenault?"

Nicholas frowned. "Yes. Who is this?"

The person on the other end cleared his throat. "This is Carl Stockard. I called your hotel in Bolivia, and they said you had left already."

Nicholas's frown deepened. So much for no one knowing he was back in the States. "Yeah, Stockard, what is it?"

"There's a security matter of grave importance that I need to discuss with you, sir."

Nicholas raised an eyebrow. "Stockard, why are you calling me, and not Paul? He's the one you should be reporting anything—"

"Mr. Chenault, because of the nature of what I've discovered and the person involved, I think I should approach you about it first."

Nicholas shook his head in exasperation. "Is that really necessary, Stockard?"

"Yes, sir. I believe it is. The future of the MC Project is involved with the information I've uncovered. I've discovered which one of our employees is working with Thomas Jordache to sabotage the project."

Nicholas drew his eyebrows together, suddenly alert and very attentive. "You know who it is?"

"Yes, sir. There's concrete evidence that can't be disputed."

Nicholas felt numb. He had hoped that none of his employees had actually been guilty of treachery. But from what Stockard was saying, that wasn't the case. Someone in his employ had been working against him. "Okay, Stockard, I'm on my way."

Paul parked in front of the Victorian-style house and thought that it suited Callie. From the first time he'd seen her, as a young woman, he'd known that she had style. She had been twenty and in her junior year of college the summer they had met. He'd been five years older, and had been working at Chenault for nearly three years.

He checked his watch again before getting out of his car and walking up to the door. It was almost nine o'clock. Most people would be up and moving around about right then. He hoped that was the case with Callie.

Callie pushed the newspaper aside and stood up when she heard the doorbell. Glancing at the clock over the fireplace mantel, she wondered who it could be. She glanced through the peephole and couldn't make out the person's identity. His back was to her.

"Yes? Who is it?" she asked through the door.

There was a pause before the man answered. "Paul Dunlap."

A tight knot suddenly formed in Callie's chest. She glanced back through the peephole, and this time she stared directly into Paul's face. There were only slight changes in his features. Overall, he looked just as handsome as he had the first time she had seen him. He had matured over the years, in a definitely good-looking away. The stubborn reserved tilt of his chin that had intrigued her when she'd first met him was still there, along with the deep-set dark eyes that had made her senses acute and full of desire whenever she was with him. His mouth, a mouth she had kissed countless times, had a masculine strength that had not been there before, and gave his features even more tantalizing dimensions. She took a deep calming breath, then pressed her lips together tightly, coolly, wishing her thoughts would not go there.

Taking another deep breath, she exhaled deeply. She had an idea of what had brought him to see her. She opened the door and came face-to-face with the man who had broken her heart over twenty-seven years ago—the man whose wrongful accusations had destroyed the love they had shared.

"Paul? What are you doing here?" she asked, struggling to keep her voice light and casual.

Paul tried to answer Callie's question, but his brain wasn't functioning. It was on overload at seeing her again. She didn't look as if she had aged much at all, standing before him dressed in an oversize T-shirt and a pair of black tights. Her body looked just as youthful, and her features just as beautiful, as he remembered. The same earthquake that had rocked him on the day he had first laid eyes on her, twenty-seven years ago, was shaking him now. He wondered if she still had those same pristine qualities, that ability to give and share with those she loved abundantly and unselfishly. He, who had always been a loner, had been touched by those qualities in her. He had needed them, and gloried in them. Those qualities, along with the most beautiful sensual face his eyes had ever beheld, had been what had attracted him to her, and later those qualities had completely, irrevocably, captured his heart.

"Paul, I asked what you are doing here."

The repeat of her question snapped his mind back in focus. "I need to talk to you, Callie."

"About what?"

"About Shayla Kirkland. May I come in?"

Callie took a deep breath. Her hand tightened around the doorknob, wondering how much he knew. "Yes." She stepped aside to let him in.

Closing the door behind him, she led him into the living room. "Please have a seat."

Paul took a seat on the sofa. Callie decided to remain standing.

"Can I get you anything to drink? Milk?"

He stared at her. Even after twenty-seven years she remembered that he didn't drink coffee, and preferred milk. "No, thanks. I've had my milk this morning already."

She nodded. "Why do you want to talk to me about Shayla?"

"You know that she's working at Chenault?"

Callie felt heat rise on the back of her neck. "Yes, of course."

He nodded. "Is she aware that Evangeline used to work for the company years ago, and that she was terminated?"

Callie stared at him for a long moment before replying. "Yes, she knows. She found out after Eva's death, when she came across her diary. She knows Eva was fired after being falsely accused of something she didn't do."

Paul's jaw clenched. He deserved that hit. He didn't want to put Callie on the defensive, and decided to word his next question carefully, but straight to the point. "Does she know that Thomas Jordache is her biological father?" He didn't miss the look of shock that flared in Callie's dark eyes.

His question hung in the air as she walked over to the fireplace and stared into the flames. The silence grew tight with tension. When she turned around her face was covered with a cool facade. Her eyes were expressionless. "And what makes you think Thomas Jordache is her father?"

Paul leaned forward. "Deductive reasoning with mathematics thrown in. I read her file, then did a bit of adding and subtracting. Unless Shayla was born prematurely, Evangeline had to have been pregnant when she left the company. Since she was involved with Thomas Jordache at the time, I can only assume he fathered her child. Did he?"

Callie stared at Paul for a long moment. She felt as if her very breath were being squeezed out of her with his question. She, Eva, and Glenn had agreed that the truth would never be known, but it appeared that would not be the case.

Taking a deep breath, Callie crossed the room to stand a few feet from Paul and met his eyes. She couldn't help remembering how fury and rage had blinded his eyes twenty-seven years ago. He had hurt her deeply, because she had loved him and he had believed the worst about her. "Yes, Thomas Jordache fathered Eva's child," she finally answered. "But he is not Shayla's father."

When she saw his confused expression she decided to clear things up for him. "Thomas Jordache is not Shayla's biological father, Paul. You are."

Chapter 26

Paul Dunlap was off the sofa in a flash. "What do you mean?" he demanded, shocked, incredulous, as he towered over Callie.

Callie lifted her chin and looked up at him. "Just what I said. You are Shayla's father. Eva lost her baby from Thomas Jordache in her fourth month. I carried mine to full term. Our due dates were about the same time, within a week of each other."

"You were pregnant?" Paul asked in a gut-wrenching voice, still in the clutches of shock.

Callie saw the pain in his features, and wondered if it was from not knowing or from him just finding out. She wanted to believe it was from both. She felt an unexpected tightness pull around her heart. "Yes, I was pregnant."

Paul gave himself a mental shake. "But—but how?"

Callie met his glare with one of her own. "You have to ask me that, after that summer? Think about it, Paul."

He did think about it. There had been passion between them from the moment he had first seen her, the day she had dropped by the office to see her sister after arriving in town. By the end of the summer, before she left to return to college in Atlanta, they had made love a number of times, a lot of those times without any protection, because everything between them had been spontaneous…like combustion. It hadn't taken much for their hormones to blaze out of control, and as much as he had tried being prepared, sometimes he had not been. "No, you're right. I don't have to ask you that," he finally admitted.

A small silence followed his remark. Then he looked down at her, his eyes turned cold, hard. "Why didn't you tell me? Didn't you think I had a right to know?"

Callie sighed one of those sighs she'd caught herself doing a lot recently. "Yes," she answered in a flat voice, "you had a right to know. That's the reason I skipped classes and caught the Greyhound bus all the way from Atlanta to Jacksonville, just to tell you," she said, turning away from the dark anger in his eyes. She looked across the room at Shayla's baby photo, which hung on her wall.

"But you didn't give me the chance to tell you. You didn't want to hear anything I had to say," she murmured softly. Her gaze returned to his. "You did all the talking that night, Paul. I had ridden on a bus for nearly six hours to see you. I was exhausted, scared, confused. I wanted you to hold me and assure me that everything would be all right, and that my pregnancy had changed nothing, that you still loved me and would be there for me and our baby."

Fingers trembling, Callie swiped at the tears that had begun forming in her eyes as she relived a period of her life she thought she had long laid to rest. But she hadn't, and the emotions, the hurt, the pain, were just as if it had all happened yesterday. "Instead you called me all sorts of names, accused me of all sorts of things. You accused me of sleeping with you to cover up Eva and Thomas Jordache's plot to ruin the company you worked for, the company you were paid to protect."

Her words slashed into Paul, into the very core of his being, because everything she said was true. He had loved her so much, and when he'd been faced with what seemed like her betrayal, be couldn't handle it. "Callie… I—"

"No," she cut in. "Please let me finish while I can." She took a deep breath, trying to reclaim her composure. "I couldn't go to Eva and tell her what you thought. I felt so ashamed that you could believe such things about me…and about her. I caught the bus back to Atlanta that night, with my heart shattered."

She hunched her shoulders, reliving how defeated she had felt that night. "I was able to finish the semester. My plans were to quit school, get a job, and keep my baby, without any help from you. Then, a month or so later, after Eva and Glenn worked out things between them and married, they gave me their support. They offered to take care of my child along with theirs while I returned to Atlanta and finished college. They felt with a college education I'd be better equipped to support my baby in the future as a single mom."

Callie's lips creased in a sudden smile. "Eva and I were happy about having our babies. We found out that we were both going to have girls, and knew our daughters would have a close relationship and would be like sisters, just like us."

Callie's smile faded. "But things didn't work out that way. Eva lost her baby. I felt really bad for her, because I knew that had been the last chance she and Glenn had at having a baby. Glenn was sterile."

Her small laugh was forced and shrill. "It's strange how things had worked out. Glenn had loved Eva enough to marry her and accept another man's child as his own, and there I was pregnant by a man who thought I was a whore."

Paul sucked in a sharp breath. "That's not true, I—"

"I know what you called me that night, Paul."

"Whatever I said was said in anger, Callie. I wanted to hurt you the way I thought you had hurt me."

"You succeeded." She walked over to the window and looked out. "Eva was so hurt, so broken up after losing her baby. Then I saw what she and Glenn could give my child, something that I couldn't, the love of two parents. I felt a child needed a mother and a father. I owed my child a chance to have a normal family life."

"So you gave *my* child away?" Paul asked in a thunderous voice.

Callie turned around to face him. Her expression was just as thunderous as his voice. "Don't you *dare* question my decision. You don't know what I went through to make it. You didn't want me. You didn't love me. I couldn't afford to give *my* child the things it should have. I was still struggling through school. It wouldn't have been fair to ask Eva to take care of my baby knowing she had lost her own, the only child her body could ever have. I loved my sister. I knew she would take care of Shayla, and give her everything I could not. I also knew that as long as Shayla was with Glenn and Eva I could see her whenever I wanted, and that I would always be a part of her life. And I have."

Tears Callie could no longer contain flowed from her eyes. "You had no right then, and you have no right now, to question me. You made your decision about me twenty-seven years ago."

Unable to say any more at the moment, Callie turned and rushed up the stairs, leaving Paul standing in the middle of the room.

* * *

Brenna stood and gazed out at the ocean. This would be her last day aboard the *Majestic.* The same time midday tomorrow she would be able to watch as the docks of New York came into view. Once she left the ship she would take a taxi to the airport. There she would catch a plane to Austin—home sweet home.

She sighed, knowing she should be overjoyed at the idea of returning home and planting her feet on solid ground and not having the constant rhythm of the ship moving under her. But she wasn't. Leaving the ship also meant leaving Trent. Although he'd made it clear that love meant nothing to him, she still loved him, and would miss him just the same.

A part of her wished things could have ended differently in his cabin that night. But, she thought as she left the window and went to sit on the side of the bed, another part was grateful that he had been so brutally honest with her. No matter how things had ended between them, in her mind and heart he would always be the most amazing man she had ever met. Every day she had spent with him had been special.

But he couldn't accept the kind of person she was. While some women were comfortable engaging in casual affairs, she wasn't. She needed more from a relationship. She needed substance, she needed commitment, she needed love.

Brenna had picked up her sunglasses and hat from the bed when she heard the soft knock at the door. Thinking it was the steward delivering the lunch she'd ordered, she crossed the cabin and opened the door.

"Trent?"

"Brenna."

She smiled wryly up at him, inwardly admitting that she was glad to see him. She had deliberately avoided him the last three days, taking most of her meals in her cabin.

"May I come in?"

She nodded and moved back to the center of the room.

He stepped into the cabin and closed the door behind him, then leaned against it. "You're all set to leave the *Majestic* tomorrow?"

"Yes. What about you? Or will you be remaining on the ship?"

"I'll be remaining for a while," he answered, not taking his eyes off her. "Probably for another day or so. Then I'm going to Chicago to check on my father." He walked over to the window and stared out at passengers moving around on deck. Although they had enjoyed the trip, it was evident that they were ready to get back home. Three weeks were a long time, but that was all the time he had needed to fall in love.

"Trent, there's something I want to say to you," Brenna said behind him.

He slowly turned around to face her. "There's something I want to say to you, too, but as a rule ladies are first."

Brenna nodded and plunged ahead. "I enjoyed our time together, and I'm going to miss you," she said breathlessly, her nerves frazzled.

Trent lifted an eyebrow as a slow smile tilted his lips. "I enjoyed our time together, too, but I'm not going to miss you. What I want more than anything is to marry you."

Brenna stood a few moments in stunned silence. "Marry me?"

"Yes."

"Why? Just so you can sleep with me?"

Trent crossed the room to her. "No, this is nothing like the last time I got engaged, when one was dependent on the other. I want to marry you because I love you."

Brenna inhaled sharply as her mind raced back. "But just three nights ago you said—"

"I know what I said. I was fighting my feelings for you then. My mind didn't want to accept what my heart was saying. There's more between us than sex. The time we've spent together on this ship has proved that. Women aren't the only ones who want someone special. Just like women want a one-of-a-kind man, men want a one-of-a-kind woman. And I believe you're that, and more. You're a beautiful intelligent woman I want to share my life with. I want you by my side forever. This is all about love. I feel it every time I take you into my arms. I do love you, Brenna. I need to know how you feel about me. Do you love me, too?"

Brenna smiled. Pure happiness showed in her eyes. "Yes, I do."

"Will you marry me?"

"Yes, I will."

"Today?"

"Today!"

"Yes, as soon as it can be arranged. Since we're still in international waters, my captain can perform the ceremony at a moment's notice. We can have another ceremony for the benefit of our family and friends whenever you want. I just don't think I can let you leave this ship without binding you to me forever. But if you prefer that we wait, then I'm willing to do that, too. You're definitely a woman worth waiting for."

He reached into his pocket and took out something wrapped in tissue paper. "This is my mother's ring. I had my father air-flight it to me," he said huskily, drawing her hand into his and slipping the ring on her finger.

Tears pricked Brenna's eyes as she looked at the huge diamond that graced the third finger of her left hand. "Oh, Trent, it's beautiful. I don't know what to say."

"Say you'll love me forever, because that's how long I intend to love you."

Brenna looked at him, smiling, then looked at the ring. "You're completely serious about all of this, aren't you?"

To prove that he was, Trent pulled her to him and kissed

her, letting her feel from his kiss what was in his heart, When his tongue touched hers, tingling heat raced through her entire body.

Moments later she pulled back, withdrawing from the hot passion of his mouth but not from the warm embrace of his arms. "This is crazy. We've only known each other for three weeks," she said softly against his moist lips. She'd never been one to act irrationally or rush into anything. She'd always prided herself on being logical and clearly thinking through any situation before acting on it.

"What you're proposing is insane, ludicrous, Trent." But then, she thought, he *had* proposed, and she was wearing his ring to prove it. And to top it off, he was ready to marry her at a moment's notice—today. Her mouth curved into a dreamy happy smile. What more could a girl ask for?

She touched her lips to his. "And if we marry here, today, you'll be willing to go through another wedding ceremony for our family and friends?" Corinthians would kill her if they didn't.

Trent chuckled against her lips. "Yes. I'll say 'I do' as many times as you want me to, and mean it every time."

Brenna's mouth curled at the comers. "I love you, Trent, and yes, I'll marry you today."

Trent pulled her into his arms, claiming her mouth and again demonstrating the depth of his love for her.

Chapter 27

Nicholas stood up from his desk and walked to the window. His heart shouted a denial of everything Stockard had just told him and shown him, but his mind was forcing him to believe what his heart didn't want to. Hurt welled deep in his throat, and anger surged through every part of his body.

Shayla was the one who was betraying him.

"Mr. Chenault, what do you want me to do now, sir?"

Nicholas took a deep breath, although his chest felt as if it would burst from the overabundance of pain that had settled there. His mind heard Stockard's question, but he couldn't acknowledge it with an answer. He didn't know what he wanted him to do. He had to think for a minute. He turned back to the man who was staring at him, waiting for his answer. "I need to think about this, Stockard."

"Yes, sir. I understand."

Nicholas's tone of voice was relatively calm in spite of

his anger and his pain when he said, "No, Stockard, I don't think you do."

"Not to be disrespectful, sir, but I *do* understand. I know there was something going on between you and Ms. Kirkland." At Nicholas's raised eyebrow, Stockard continued. "You pay me to be observant, sir."

Nicholas nodded slowly. He couldn't dispute that.

"That's why it was hard for me to bring all this to you, but I felt you should be told as soon as possible. I hope I didn't do anything wrong," Stockard said, laying it on thick in his role as the efficient security man.

"No, Stockard, you did everything right. Your efforts at finding out who's working with Jordache are to be commended. I appreciate what you did, and I won't forget it."

Stockard smiled brightly. That was what he wanted to hear. Mr. Chenault was playing right into his hands. All his scheming, and plotting, arranging the fire and the break-in, had been worth it. "Thank you, sir. I was just doing my job. Is there anything else I can do?"

"No, you've done more than enough. You don't know how appreciative I am. I'll call you once I make my decision on how I'm going to handle this."

"Yes, sir." Stockard then walked out of Nicholas's office, closing the door behind him.

Nicholas went back to his desk and picked up the items Stockard had presented to him. First was the page Stockard had ripped out of Shayla's planner, an entry she had made while in China. She had written, *"I'll do whatever I have to to get Nicholas to lower his guard and trust me. Tonight at dinner I'll put my plan into action, and begin working toward that goal."*

Nicholas reread the entry a couple more times and each time he read it fury and anger poured through his veins.

After putting it back down, he picked up a copy of the company's telephone log, which listed all incoming and outgoing calls. Jordache had called the office twice in the last three weeks, and both times he had spoken to Shayla.

Nicholas then picked up the photo that Stockard had taken of her getting into Thomas Jordache's limo. According to Stockard, this had been her second meeting with Jordache, and the photo was taken yesterday.

Yesterday.

While he'd been in a frantic rush to get back to the States to see her, she had been planning the downfall of his company with Thomas Jordache. The rage Nicholas was beginning to feel at Shayla's treachery was so thick it all but clouded his mind.

He had trusted her. He had loved her.

He still did.

His heart began to ache. He was a pitiful soul to admit to still loving a woman who had betrayed him. A part of him cursed the day he'd met her. He felt that his whole life had suddenly fallen apart, and all because of her.

He sighed when his anger became thunderous, almost unbearable. He would not let her and Jordache get away with this. He did not have enough evidence to bring legal charges against her, but he would make sure she remembered this day as long as she lived.

Another thought occurred to him. The two times there had been incidents at the office in Jacksonville and here, he had been with Shayla when he had gotten the calls. Had she acted as a diversion? That possibility made his anger reach the boiling point.

Picking up the phone, he dialed Leanne's extension. He was so furious he could barely get his words out. "I gave Shayla Kirkland the day off. Call her at home and tell her something has come up and I need her to report to my office immediately. Then I want you to find Paul and tell him to get here as soon as possible."

Nicholas inhaled deeply, then added, "And Leanne, I want you to process Ms. Kirkland's termination papers. I want them ready when she arrives."

Paul thought about following Callie upstairs, but changed his mind. She needed to be alone for a while. But he had no intention of leaving. He had more questions he wanted answered.

He walked over to the window Callie had just left and looked out. Her announcement had been a blow to his mind. Shayla Kirkland was his daughter. Was that the reason he'd had this strange feeling every time he'd been around her? Did she know? And if she did, did she hate him? Was that the reason she'd always acted uncomfortable around him?

He swallowed. That ill-fated night of twenty-seven years ago had happened just the way Callie had said. He hadn't taken the time to ask how she had gotten to Jacksonville, or why she'd shown up in the middle of the semester—on a week night, at that. Earlier that day he had discovered Evangeline's involvement with Jordache, and evidence indicating she'd been passing him information. He'd figured Callie had to have known, since she and her sister were so close. And if she had known, that meant that the two of them were working together with Jordache.

He had been wrong—totally off base.

Once he had discovered the truth that both Evangeline and Callie had been innocent and his charges groundless, he'd wanted to go to Callie and ask for her forgiveness. But he'd known she would never be able to forgive the things he had said to her. So he had accepted his fate, losing the only woman he'd ever loved. And now, to make matters worse, he knew that his actions on that night had also cost him knowing about his daughter. For twenty-seven years he had not known of her existence. A part of him knew he deserved the crushing blow he'd just been given.

When he heard movement in the room, he turned around. Callie had returned. She had changed into a fashionable skirt and blouse, and stood across the room from him, twisting the strap of her purse in her fingers.

"I know you have more questions, Paul. I have another couple of hours before I have to open my dress shop if you want answers now," she said quietly. All traces of the tears were absent from her eyes. He felt the barrier she'd placed between them.

"Yes, please. Can we sit down," he asked in a subdued voice.

She nodded. When he returned to his spot on her sofa she sat in the wing chair across from him.

"First of all," Paul began as he locked his gaze with hers, "I know this comes twenty-seven years too late. But I want to apologize for that night. I know I acted unforgivably. I loved you, and I should have trusted you and believed that you wouldn't betray me. I had spent enough time with you that summer, and had made love to you enough times to know there wasn't a dishonorable bone in your body."

He held his head down for a second, then raised it to capture her gaze once more. "But instead I was quick to think the worst, quick to be blinded by fury, because the evidence seemed so clear, and because I loved you so much. I said a lot of things to you that night. Some of them I remember, some I don't. I wanted you to hurt the same way I was hurting. I'm so sorry for what I did to you, and to us."

He dragged in a deep breath. "After I found out the truth I knew that losing you would be my punishment for the rest of my life. Now I realize that having lost my daughter, as well, was another price I've paid, and deservedly so."

Callie said nothing. She just continued to look at him. She'd known from the moment she'd met Paul that he was proud, often stubborn and tenacious, but that deep down he was a good man. It had taken her a long time after that night to face the fact that he also was human, and that given the set of circumstances he'd reacted the way most men would have, with his head rather than his heart. Had he listened to his heart that night he would have known she was innocent. But talking about it now wouldn't change what happened, nor would it erase the hurt. They had to move on, and right now Shayla was their main concern.

"What brought you here, Paul? Is Shayla in some kind of trouble at work?"

Paul leaned back on the sofa, noting the smoothness with which Callie had brought the conversation from out of the past and into the present. He also noted she had not said whether she accepted his apology. "No, she's doing a fine job. It's just that every time she was around me she acted uncomfortable, as if she thought I knew something, and I couldn't understand why. I got suspicious of her actions, and reviewed her file. Does she know I'm her father?"

Callie shook her head. "No. Like you, she's convinced Thomas Jordache is. Eva's diary told what happened to her at Chenault, and her brief affair with Jordache. Shayla assumes she's the result of that affair."

"Why didn't you tell her the truth?"

Now it was Callie's time to briefly look away. When she met his gaze again she said, "Because Eva had just died, and Shayla had read information in that diary that revealed Glenn was not her natural father. That in itself was a blow to her. I wasn't going to hurt her any more by telling her that Eva wasn't her mother, either, that the two people who raised her, who she assumed for twenty-six years were her natural parents, were her adoptive parents."

Paul nodded. "Why did she come to work for Chenault?"

Callie hesitated only a moment before answering. "To get back at them for what they did to her mother. After reading Eva's diary she felt her humiliation and her pain. She wanted someone at Chenault to pay."

"Nick?"

A faint smile touched Callie's lips. "Yes, Nicholas Chenault. Or so she thought, until she fell in love with him, which didn't take her long. She left for China with revenge on her mind, and returned a week later with love in her heart."

The hint of a smile threatened on Paul's lips. "Nick loves her."

"That's good to hear."

Paul struggled to stay focused, but with Callie sitting across from him it wasn't easy. She could still make his throat feel dry, and his lower body simmer. She looked so darn good. He shifted positions in his seat. "Did she mention to you that she got a glimpse of Thomas Jordache while she was in China?"

Callie nodded. "She also met his son Trent. Shayla thinks he's her half brother. It took all my will not to tell her he was actually her first cousin."

Paul's thoughts drifted back to Thomas Jordache again. "I'm glad Jordache doesn't know anything."

"I'm afraid he does. Shayla has met with him twice."

Paul gritted his teeth and leaned forward in his seat. "For what reason?"

Callie told him what Shayla had told her about her two meetings with Jordache. "So, as you can see, he's convinced Shayla he's dying, and that someone who works for Nicholas Chenault is trying to make it seem as if Jordache is behind all those things that have been happening at Chenault."

Paul nodded. "I don't know if Jordache is actually dying, but I do know that someone who works for us by the name of Carl Stockard is making it seem that Jordache is up to no good. At least, that's his plan. I only found out about it last night. I'm going to wait and see just what his next move is before I do anything."

At that moment Paul's beeper went off. Standing, he pulled it out of his pocket and checked it. "May I use the phone? It's the office calling."

Callie nodded. "Yes, it's on the desk over there."

She watched Paul cross the room, thinking that he still walked with purpose in his stride. She also couldn't help but notice what great physical shape he was in. He'd taken off his jacket, and as he picked up the phone and began dialing, his muscular shoulders flexed beneath his white dress shirt in a way that made her draw in a deep breath.

"Leanne, it's Paul." After a few moments he exclaimed. "What!" Then a few seconds later. "When? Where's Nick now?" He released a deep sigh of disgust before saying, "Leanne, I want you to find Howard Reeves. I'm on my way."

After hanging up the phone he crossed the room back to Callie, his face filled with rage. "Stockard has made his move. Nicholas returned to the States earlier than expected, and Stockard presented him with evidence that Shayla is working with Jordache and supplying him with secret information."

Paul heard Callie's sharp gasp, and understood. It was like history repeating itself. The same charges had been made against her sister twenty-seven years ago. Callie was on her feet now. "Where's Shayla?"

The muscle jumped at the base of Paul's jaw at the thought of what Stockard had done, and how far he'd gone to get a higher position in the company. And to make matters worse, he was going to use his daughter to accomplish the feat.

His daughter.

The thought washed over him. Shayla Kirkland. His

own flesh and blood. A daughter he'd created with the woman he had loved.

"Paul, where's Shayla?" Callie repeated, reclaiming his attention.

"She's on her way into the office." He decided not to tell Callie that Nicholas had ordered that Leanne type up Shayla's termination papers.

"I have to get there immediately," he said, putting his jacket back on.

"I'm going with you."

Paul stopped what he was doing and looked at her. "Why?"

"To make sure Shayla's okay."

Paul shook his head. "Nick loves her. If she makes it into the office before I get there, once she explains things to him he'll—"

"Refuse to listen to anything she has to say, just like you refused to listen to me that night. Your anger overshadowed your love, and so will his."

Paul inhaled deeply, hoping with every breath he possessed that she was wrong. He hoped that Nicholas proved to be a better man at love and trust than he had.

"But I wouldn't want to be in Nicholas Chenault's shoes if he doesn't believe her," Callie added.

Paul raised a brow. "Why's that?"

Callie looked up and shrugged before saying, "One thing Shayla inherited from you, Paul, is your stubbornness and tenaciousness. Unlike Eva and me, she'll stand up for herself. She won't let Nicholas or anyone else accuse her of something she didn't do. And if he tries, all hell's gonna break loose."

"That should be interesting," Paul said, heading for the door and thinking about anyone giving Nicholas hell about anything. "I think it's time we cleared things up once and for all, and that includes telling Shayla I'm her father, not

Thomas Jordache. That means you'll have to tell her you're her mother, as well. It's time she knew the truth, Callie."

Callie nervously bit her bottom lip as she followed Paul out the door. He was right. It was time. But she couldn't help worrying how Shayla would handle it all when she found out.

Chapter 28

One of the first things Shayla noticed when she reached Nicholas's office was the number of security men sitting in the lobby. She raised an eyebrow when Carl Stockard looked at her with what appeared to be a smirk, then she frowned. She'd never liked the man since the first day he had introduced himself to her.

As she approached Leanne's desk she couldn't help wondering why Nicholas had changed his mind and decided to come into the office, and why he wanted to see her. Something must have happened. Had there been another break-in?

"Good morning, Leanne. You called and said Mr. Chenault wanted to see me."

"Yes, go right in. He's expecting you."

Shayla frowned at the briskness of Leanne's response. "Thank you." She crossed the lobby to Nicholas's office, opened the door, and walked in, closing it behind her.

He was standing with his back to her, looking out of the window as if deep in thought. Light snow had fallen earlier, and now everything was bathed in a beautiful white frosting. At any other time she would have thought Nicholas's musing was about the scenery, but something about the stiffness in his stance dismissed that idea.

Something had happened.

She immediately crossed the room to him, stood on tiptoe, and kissed him primly on the cheek. He automatically jerked back, recoiling from her touch. "Nicholas, what's wrong?" Instead of answering, he turned to face her. The eyes that looked down at her were filled with anger. They were cold, brittle, and hard.

"Ms. Kirkland, now that you're here we can get started," he said in a very clipped tone.

Shayla glanced around, making sure they were alone. Why had he called her Ms. Kirkland, when there was no one else in the room? "Nicholas, what's going on?"

Nicholas's eyes glittered stone. "What's going on is that you're about to be fired."

"Fired!"

"You heard me. And if there was any way possible, I'd make sure you'd never work in this city again."

Shayla closed her eyes, certain she was hearing things, certain when she opened them again this would all be a bad dream. However, when she did reopen them, she saw Nicholas standing in front of her with a face of stone. "I think you'd better tell me what's going on," she said in a strained voice. "You owe me an explanation."

Nicholas stood silently, all his attention on the woman standing before him. She was a consummate actress. Sterling ought to put her in one of his movies. Here she was standing before him looking innocent…and so beautiful. It hurt just to look at her, but he couldn't take his eyes off her.

He had loved her deeply, physically and mentally, and she'd only been using him.

"I don't owe you a thing, Ms. Kirkland," he was finally able to say through clenched teeth. "But you do owe me. We never got around to doing it on the desk, did we? Since you were willing to sleep on your back to get information for Thomas Jordache, you might as well have gone all the way."

Shayla froze, and the color drained from her face. "Jordache?" she asked in a painfully soft whisper.

"Yes," Nicholas snarled as rage engulfed him. "Did you think I wouldn't find out about your lover? How much is he paying you, Shayla? How much were you getting to sleep with me? What does one earn for pillow talk these days? You weren't so bad in bed. I could have beat his price."

Shayla swung and slapped Nicholas full force on his face. "How dare you! How dare you insinuate that I'm a whore," she hissed, eyes blazing with the same fury as his. "You're the only man I've ever slept with."

Nicholas rubbed the cheek that was still stinging from her assault. His entire body shook with exploding violence. Never in his life had he been this angry. "That's right, you were a virgin, weren't you? I'm sure that must have increased your value."

When Shayla raised her hand to slap him again, he caught it in his. "I wouldn't advise you to try that a second time, unless you want to spend the night in jail. I'll press charges against you so fast it'll make that pretty head of yours swim."

When he let go of her hand Shayla jerked it down and balled it into a fist at her side. "There's been a mistake, Nicholas. You're wrong about me," she whispered. The tightness in her throat made the words hoarse, ragged. "Please let me explain."

Nicholas heard the raw pleading ache in her voice and

felt a part of him beginning to melt. But then, just as quickly, icy coldness covered his heart again. He would not succumb to her innocent act. He had loved her. He had trusted her with his heart. He had cherished her with his body, mind, and soul.

His jaw tightened as he reached on his desk and picked up the paperwork Stockard had presented to him. "Can you explain these, Shayla?" he asked in a voice tinged with fury and pain.

It was the pain more than the anger that Shayla's mind suddenly latched on to. She took the papers he was handing her and studied each one, realizing how he could think what he did, but hurt nonetheless that he had. "Yes, I can," she said quietly.

Nicholas's gaze held hers, once again feeling his anger trying to dissolve. He fought to retain his pride, his dignity, and respect. "Can you also explain why both times there have been incidents with my company I just happened to be with you?"

Her gaze never leaving his, she shook her head and said softly, "No, *that* I can't explain, other than to say they were coincidences."

His eyes darkened even more. "Coincidences like that don't just happen." Summoning the last vestiges of his control, he once again hardened his mind and heart against her and her claim of innocence. He took the papers from her hand. "I don't want to hear any explanations you claim you can give. You're fired. I'll have my security men escort you out."

By determined will and sheer stubbornness, Shayla refused to let him believe the worst about her. She refused to be put in the same position her mother had been placed in by this same company twenty-seven years ago. She refused to let Nicholas dismiss her from his life. She loved him. He was wrong about her, and she was going to make him see it.

"I won't let you fire me, Nicholas, without hearing me out first," she said, tilting her chin and folding her arms over her chest.

Nicholas frowned. For one heart-stopping moment when he looked into her eyes he thought he saw the same pain and hurt he knew were reflected in his. "I don't want to hear anything you have to say, Shayla. And if you insist, I'll have my security men carry you out of my office."

Shayla held his gaze, the look on her face furious. "I'd like to see them try. Call them, and see how big a scene I'll make. Then I'll leave here and go to the authorities and claim sexual harassment. You've slept with me a number of times, and you can't deny it. Just think what the price of your stock will look like in the morning after such negative publicity."

Nicholas stilled. His face hardened. His anger deepened. He was so mad he could have strangled her.

But, amazingly, a part of him wanted to make love to her, instead.

He drew back. The woman had him crazy, demented, foolishly in love. From the very beginning she had found a vulnerable chink in his armor, and now she was using it. He dragged in a deep breath, feeling hopeless against her. Her pull on his heart was too strong, too tight. But still, he refused to weaken, refused to let emotions get in the way of common sense and self-control.

"Say what you want to say by way of explanations. Then I want you out of here. After today I never want to see you again. And if you're ever seen on these premises for any reason, you'll be arrested."

Shayla swallowed hard, and part of her composure almost slipped, but she stopped it from happening. She would not let Nicholas bring her to tears, at least not in his presence. "Fine, and if you still feel that way after I've explained things to you, then you won't have to worry about seeing me again, because you'll be the last man I'll want to see."

Nicholas watched as she slowly walked over to the window as if to collect her thoughts. He wondered if he was making a mistake by letting her remain in his office and listening to her.

He was going through a slow burn as he watched her, feeling tightness in his groin area. Exhaling slowly, he allowed his gaze to move over her when she reached the window and stood with her back to him. Her pose gave him an ample view of her soft curves and her shapely backside, which the skirt she wore couldn't hide.

Just looking at her curvaceous backside made him recall the wee hours of the morning, right before dawn, when he'd passionately kissed her awake before easing her onto her stomach then settling his body over hers, lifting her hips with his hands and then smoothly easing into her, finding her moist and ready. His body had fit hers snugly as it spooned her backside and then after they'd established their rhythm, the primitive sounds of their mating had driven them to frantically increase their pace. The only sound in the room had been the slap of flesh against flesh as he repeatedly smacked against her backside with the hardness of his thighs, plummeting into her with a desperation that bordered on mania. The force of their climax when it followed was gripping, compelling, overwhelming, and had left them gasping, luxuriating in the aftermath of such perfect and profound lovemaking.

Nicholas snapped out of his thoughts when Shayla turned around to face him. Her features were a mask of remorse and regret. Her voice was menacingly soft when she spoke.

"Thomas Jordache is not my lover, Nicholas. He's my father."

Chapter 29

Nicholas blinked twice, thinking he had not heard Shayla correctly. "Come again?"

He knew those two words were a mistake the moment they had left his lips. They were the same two words he had passionately whispered in her ear last night while making love to her, coaxing her into a second climax.

"Could you repeat that?" he quickly clarified, dragging in a deep ragged breath.

"I said, Thomas Jordache is my father."

That's what he'd thought she'd said. Did she actually expect him to believe that? His lips pressed together, still hard and untrusting, he looked at her and said, "That's a good one."

Shayla flashed him a look of irritation, then paused. Liquid gold eyes held hers in a challenge, but she refused to let him bait her. She owed him the full story. "I need to start from the beginning."

Nicholas leaned against his desk as if bored. "Then by all means please do, Ms. Kirkland."

Hauling in a quick breath, Shayla began. "My mother used to work here, for this company, over twenty-seven years ago."

Raising an eyebrow, Nicholas said nothing.

"I found her diary a week or so after her death, while going through her things. While working here she met Thomas Jordache and began dating him, not knowing that he was one of Chenault's biggest competitors."

Shayla looked down for a second, remembering the words her mother had written and how they had affected her after reading them. "During that time someone was spying on Chenault for company secrets to pass on to Jordache, and when my mother's involvement with him became known, it was erroneously assumed that she was the one doing it. She got fired because of it."

She lifted her head and boldly met Nicholas's eyes, forcing him to see the similarities in her and her mother's situation. "She was innocent. She also discovered a week or so later that she was pregnant. The one night she had slept with Jordache had resulted in that. When she told him about her condition he told her to get an abortion. Instead she left Jacksonville and went to Atlanta and married her childhood sweetheart, who willingly agreed to accept the child as his." Shayla looked down again, to retain her composure.

Straightening, Nicholas frowned as he pushed away from his desk. Something in the tone of Shayla's voice was compelling, almost believable...but still. "Go on," he said stiffly.

Lips compressed, Shayla met his gaze, then continued. "After reading her diary I became furious at the humiliation my mother suffered from the false accusations at Chenault Electronics, and from Thomas Jordache's total disregard of her. So I decided to make Chenault and

Jordache Electronics pay for what they'd done to her. I was going to ruin both companies."

Nicholas's eyes flashed with anger. "Is that why you came to work here?"

"Yes," she replied honestly. She drew herself up, clasping her hands in front of her. "I had intended to succeed at my goal until I met you. Until I really got to know you." And she added, in a soft voice while his gaze was heavily on her, "Until I fell in love with you."

"Really? How touching," he snapped sarcastically.

"Yes, it was touching. Actually, Nicholas," she said in a near whisper, her gaze still locked to his, "it was more than touching. It was everything I ever thought true love would be." For one instant, Shayla thought she saw some emotion pass through Nicholas's eyes but when his expression didn't soften she thought she had imagined it.

"Once I realized that I'd fallen in love with you, knowing that I had not been completely honest with you about my reason for seeking employment here, I knew I couldn't work here any longer. That's why I gave you my resignation. But you wouldn't accept it."

That much, Nicholas thought, was true. He hadn't accepted it. He had wanted to keep her around, and had been willing to break every rule he'd ever put into place to do that.

"One day I received a phone call from Thomas Jordache requesting to meet with me," Shayla said. "The first time I'd ever laid eyes on him was at the Mings' dinner party. As far as I was concerned, he and I didn't have anything to talk about. In fact, I was surprised he'd figured out who I was, since the truth about me not being Glenn Kirkland's biological child had been a closely guarded secret."

Nicholas raised a brow. "Indeed?" he taunted.

Shayla met his gaze with narrowed eyes. "Yes, indeed. The only people who knew the truth were my mother, my father, and my aunt. But when Jordache saw a picture of me and my mother together in a newspaper article shortly after my father's death, he put two and two together and figured she had not gotten the abortion he'd told her to get."

"Why did Jordache want to meet with you? To offer you compensation to spy on us?" Nicholas's words were asked through clenched teeth.

"No, actually he was concerned with the recent incidents at Chenault. They pointed to him as being the person behind them. He claimed he was innocent, and was concerned that Trent would believe the worst and he didn't want that. He's convinced that someone at Chenault is behind those incidents. He asked if I had noticed anyone suspicious."

Nicholas shook his head. "You were so gullible you believed him?"

"Yes, I believed him. Because he's dying, Nicholas. Thomas Jordache has terminal cancer, and has less than a year to live. He wants to die with his son believing he has changed. Yes, I believed him, because my father, Glenn, died of the same type of cancer. The same symptoms were there—the dry cough, the wheezing, and the raspy sound of someone barely getting by on one good lung."

Nicholas frowned. He remembered his last conversation with Trent, the one they'd had before Trent had left on his cruise ship, and the favor he had asked of him. He had been concerned with his father's health. But still Nicholas wasn't ready to buy Shayla's story. "If you were convinced that someone who worked here was actually behind those incidents, why didn't you come tell me or Paul?"

"Because I knew the two of you were distrustful of Jordache. I felt the least I could do was to keep my ears and eyes open. I haven't noticed anything or anyone suspicious, and when I met with Jordache again yesterday that's what I told him."

Nicholas studied her, her eyes, her face. He wanted to believe her, but… "That was a pretty tidy story, Shayla. It may explain this page torn out of your planner, Jordache's two phone calls to you, and your two meetings with him, but it doesn't explain why I was with you every time there were incidents at my company."

Shayla frowned. "They were merely coincidences, nothing more. Think about it. Were any of those times calculated planning on my part, Nicholas?"

Her words, which had been quietly spoken, hung in the air between them, raising several questions in Nicholas's mind. He couldn't help remembering those two times in question, and she was right. There hadn't been anything calculating on her part. If anything, there had been on his. He had wanted her, and had deliberately set out to seduce her. His chest tightened, and his thoughts began whirling. What if everything she had just told him was the truth?

Shayla bit her lip when Nicholas didn't answer, although she saw signs of wavering in his features. She knew he was weighing what she'd told him, trying to decide whether to believe her. Taking a chance, she crossed the room to stand in front of him. She had to make him believe her.

"I admit I'm guilty of coming to work here for the wrong reason, and you can fault me for that, if you want. But I won't let you fault me for something I didn't do. You don't know how confused I was when I had the perfect chance to ruin your company and made a decision not to. I could have screwed things up for you big-time with the Ling Deal…but didn't. It was only later that I accepted the reason why. I had fallen in love with you."

She took in a shaky breath. "That's why I knew I had to leave here, Nicholas. That's why I gave you my resignation. If Jordache was paying me to spy on you, why would I have turned in my notice?"

Nicholas knew that he should back away from her and give his mind time to sort through everything she had told him. He needed to remain objective. He owed it to her and to himself to be fair in his reasoning. But how could he be fair and objective when his heart was all into it? How could he be fair and objective when the person he loved more than life was standing before him, pleading with him to believe her?

"If what you've told me is true, Shayla, then why didn't you come to me after we became intimate and tell me the truth about why you came to work here?"

Shayla's eyes became misty. "I was going to tell you the truth. Today, in fact. The reason I didn't tell you before was because I didn't think the time was right. I thought if I told you I'd push you away."

His eyes searched hers for a better understanding. "What made the time right today, and not before?" he asked, still holding on to that one piece of doubt, wanting to let go but afraid to.

Shayla took another step forward, bringing herself toe-to-toe with him. She looked up and met his gaze. It was still distrustful, but not as much as before. "Because," she said in a soft shaky voice, "last night, for the first time, you told me you loved me."

Tears pricked at Shayla's eyes. She tried holding them back, not wanting Nicholas to see her cry, but failed when water gathered in her eyes. "You once told me that you believed that true love could overlook a multitude of faults." She swiped at a tear. "I admit I wanted revenge on your company, Nicholas. Go ahead and fault me for that, but if you truly love me you'll find it in your heart to overlook it. However, I won't let you fault me for something I didn't do. I didn't betray your trust, Nicholas. I could never do that to you. I love you too much. If nothing else, you have to believe that."

Nicholas's golden eyes held Shayla's dark ones for the longest time. Over the past thirty minutes or so, he had heard what she'd said. He had listened to her explanations and the one thing he couldn't discount was the fact that she *had* come through for him with the Ling Deal, a fact that had somehow gotten lost in his rage. If she had been working with Jordache from the first, why would she save a big deal for his company? Everything with the MC Project had hinged on that deal. She had read the reports, and knew that. Yet, she had miraculously pulled it off for him.

Then there was something else. As much as he wanted to believe she was a consummate actress, he knew that wasn't true. The hurt and pain he'd seen in her eyes when she'd told him about finding out about her mother's past had been real. He had felt it, because he had suffered a similar experience with his own mother last year.

He inhaled deeply. He believed that someone from inside the company was working against him, but now, at this very moment, a part of him refused to believe it was the woman standing before him, waiting for him to decide their fate. The decision of whether they would have a future together rested in his hands…or so she thought.

In reality their fate had been sealed the moment she had walked into his office for that interview. He had loved her from that moment. And she was right. He did believe that true love overlooked a multitude of faults.

Reaching out, he tenderly wiped a tear that flowed down her cheek. His finger lowered, then drew out the chain, lifting the pendant from its hiding place beneath her blouse. Clasping it in his hand, he fingered it for a few seconds before releasing it. Their eyes locked, and the silence stretched. Then he spoke. "Have you finished explaining everything now?"

His voice had deepened to a smooth tender sound and

that, along with his touch, slowly eased the tension from Shayla's body. The tension was gone, but the heat remained. She nodded and drew in a deep breath. "Yes."

He leaned closer to her. "Promise me that you won't keep anything from me ever again. We are to share everything."

"I promise."

When his mouth was mere inches from hers she whispered softly with her gaze on his face, "I love you, Nicholas, and I'd never deliberately hurt you."

"I know," he murmured, pulling her into his arms. "I know that now." His mouth captured hers. His kiss was possessive, ravenous. It took all that she was offering, and more. They had come close to losing each other, but were back in each other's arms. For the moment that was all that mattered.

Nicholas dragged his lips from hers only long enough to whisper on a long-drawn-out sigh, "I love you, too." Then he drew her back to him for another slow, passionate, intimate kiss.

Outside Nicholas's office Carl Stockard checked his watch for the hundredth time, nervously wondering what was going on behind the closed doors. How long did it take to fire somebody? Why was it taking so long? Mr. Chenault had been furious when he had reviewed the documents given to him. Surely he wasn't letting the woman talk her way out of it.

He nearly jumped when the phone rang on Leanne's desk. Moments later she hung up, gave him a quick glance, and said, "Mr. Chenault wants to see you."

Stockard smiled, thinking it was about time. He would take pleasure in escorting Shayla Kirkland out of the building. He didn't hesitate in crossing the lobby and entering Nicholas's office. Then he stopped dead in his tracks.

The boss was smiling.

Still holding Shayla in his arms, Nicholas turned to Stockard. "It seems a mistake was made. Ms. Kirkland is not spying on us for Thomas Jordache."

Stockard heard him, but didn't believe him. "But what about the evidence? I saw her meeting with him twice."

"She has explained everything."

Stockard's hands were balled into fists at his side. "And you believe her?" The words came out abrupt and loud, laced with disgust and incredulity.

Nicholas stiffened. His hold around Shayla's waist tightened as he brought her closer into his arms. His eyes narrowed, and he considered the man steadily. "Yes, I believe her. You have a problem with that, Stockard?"

"Yeah, he does," Paul Dunlap said, walking into Nicholas's office with an attractive lady at his side. "And I know the reason why."

Shayla's features registered her surprise. "Aunt Callie! What are you doing here?"

Chapter 30

It took less than an hour for Paul to reveal Stockard's duplicity. It might have taken longer if Cindy Davenport, fearful of maximum jail time, had not willingly spilled her guts. She admitted setting Harris up, following Stockard's orders. After all the videotapes had been confiscated and destroyed, Stockard, with Cindy at his side, had been escorted from the building by security men and the Chicago police. They still needed to be questioned about the fire at the Jacksonville office and the break-in.

Due to the possibility of the scandal it could have caused Silas Harris and his family, Nicholas decided not to press charges against Stockard and Cindy regarding the blackmail scheme. However, after terminating them, he issued a warning that if they were seen on the premises of Chenault Electronics, in Chicago or Jacksonville, charges of extortion and blackmail would be added.

"You were working undercover?" Shayla asked Howard

Reeves after Stockard and Cindy had been taken from the building.

"Yes," he replied, smiling, "Nick, Trent, and I are childhood friends who spent most of our summer months together at camp. With Paul's retirement fast approaching, Nicholas wanted Paul's replacement to be someone he knew he could trust, and he didn't feel completely comfortable with any of his top contenders. He offered me the position around six months ago, but wanted me to secretly be his eyes and ears for a while. He needed to know which of his employees were loyal."

Shayla nodded, understanding Nicholas's strategy. The MC Project required complete loyalty and trust from his employees. Too bad Stockard hadn't known Nicholas had already chosen Paul's replacement. All of his underhanded plans had been for nothing, since he wouldn't have gotten the job anyway. "Is that why you constantly made negative comments about Nicholas, to filter out disloyal employees?"

Howard smiled ruefully. "Yes, I was testing you."

Shayla returned his smile. "Did I pass?"

Howard couldn't keep from grinning. "Yes, with flying colors."

Hours later, after things had gotten back to normal, Nicholas and Shayla sat in his office along with Paul and her aunt. Shayla suddenly remembered something. "Aunt Callie, you never did say why you're here. How did you know what was going on?"

For a few minutes Shayla's question hung in the air. Then Callie finally answered. "Paul came to see me."

"Paul?" Shayla shifted her gaze from her aunt to Paul Dunlap, surprised her aunt was on a first-name basis with him. "You two know each other?"

Again Shayla's question seemed to linger in the air

before her aunt responded. "Yes. When Eva worked for Chenault, I spent the summer with her during break from college one year." She glanced at Paul, then met Shayla's gaze once more. "I met Paul when I dropped by to have lunch with her one day."

Shayla nodded. "Oh, I see."

Nicholas shifted in his chair. He didn't think Shayla really did see, but he was beginning to. Only someone close to Paul could detect that at one time Callie Foster had meant something to him. He would not be surprised to discover that they had once been lovers, and even figured it was a good possibility that she was the one Paul had lost after accusing her of something she had not done. He shuddered at the thought that he had almost lost Shayla the exact same way.

"Shayla, there's something I need to tell you," Callie said softly.

Shayla lifted her brow. Her aunt's tone made her alert. Something was wrong. "What is it? What's the matter?" she prompted softly.

A tense silence followed. Then her aunt spoke in a ragged low voice. "I lied to you. We lied to you," she said as tears suddenly washed across her eyes.

Shayla's throat tightened. She was confused. "Tell me, Aunt Callie. Who lied?"

"Glenn, Eva, and I."

Shayla frowned, still not understanding. "What lie are you talking about? I already know that Glenn's not my father, and that Thomas Jordache is."

"He's not your father, either."

Shayla caught her breath. "But I—I thought he and Mom…" Shayla stared, bemused. "I thought he was the one who got Mom pregnant. Her diary said so."

Callie wiped at a tear. "He was."

Now even more confused, Shayla lowered her head for

a brief moment. Lifting her head again, she met her aunt's tear-filled eyes. "Then I think you need to explain things to me, Aunt Callie, because at the moment I'm totally confused."

Callie stared at Shayla as if what she was about to say could make her lose her forever. She took in a deep breath and said, "Eva lost her baby from Thomas Jordache. She wasn't your mother. At least, she wasn't the woman who gave birth to you."

Shayla's head reeled from her aunt's statement. She felt blood slam urgently through her body. Her turbulent senses reached out to Nicholas. As if he felt her anxiety, he walked over to where she was sitting and stood next to her. She looked up and met his attentive gaze, then leaned her shoulder against the lower part of his body, needing a connection to him, needing to rely on the comfort of his strength.

Her breathing was coming too fast, and she willed herself to slow it down. Inwardly shaking with the effort to remain calm, she turned to her aunt. "If I'm not Thomas Jordache and Eva's child," she said in a voice barely above a whisper, "then whose child am I?"

Out of the corner of her eye, Shayla saw Paul come into view. She watched him cross the room and sit down next to her aunt on the love seat in the office. She watched as his hand closed firmly around hers, protectively and endearingly. They both met her gaze. Then she heard them answer her question simultaneously in torn ragged voices. "Ours."

Shayla stared at them—then everything went black.

In the deep recesses of her mind Shayla heard Nicholas softly calling her name. She felt the warmth of his hand gently rubbing hers, felt the tender butterfly kisses he was placing around her lips. She slowly opened her eyes and discovered she was lying on the love seat, with him hovering over her. His face was lined with worry. She blinked. "What happened?"

"You passed out on us."

Shayla nodded, remembering. She tried to sit up and felt the force of Nicholas's arms holding her down. "Just lie still for a minute, sweetheart."

Shayla nodded and settled back down, but not before she glanced around the room. "Where are they?"

Nicholas rubbed her forehead. "Outside the door. I wanted you to myself for a while." He stood and lifted her up in his arms, then sat on the love seat with her cradled securely in his lap. He looked down at her. "I know hearing that was quite a shocker. You okay?"

Shayla shook her head. "I don't know. I can't believe it. I can't imagine anyone being my mother but Eva."

"Then you shouldn't. Callie loves you, Shayla. You know that, don't you?"

"Yes. But she didn't tell me the truth."

"Only because she loves you, and didn't want to hurt you," he said softly.

"She gave me away, Nicholas."

Nicholas leaned over and kissed her lips. "No, she didn't give you away, Shayla. She shared you. She shared you with the two people she loved and trusted most. Has there ever been a time when she wasn't there for you?"

Shayla heaved a sigh, then shook her head. "No." And that was the truth. Her aunt had always been a part of her life, a major part. She'd always been like her second mom. Even when Glenn had gotten a huge job offer to head the pediatrics department of the largest hospital in Chicago, Callie had made the move from D.C. with them.

"The way I see it," Nicholas was saying, "the person who's gotten the short end of the deal is Paul. He just found out today that he has a daughter."

"Oh." Shayla had forgotten all about that.

"You're blessed, you know. Some people have only one set of parents. In your lifetime, Shayla, you've had two."

Resigned, Shayla nodded. That was true when presented that way.

"So, what do you want to do about it? Callie thinks you hate her, and poor Paul is a basket case, because he isn't sure how you feel about him one way or the other."

Nicholas's hold on her tightened securely. "I know you love your aunt, and I tried to assure her that things would work out. I know that, like me, you believe true love overlooks a multitude of faults. And that would include any she has. Right?"

Shayla blinked away her tears, then raised her eyes to Nicholas. "Right. Can I see her now?"

"What about Paul?"

"I'd like to see him, too."

Nicholas smiled down at her. "Later. It's been one hell of a day, and right now I think we both need this." He leaned down and captured her lips. The heat in his kiss warmed her soul, repaired her torn heart, and promised her many tomorrows with him. It also made her thankful for the day Nicholas Chenault had walked into her life.

Shayla was standing at the window when she heard the sound of the door to Nicholas's office opening. Taking a deep breath, she turned around to face the older couple who had walked in behind Nicholas.

Her gaze immediately lit on her aunt's broken features before moving to Paul's stiff and uncertain stance. They were the two people who had created her. She could imagine a young, handsome, self-assured Paul Dunlap falling in love with the beautiful, vibrant, and classy Callie Foster. Seeing them now it seemed that was how it was meant for them to be—together.

Slowly walking over to them, Shayla leaned over and kissed her aunt's cheek. Then she reached out and took Paul's hand in hers. Through misty eyes she looked up at them. "Nicholas is right. Not everyone gets the chance to have two sets of parents. I feel blessed that I'm lucky enough to get that golden opportunity."

She then pulled the two of them to her, holding them close and feeling the tension leaving them, appreciating the value and importance of true love.

Chapter 31

Shayla slowly opened her eyes, and her gaze drifted up to the hard masculine body that had just moved on top of her.

"You're awake," Nicholas said softly as his gaze locked dead center on her mouth.

The intense look in his eyes as well as the hard body that settled gently over hers shot immediate heat through her bloodstream. She blinked the sluggishness from her eyes and smiled up at him. "It seems, Mr. Chenault, that you have great timing."

Nicholas chuckled, and when he did his entire face radiated just how happy he felt. "That's not all I have. Feel."

Shayla sucked in a quick breath when she felt his hardness against her thigh. Her smile widened. "And I guess you want me to do something about it."

"I was hoping that you would, but first I think we need to talk about our future."

To be quite honest, Shayla didn't think she would be able

to talk at all, not when the evidence of his desire was resting in an area of her body that was too close to home. "Talk?" she asked simply.

"Yes."

"About our future?"

"Yes."

"Why? Do you have any suggestions?"

Nicholas's gold eyes glittered with love when he said, "Yeah, I have quite a few, but I think we should start off with marriage. Your father's orders. And Paul was pretty adamant about it, too."

Shayla couldn't help but smile. She had to get used to the fact that Paul Dunlap was indeed her father. "So he wants you to make an honest woman of me, huh?"

Nicholas chuckled. "Sweetheart, you're already an honest woman. Regardless of what Paul wants, what I want is to give you my name, my love, my babies."

"Umm, in that order?"

Nicholas shook his head, grinning. "No. In fact, after last night and not using a condom that one time, it just might be that a baby is somewhere in our future."

"I'm game if you are."

"So, it's settled, then," he said, giving her a smooth smile. "We're getting married."

"Are you sure you really want to, and not because Paul wants you to?"

He bent his head and his lips grazed hers softly, feeling the quiver that touched her body. "Yes. I'd planned to ask you, anyway, before all that mess with Stockard came up. That's why I'd wanted you to take the day off to spend with me. I was going to take you shopping for an engagement ring."

Nicholas's words filled Shayla's heart. She couldn't seem to quit smiling at him.

"So I'll let you set a date."

"Do you have a preference?" she asked, still smiling.

"What about next month?"

Her smile vanished immediately. "That soon?" Her mind began whirling with all the things she would have to do to pull off a wedding in a month.

"Sweetheart, if I had my way it would be sooner than that." He captured her mouth in his, kissing her deeply and thoroughly as a flood of hot sensations ignited passion between them. Shayla wrapped her arms around his neck and tightened her hold.

"Well…I guess that settles it," she whispered when he released her mouth.

"Yes, I guess it does." His lips quirked when he saw her smile return. "Besides, you aren't in any position to argue right now."

Shayla's smile widened as she realized just what position she was in. She was flat on her back beneath him, definitely a position she liked.

"I love you, Nicholas," she said, lifting her hands to capture his face and trapping his gaze.

"And I, you. You're my one true love," he whispered as he leaned down and captured her mouth. He shifted and smoothly united their bodies, the same way they had promised to unite their lives. As one.

Epilogue

One month later

Shayla had been vaguely aware of the people who had been invited to her and Nicholas's wedding. She'd only had eyes for the groom. However, as she circulated among the guests she realized just how many people had attended what was supposed to be a small and private outdoor wedding on Sterling's mountain.

Out of the corner of her eye she saw Trent in deep conversation with his wife, Brenna, a beautiful woman he had met, fallen in love with, and married on his African cruise. Trent and Brenna would be having another wedding ceremony in June for the benefit of family and friends who had missed the first.

Shayla glanced around and saw Angeline Chenault, mother of the groom, standing by the pond, looking ravishing on the arm of the man she was currently seeing, Jessup Baron.

After stopping to hold conversations with Sterling's wife, Colby, the Garwoods, the Wingates, and the Madarises, Shayla scanned the crowd looking for Nicholas. She saw him standing next to her parents.

Her parents.

She inhaled a deep breath of mountain air, still feeling happy and blessed. Callie and Paul had told her everything, including what had driven them apart twenty-seven years ago. Nothing would make her happier than to see them put the past behind them and get together again. She knew they were pretty close to doing that, since they were now seeing a lot of each other. Aunt Callie had gone sailing with Paul on his yacht for an entire week. And there was also talk of expanding her business and opening another dress shop in Jacksonville. Anyone who saw them together could quickly see that they were still in love, even after twenty-seven years of separation and misunderstanding.

Shayla's own relationship with Paul was growing. They had both agreed they would take one day at a time. She knew she had made him happy by asking him to be the one to give her away to Nicholas today.

Shayla was about to walk off in Nicholas's direction when she happened to notice Thomas Jordache standing alone near a group of oak trees. She walked over to him. She and Nicholas had made a decision to invite him. It was time to forgive and forget. "Mr. Jordache? Are you enjoying yourself?" she asked, trying not to notice how much weight he had lost.

"Yes, I am. Thanks for inviting me."

Shayla looked at him before asking something that had been nagging at her for a while. "You knew all along that

I was Paul's child, didn't you? That's why you didn't acknowledge me as your daughter that day we met."

He looked up at her and smiled warmly. "Yes. That day I met with Eva she told me the truth. Even if she hadn't, it would have been obvious to me after seeing you up close."

Shayla lifted a brow. "Why?"

"Because you and Trent look so much alike. The two of you can pass for brother and sister. Trent has a lot of Paul's features, and so do you—only you're a lot prettier than Trent and Paul."

Shayla smiled. "Thank you." She glanced over at where Trent and Brenna were standing. He had whispered something in her ear, and whatever he'd said had brought a warm blush to Brenna's features and a huge grin to her lips.

Shayla grinned, as well, seeing how happy the couple were. "So, what do you think of your new daughter-in-law?"

Thomas Jordache followed her gaze and smiled. "I think she's a wonderful person who's truly made my son happy. He's blessed to have found her. I'm glad that when the time comes, he won't be left alone. Trent is all I have, but now, for my remaining days, I'll have a daughter to love, as well."

Moments later Shayla was finding her way toward her husband again. He happened to look up and see her approach. Instead of waiting he excused himself from her parents and began moving toward her, to meet her halfway.

Smiling serenely with love in her eyes, she took his hand in hers. She glanced around the crowd, then looked up at him. "Well, it's over."

Nicholas pulled her to him, closer in his arms. "No, sweetheart, the best part is just beginning. Besides getting a brother-in-law who's a famous movie star, a sister-in-law who believes in doing everything properly, a beautiful niece, and a pretty nice mother-in-law, you'll also share ownership of that desk in my office. We haven't tried it out yet, you know."

Shayla grinned. "And you get a father-in-law you've known all of your life, a mother-in-law who I think is the greatest, and marriage to your best friend's cousin. What more could a man want?"

Nicholas released a deep chuckle before leaning closer, bringing her lips mere inches from his. "I can think of one other thing."

In the sight of everyone, Nicholas kissed his beautiful bride for the second time that day.